LINDA MCKOWN

I0659541

WHITE

BOOM

AND

THE

SEAGULLS

BY

LINDA MCKOWN

Publisher LindaMcKownAuthor LLC
Scottsdale, AZ

1

WHITE BOOM AND THE SEAGULLS

White Boom and the Seagulls

ISBN-13: 978-0-9997357-9-4

Library of Congress Control Number: 2019913851

Author:
LindaMcKownAuthor LLC
11574 E Running Deer Trail
Scottsdale, AZ 85262
https://www.lindamckown.com

Any names of people and entities are fictitious in this story having been created by the author's imagination.

Front Cover Photo of the book was purchased from Shutterstock. Book title manipulation was done by Joseph McKown

This book was written for those readers who love to play around boats and water. Having lived in the Northern part of the United States, there are large bodies of water readily available for vacation time.

Sailing in the Apostle Islands on Lake Superior is an experience I won't forget. Sometimes a person lives on the wild side.

Table of Contents

1 Sailboat Brochure

No one is ever prepared for what comes next.

Emily Erin closed her journal after writing the sentence. This was her last day at work. Cleaning out her desk, she stumbled upon a brochure tucked in the corner. The loss of her job added to the inevitable change coming her way. She turned the brochure over. There was something about the pictures. She read the pages. A sailing vacation cruise would put her on top of the deepwater per the colorful four-page brochure she held in her hands. She touched the white sailboat on the blue water. The magnificence of the picture entranced her. The scenic beauty caught her breath. Memories flooded from her past.

"I saw this place."

Emily felt the tug on her heart. Sailing was a mystery she could master. At age eight she also wanted to learn to swim after her accident. Being on a sailboat cruise might be like stepping off the grid.

"Or falling off the grid."

She read the words aloud.

"Water surrounds the boat, miles of beautiful shoreline await, and only the seagulls disturb the evening glow."

If she could relax on a boat cruise, her real feelings might take over and make her feel more alive. The knowledge gained from sailing could be very useful. She opened her journal. Speaking softly, Emily wrote.

"The sun looked down and created warmth over cooler water. Clouds and other masses developed. Ripples appeared on the water as kisses. The boat headed straight toward the ripples and the miraculous wind moved the craft forward. The hull's shape enhanced the movement until the ship's wheel steered us toward paradise. We were beyond virtual reality, aka VR."

She picked up her cell phone to call the 800 number. Emily stopped. She touched the gold chain necklace around her neck. A lifeguard gave her the special necklace years ago. Encouraged by the warmth of the chain, she made the call to the Shane A. Hanigan Company regarding the sailboat cruise on Lake Superior. She wanted the words in her journal to come true. In her imagination, the trip was possible. The dullness of her life could be wiped out if there was a spot for her on the boat.

She sent her application and a picture of herself. A week went by and there was no call from the Shane A. Hanigan Company booking agent.

In desperation, Emily spoke to the stars one evening asking fate or someone to open the magical door. She didn't care about which door.

"Well, maybe a good-looking guy or two on the sailboat wouldn't hurt. Oh, and some excitement, too."

Her best friend, Cari Higgins, would have told her to be careful. Wishes sometimes are answered.

Emily took matters into her own hands. She called the direct phone number for the company. A secretary put her on hold.

A man came on the line, "Dad?"

Emily stammered, "No, this is Emily Erin. I'm waiting to find out if my name made it as a guest crew member onto your next sailboat cruise."

"Thank you for calling. I see your application on my computer. I'll have my secretary contact you."

Fifteen minutes later, Shane Hanigan's secretary called her back. An opening on the cruise did occur. Emily gave them her credit card number.

Emily excitedly called Cari to let her know she was accepted for the beautiful sailboat cruise on Lake Superior.

"Are you sure you want to go sailing?"

"Yes, I am so excited, I can hardly wait! A door has opened," said Emily.

"Oh, no, not a door. You didn't talk to the water again?"

"Yes, maybe. Then I became frustrated when no one from the Shane A. Hanigan Company called after I sent my application. I called their business directly. I think I talked to the owner."

"You talked with Shane? Emily, go look at his profile on the company website."

Emily pulled up his image and read his biography.

"Wow, one good-looking guy, lots of degrees, and sandy color hair. He has nice eyes, too."

"Well, then you must absolutely buy some gorgeous sailing clothes. You know drip-dry, crushable clothes that you can handwash. Also, you need to get your medicine refilled."

Emily went shopping. Along with the rest of her clothes, she bought two swimsuits, a black one-piece, and a red bikini. She called back Cari for help in making a choice. Emily texted pictures of her new clothing items. Her friend encouraged her to take both swimsuits and dump the baggy sweats. At the last minute, the red bikini was left at home because her backpack was full.

"Shane won't be on the cruise."

She laid her sweatpants out to wear the first day. The rest of the nice clothes would suffice for the trip. Emily didn't know she would get to step out of her comfort zone. She didn't realize she was headed into experiences that were way beyond the normal and would test her limits.

Never in her wildest dreams would she believe a murderer could ride into her midst. A boat stalled in the water would become an unpredictable event. Love could approach faster than a powerful gale in a Great Lakes storm if a person wasn't prepared. Not in any order, she would feel fear, chaos and stress enter her life besides a great adventure.

After her cruise ended, Emily's course would be permanently altered. She would again write in her journal,

"I touched paradise."

2 The Water

People will tell you their most intimate and traumatic experiences. There are those who boast and others who won't ever mention the events. Some stories are emotional or difficult to recall. The brain blocks the memory permanently or the memory resurfaces later.

There's always a question among critics. Some say there is a fine line between living and dying. Others believe the whole idea is false. A person either breathes or doesn't. There are the few who realize stepping off the grid can happen.

Emily Erin is one of the few who've disappeared and came back. She has walked the plank, stared at the water, and fallen into the deep.

Her story truly began when she was eight years old. Her babysitter should have paid more attention.

The home Emily lived in was a well-to-do neighborhood in Los Angeles, California. The walls inside her home were white with white drapes and carpet. Even the couch was white. The only color was an occasional eggshell-colored throw or blue-black pillow. There were no frills or tassels allowed in the home. The outside was eggshell white with brilliant white trim and black shutters. There was a landscaper who took care of the lawn and pool.

Her parents believed their world was safe from the outside elements by keeping their living space pristine. Neat and clean was their mantra.

Emily came along into their sterile world and was expected to be the perfect child. They were currently on their vacation to Greece staying in a white-washed hostel near the sea. Most of their vacations didn't include their only daughter.

Emily looked at the pale-yellow roses on the back patio. When they opened, their color faded to match the siding. She smelled one of the small and more perfect rose flowers. The flower belonged on the bush. She liked the center reaching for the sun.

She held her thin arms over her head in a cup-like fashion pretending to be the flower. She felt alive and healthy. She closed her eyes feeling the red heat from the sun. Next, she tapped her feet pretending to be a ballet dancer. She turned to see her babysitter texting on her phone. She picked the small bud and came inside.

"You missed my dance because you weren't paying attention. Can we go to the big pool?"

The kid was bored with her home pool and no friends were allowed over to play while the parents were gone. The babysitter was bored. All this kid did was talk. The yellow rose made her sneeze.

"There's the game board boxes in the closet."

"Board games."

Emily wasn't excited about games. She hated the games. Her mom bought the stupid board games. She opened the boxes so her mom would think she played with them. When her mom was in a better frame of mind, Emily received her own cell phone. She could play games on an app. She looked at her babysitter.

"My mom said we could use our car for emergencies. Do you know how to drive?"

The babysitter was exasperated at being disturbed.

"Of course, I'm an adult. Adults take tests and get a license."

"What's a license?"

The babysitter showed her the laminated card.

"Oh, I thought the picture was for identification. My parents have to show the card when we fly."

"Dah!" responded the babysitter.

Emily scrunched up her face. Kids in school said the three-letter word frequently. She knew stupid was a good synonym.

The babysitter found the keys on a hook in the kitchen cupboard and agreed to take her to the pool. There were good looking and much older boys at the one in Los Angeles. The babysitter believed watching gorgeous hunks of half-naked male torsos was an emergency. Speaking to one was the optimum reason for the adventure.

Emily jumped up and down.

"Yes!"

The babysitter drove carefully on the freeway. Emily kept quiet. She didn't want to distract the babysitter and cause an accident. Her mom was fussy about her car. Scratches meant imperfection. Dents were a brand-new car.

After an hour of swimming, Emily noticed the line to the small diving board was shorter. She stood in line. She watched the kids in front of her jump off the diving board. A red-headed boy with a light sprinkling of freckles turned after he saw Emily.

"Jump as far out as you can."

She was next. Walking to the end of the board, she used her fingers to plug her nose. Without hesitation, she backed up and took a run. She jumped into the air.

There was a splash. Emily was surprised the water was colder in the deep end. She opened her eyes and saw massive bubbles. Her feet touched the bottom of the pool. Her arms were extended, and her legs wouldn't move. She watched the bubbles disappear. The water surrounded her. She felt strange. A leaf drifted by her face.

The lifeguard saw the kid not moving and immediately dove in the deep end after her.

Emily closed her eyes. The quiet lulled her to sleep. She dreamed. She could touch the sky and see clouds. There were waves crashing on the shore. The scenery was brilliant green and the water a deep blue. A sail flapped. She turned to watch. The sail tightened and she was flying over the water. There was no sound. She felt warm and excited. Then, she heard a voice. Someone whispered, *Wait for me*. Emily opened her eyes and tried to speak. Water rushed into her mouth and she was awake. Her brain clicked a word in neon red, *drowning*.

A person pushed her toward the surface. Another lifeguard caught her arm and pulled upward.

Coming through the warm layer of water, she surfaced. Taking gulps of the sweet lifesaving air, Emily was guided to the ladder where the two lifeguards helped her to the cement deck. They laid her down. She was coughing up water and the lifeguard stopped CPR. She tried to sit, and they told her to stay down. They waited until she was breathing better. They helped Emily into a sitting position.

"Are you all right?"

Emily looked at the lifeguard. He was handsome, strong, and sounded nice.

She looked at the kids at the diving board staring at her. They looked mad. She was their target. Kids couldn't swim until the lifeguards gave the whistle signal.

Emily started to cry.

"No, no, ignore those kids. There isn't anyone at the pool who can hurt you. I'm here. Please don't cry."

Emily hiccupped. She wiped her face.

The other lifeguard left the two of them alone. He blew his whistle and waved the kids in the water. Tanned bodies jumped into the pool. Water splashed. The noise level increased.

"I don't know what happened. When I get anxious, I freeze. I guess I shouldn't have tried the board. The other kids were having fun."

"What's your name?"

"Em, I mean Emily."

The lifeguard looked around. The kid should be with an adult. Those were the rules.

"Em, where's your adult?"

"My babysitter went to get a cola. She's been gone a long time."

The lifeguard spotted someone running toward them.

"Oh, my gosh, Emily, why are you in the deep end?"

The lifeguard appraised the babysitter and frowned.

"She seems to be fine after her mishap off the diving board. I would take her home. This day has been too much."

The babysitter said, "Sure, come on Emily."

They helped Emily to her feet and wrapped a towel around her shivering body. She staggered. The lifeguard signaled for his relief person, picked up Emily, and carried her to their vehicle.

Emily was in awe. The lifeguard was warm to the touch. His body was firm. He wore a gold chain with a lifesaving symbol. She asked him a question.

"Are you a pirate?"

The lifeguard was caught off guard. He noticed how bright Emily's brown eyes were. He wondered if she should have seen a doctor. He realized she was in a state of mind that young girls at the pool found themselves. The lifeguards became sun gods. Emily was caught in immense-like mode.

Relief spread over his face. She was sounding like a normal kid.

"I might be. When you're older, I hope I run into you. You will be a beautiful and sweet woman. Take your time picking someone and stop feeling anxious especially when you're in the water. A few swimming lessons are necessary. And remember, you're not indestructible." He put his gold necklace around her neck.

"Be brave."

The lifeguard spoke privately to the babysitter.

"Goodbye, Em."

Emily went home. The babysitter told her no more emergencies. The rest of the week was long and super quiet. Her parents arrived home. The babysitter didn't tell them about the swimming incident. Emily suppressed her memory regarding the deep-water part.

She wanted to go back to the large pool and see the lifeguard again. Emily forgot to thank him. The bus didn't come to their neighborhood. She was stuck.

This was her first anxiety attack. There would be more. The timing of her attacks would place her in harm's way.

Emily decided she should learn how to swim properly. Her mom took her to classes at their country club. In school, there was a pool. Emily joined the swimming club. The most exciting part of her childhood was winning medals during the swim meets. Her confidence grew. She knew if anyone asked her about her childhood, Emily would have told them it was a wasteland of boredom except for swimming.

In her teens, she turned into a beautiful woman. Then she met her friend, Cari Higgins. The two became inseparable best friends. Water would be their favorite place to play. They agreed water wasn't as dangerous as other people.

Emily told Cari about her swimming accident. Cari told her fate or angels were in the water. Angels could certainly jump off a diving board and swim. Emily realized Cari didn't say angels could talk. She wondered, "Who was in the water with me?"

Both girls acknowledged they were smarter than the other girls in their college classes. They raced each other to their classrooms and helped each other with assignments. Both girls finished college in record speed.

They drifted apart after graduation. Emily moved to Minneapolis and was on her own. Cari stayed in LA. They called each other occasionally. Both girl's futures seemed bright until Emily lost her job. The sailboat cruise loomed on Emily's horizon.

3 Bayfield Shores Launch

Emily Erin arrived at the Bayfield Shores Marina in Northern Wisconsin. She was there early having taken a bus to the small port city the day before. She had nowhere to go and this was her only future destination.

Her backpack and large duffle bag were all she possessed for the moment plus a post office box and checking account. There probably wouldn't be too much mail in the three weeks that she would be gone.

There was no one who would truly miss her if something happened.

"Maybe Cari would miss me."

Her parents were on a trip again. They were always gone. This time was the Caribbean. She was on her own. There was no job to return to when her vacation was over.

The twenty-four-year-old woman felt sad and a little lost. She shivered and took her sweater out of her pack.

Her company moved her job from Minneapolis to Chicago. They were given the opportunity to transfer. She chose the ten-thousand-dollar buyout program. Emily thought the money was a good deal after three years of employment. Her confidence level was high at the time she submitted her resignation. Now, she was rethinking her overly quick decision.

"Perhaps I should have stayed with the company. Maybe I would have liked Chicago. No, it was time to try someplace warmer. Before I move back to California, I'm going to have fun on a sailing cruise on Lake Superior."

She read the brochure again. The brochure touted sailing lessons for beginners and more experienced people. Emily hoped some of the crew would be knowledgeable because they would be sailing in deep water. The waves could get high if they ran into a storm. Emily rechecked the weather for the next week on her cell phone app. The weather looked grand.

A large noisy old van pulled into the marina parking lot and four people climbed out. The driver sat in his seat smoking a cigar. Two women and two men assembled their gear outside the van. The driver waved and drove off. The four people moved toward Dock 13, sat down, and waited for the sailboat to arrive. Emily decided to remain where she was sitting until the boat docked.

An hour went by and the sailboat didn't appear. Emily rechecked the note she received for the correct boarding time and location.

"Dock 13, slip 1. This is the place."

She saw the four people were walking back and forth on the dock and were peering toward the water entrance to the marina. A few powerboats arrived and pulled into their slips. Emily sat down again.

After a second hour passed, Emily felt the urge to use the restroom facilities.

"No sailboat. There should be enough time."

She walked to the Marina building and quickly ducked inside.

Upon exiting the restroom, she bought a cherry popsicle. The cold felt good and made her lips pink. Turning around, she saw the large sixty-five-foot sailboat. A man in a captain's hat threw the boat's lines to the four people on the dock. The men quickly tethered the black ropes in the cleats and positioned the large cylindrical-shaped white and black fenders. The side of the dock didn't rub on the boat frame. The marine-grade vinyl fenders worked as designed.

Emily decided to join her sailing teammates.

Another young couple reached the dock before her and stood in the line to enter the boat. A young man with red hair and a red beard appeared behind her.

22

"I'm glad to have arrived safely. My name is Duane Ramsey, a math teacher at a Wisconsin university. Sometimes I do a little DBA work on the side. My hobby is tinkering with databases and software. What did we ever do without computers, huh?"

"Hi, I'm Emily Erin, currently looking for a new job. This is my first sailboat cruise. My friend, Cari, sometimes calls me Em. Her cat Daisy calls me Meow."

"You're funny. I like your sense of humor. Let's use Emily."

"Oh, your other question. Yes, I brought my computer and phone. They are a necessary connection. I brought a small flashlight, too. How about your experience with boats?"

"I'm an old hand at sailing. My navigation skills are spot-on. Good luck with finding a job. I can show you an app. The flashlight will work on your phone."

"Thanks. That's a good idea. The flashlight should be saved in case we get stranded. Imagine my relief about your navigation experience. Maybe the captain will let the two of us crew together. I know a little bit about stars, but I'm not sure how those skills will help."

"Stranded like in shipwreck?"

"Oh, no."

"Trust me, stars are important. I'll mention the crewing idea to our captain," said Duane.

Emily smiled. She saw the ring on the young man's hand and wondered why his wife didn't come along.

The throng settled on the back of the boat. It appeared there were eight people on the cruise and one captain. Emily was disappointed there wasn't more crew from the company. She wondered if there was a chef on board or if they were going to cook their own meals.

The brochure only referenced briefly the meals and showed a picture of a small barbeque where someone cooked fish. Another picture showed an island with a large campfire. The people were holding sticks of hotdogs or brats.

The captain introduced himself as Aiden Hanigan.

"Call me Captain or if you must, Mr. Hanigan. I hate the name Aiden."

He told them about the company and mentioned Shane Hanigan as the owner. He explained when the boat was in the water, he was in command.

The captain apologized.

"Our chef couldn't make the cruise due to stomach flu. I'll be cooking breakfast after our first morning. The cruise guests or crew would need to make lunch and cook dinner."

The captain told the others that the meals were all planned. They should be able to handle the other recipes with ease. Many of their meals were already prepared and frozen. Some of their stops would require their ingenuity in finding produce and fish at the local markets, especially if they didn't catch any. He would request a fifty-dollar refund from his management team to compensate everyone for the cook's absence.

The team clapped their approval.

Next, he handed the crew their bunk numbers and a packet for them to read about the rules on board the boat.

He showed them safety features of the sailboat, the location of life vests, how to unhook the lifeboat, manually lift and lower sails, the anchor crank compartment, and the ship-to-shore radio.

Moving toward the helm, he showed them how the items worked with the computer. They were amazed at how easily the boat mechanisms worked.

"We'll be manually hauling the sails and anchors the first week, so everyone gets familiar with the equipment. A computer is nice to have for sailing a ship this size. However, we shouldn't rely on electronics."

The team groaned.

He told them they were clear for fifteen minutes to store their gear and they were to come topside.

"A catering company is bringing boxed sandwiches and fruit with beverages for our evening meal. The egg cheese or egg sausage sandwiches, and orange juice with coffee would also be brought on board by the catering firm. The boat will set sail after our egg breakfast in the morning. We leave at nine o'clock sharp."

The captain dismissed them to their quarters.

The crew spent the rest of their evening time introducing themselves.

The single people from the van were Nick Kent, a student from Chicago and Nancy Smith, an accountant who was also from Chicago, Illinois. Nick mentioned he knew how to sail. He winked at Emily. Emily was single. Nick liked single women. Her blonde hair was soft. Her lips were shiny pink.

Seth Moran, grocery store manager and Dell Cameron, secretary, lived around the Wisconsin area near Milwaukee.

The couples were Lucy and Mic Erickson. They were scuba diver instructors from Green Bay, Wisconsin. The Erickson's were no stranger to boats and sailed with friends on occasion around Lake Pepin,

26

Wisconsin. They brought their own scuba tanks and gear.

Duane introduced himself as did Emily. Duane was also from Green Bay and worked in Sheboygan.

Emily was the first one to reappear from her bedroom bunk. She went to the front of the boat where the captain sat. She squatted down and sat with her legs crossed.

"Hello, you are the Emily person originally from Los Angeles. Your blonde hair was my first clue. You look very much like your picture. Normally people don't send us their photos. Optional means don't comply."

Emily wondered how many didn't include their photo. The captain read her mind.

"Duane Ramsey sent his photo. I read your application request. You are the least experienced one of my crew."

"Yes, I did bring a book to read about sailing to help in my training."

"Good for you. I hope the book contains lots of pictures. Pictures tell the story about a great many things."

Emily saw the batch of seagulls flying off the bow of the boat searching for minnows in the water.

"Captain, how long have you been sailing?" asked Emily.

"Over thirty-five years, I think. Time drifts by and the days blur into each other. The number of people that have taken sailing lessons from me is many. You will be in good hands unless a storm hits and breaks our white boom. It's hard to sail in rough water with no boom. That only happened once. The lakes are large with long rocky shorelines. Boats our size do sometimes get lost."

The captain was silent and didn't explain what situation occurred. Emily felt a stirring of alarm. She needed to ask the question.

"The boat and people made it to shore?"

The captain remained quiet. He stood up and waved his hands at the seagulls.

"Darn birds, they follow me everywhere. Scat or this boat will plow through all of you scoundrels."

He turned to Emily.

"They aren't smart like the eagle. Now the eagle is a fine specimen of a bird and finds his own fish. My son is like the eagles. He soars on an airplane. Shane runs a floatplane business delivering supplies. His offices are in Sault Ste. Marie."

"Ontario?"

"No, the other twin city in Michigan. He does deliver to places in Canada."

"How nice? Does he ever sail with you?"

The captain scratched his beard.

"Shane used to sail. We've sailed Lake Superior and Michigan, but he has been too busy recently. I tried to get him to work with me on my last sailing trip. The words too busy get old. He told me that I must slow down. Retirement seems to have caught up with me. I rarely see my son. He will someday find someone else to captain this vessel."

"Your son is Shane. Shane Hanigan's name is on the website. The last name should have been a clue. This boat is a nice one."

"Aye, sleek and swift. We put a brand-new canvas on the boat last year. We went for black. Shane wanted red. I hate red. The color reminds me of a pirate ship on a board game. How do you like the color?"

"Very sophisticated. Red is always on the cover of board games. The games are not my favorite either, except for chess," said Emily.

"Good for you, Emily. We have something in common."

The captain stood up. "The seagulls here in this marina only want handouts. The tourists are to blame."

He swore, threw the rest of his apple core at the seagulls, and left the bow of the boat.

Emily's impression of their captain dropped a notch. Seagulls meant a person was close to land. She liked listening to their chatter and watched their diving antics. The birds reminded her of children on a playground. They were noisy and free in spirit. The sun was beginning to set.

Emily wondered if she could find something about their captain online and any of his previous jobs. She worried about his comments regarding a storm and his age.

"Should she tell any other members of the crew?"

There was no evidence that any prior cruises ran into trouble. The crew could see the man sometimes appeared stiff with arthritis.

"The captain didn't answer my question about his crew with the broken boom." She wondered if the accident was this very ship.

"Wouldn't a prior accident be considered a bad omen?"

Her mind was racing with anxiety. "Did he want to scare me or is that the way the captain normally talks. He seemed obsessed about seagulls. Should I leave this boat? I don't think they will give me my money back. The money won't matter if my life is in danger."

She looked at the white boom in the dark on their boat and touched the metal. The boom felt solid enough. There were no scratches or dents. She inspected the sheets and cables.

"Maybe they put a new one in and patched the holes."

Emily looked toward the array of stars overhead. The night was quiet. The other boaters in the marina turned in for the Sunday evening. She sighed and shook herself.

"Now, who is being the paranoid one. Maybe I'm not assessing the conversation correctly. Besides, the weather looked fine for the first week on my phone and I checked the national weather map."

Emily went below and slid into her bunk. She hoped the food onboard was safe to eat.

"Stop the fear factor now or you will have a terrible trip."

She chastised herself. "That is not what this vacation is about. Get a grip, girl."

Despite her anxiety, the mind ran its course amuck with elements of water. Her dream of bubbles, white foam and waves crashing into rocky ledges made for a fitful night.

In the morning, the sailboat left the safety of the Bayfield Shores Marina. Emily sat in the front seat watching the spray on the side of the boat as the engine purred. She took a muscle relaxant pill and felt better.

The others stayed with the cruise. Emily would do the same. It was one of those times when she should have listened to her gut. There was danger coming and she would be smack dab in the middle.

She glanced toward the Bayfield Shores launch. A sailboat was waiting. The outside of the boat looked battered and the sails torn in places. The sailboat strapped tight was lifted out of the water. As the battered boat lifted, a hole shown in its side. Emily gasped. She looked at her ship's captain. He was smiling.

Now Emily became afraid.

4 Day One

The sailboat engine was stopped, and they were drifting on crystal clear water. Some small islands dotted the distance.

"The Apostle Islands were interesting. I remember Otter Island and Cat Island. The trees are brilliant green, and the water is deep blue. In the fall there are probably lots of colors."

Emily couldn't see the marina which was a few miles away.

The captain took over the main deck. He explained they would practice sailing around the grouping of islands for the day and moor briefly at a dock on one of the larger islands.

"Tonight will be our bonfire party. People usually like a large fire. Some think a fire is romantic. Just don't get too close. We've had a few people's shorts catch on fire. Ruins the evening every time."

He raised the fire extinguisher in the air, held the object high like a warrior entering battle, and secured the item in the holder.

"We can put out little fires with the gadget on the wall. The coast guard fireboat is for the big stuff. Let's try not calling their phone number. The fine is a killer."

Everyone on the boat cheered and laughed.

The captain partnered the people into groups of two. They were going sailing. Each person was given stations and tasks. The first group made sure the lines and anchors were secured, and all safety equipment was in place. The second team made sure the jib or front sail unfurled properly. The boat lightly tilted and moved.

Holding onto the wheel, the captain pointed the instrument heading on the display screen. He positioned one of the men in front of the wheel while he grabbed onto the railing that surrounded the large steering device. The others helped with the crank to raise the mainsail.

He pointed at the sails.

"Watch my actions."

The captain watched the sails fill, looked at the wind direction indicator on the top of the mast, and readjusted their heading. He told them how to tighten the mainsail to make the luffing quit. They couldn't sit down until the sails were perfectly trimmed.

The crew finally scrambled back to sit down and enjoy the ride. Everyone was exuberant to be in the sunshine and outdoor air. The sleek boat slipped silently through

34

the water, making the larger landmass disappear.

Quickly they reached their first heading and would need to tack or turn the boat. He demonstrated. He talked about the difference between tacking and jibing.

The captain explained wind to his crew and the importance of sailing safely. He showed them how to slow their speed and they watched as the boat's sails luffed. The boom slowly moved around, the sails refilled, and the boat moved in a new direction.

They sailed in crisscross fashion on their plotted course around the islands, taking turns steering, and manipulating the sails.

The captain used the computer to help reef and lower the mainsail and each person was given the chance to sail with only the jib. The crew learned to manually crank the jib sail in and out. The sails were adjusted a third so they could understand the importance of a full sail versus a lowered sail.

They learned the color of each rope line. The white was for the mainsail, sheets, and halyard lines, blue for the jib, red for the spinnaker, green for the guys, and black for the vangs and travelers. He talked about the docking lines which were made to stretch while the anchor line was made to sink.

He talked about storms and weather advisories. The importance of knowing how much sail was enough in a storm was discussed. They talked about the wind and direction of the wind.

"Better to spill the wind from your sails if you get in trouble. A storm can produce crosswinds, so you don't know which direction to take. Always reef early than be the boat that makes the news. Waiting until your boat heels over beyond normal is never a smart move."

Seth asked, "What is the purpose of reefing?"

"Reefing is lowering your sails. There will be less wind in a flat sail. You'll know you've waited too long to reef when she takes on water and your body registers cold shock."

The crew agreed and said, "Absolutely, *trim early*."

They felt the water before they boarded. Swimming in this cold water was only enjoyable for the first fifteen minutes.

The mention of storms brought up tons of questions from the crew. Emily listened intently, storing the words in her memory. Duane sat down next to her.

"Having a good time?"

"Yes, I find the captain's answers interesting. You did correct him on a few points."

"I find it hard to escape from the classroom. I've been told that I correct my students too much. Like my students, the captain was almost resentful."

Emily previously noticed the cranky look on the captain's face.

"Perhaps you need to be careful in speaking. A boat only has one master."

"Amen to that. My glib words might have come across as a know-it-all?"

Emily smiled, "Hmmm. I'll be glad when we dock. I need to feel land and sand between my toes."

Duane's hand gently touched hers. Emily frowned.

The captain called Emily's team to work the anchor. They were going to release the anchor from the front of the boat rather than use the computer to electronically lower the device. After lowering and raising the anchor by each team, they lowered their sails, turned the engine on, and docked the boat. The crew took turns with the engine and docking. The next day they would learn to sail up to and away from a dock.

The captain told them they would anchor a distance from shore for the evening and ferry the crew with the dinghy to the island. He told them for insurance purposes, they weren't rafting with the other boats on the dock.

"We can't have unknown people skipping across tied-together boats to walk on our deck. There's also too much valuable food and gear that goes missing when strangers come aboard. Usually, the steaks and hamburgers disappear first. The turkey legs are the last to go from the freezer. I guess turkey legs take too long to cook over a campfire."

Duane hopped around the boat as a stiff turkey with a wooden leg. Everyone cheered.

The captain was enjoying his tale of woe.

"If it's raining, the raingear mysteriously vanishes. Our company decided to put our logo on items. We stopped doing the logo because the items were too popular. Yellow life preservers with a logo were a real problem."

The captain handed each one of his crew a patch logo.

"If you are brave enough to stick them to your raingear, be forewarned of the danger. I'll stay with the boat as security for our first campfire. Duane will ferry everyone to shore. That is if his turkey legs are working properly."

Duane flapped his arms in assent. The men helped him with lowering their dinghy.

Tonight was going to be party time. The coolers of food and drinks were brought out with mats to sit in the sand. Everyone talked about the day and how they felt sailing. They were disappointed there was no cell phone reception on the tiny island.

Several other boats tied to the dock and the congregation of people onshore increased. Emily avoided Duane. She wasn't in the mood to connect with him.

She disappeared into one of the other boats with a woman who could get her internet access. Emily spent the next hour searching for information about her group's captain. After an hour, she gave up and rejoined the throng.

Duane saw her and approached.

"Hi, Duane, it's getting late. We crewed a busy one today. My brain is full of facts, and I need to rest. Can you return me to our boat?"

"Sure, no problem. Let me grab some of our equipment. No need to waste an empty dinghy."

After she disembarked, Emily waved, "See you in the morning."

Going to her bunk, she stowed her phone. Then she dug the object out and deleted the screens of her previous views. She opened her notepad and typed a few lines. The notepad was her journal about each day. Satisfied with the brief description, she opened the tiny window near the head of her bunk and looked at the dark water below.

"I should have gone swimming when we first arrived at the dock. I didn't want anyone to see me in my stretch one-piece swimsuit. Unfortunately, the color is black. I've been told black gives me a great wow-factor against my tanned skin. My teammates have only seen me in bulky gray exercise clothes."

Emily shifted on her bunk bed.

"The Erickson's might let me borrow their snorkel suit? The water in the morning will be cold. My turn to shower is in two more days. Maybe I can switch with someone or brave the cold in my swimsuit tomorrow."

A seagull dropped onto the small glass and looked at Emily in the slit. The wind picked up a little and fluffed the bird. She talked to the seagull.

"Are you afraid of cats? There probably aren't many cats on a sailboat. They don't like water."

The bird listened and when she stopped talking, the seagull looked in the window. Emily was gently snoring and fast asleep. The seagull flew away.

5 Duane's Mishap

The teammates awoke to gray skies and a fine mist began settling over the small islands which made the upper deck slippery. A canopy of the black canvas was snapped to the back deck so they could stay dry during breakfast. Jackets were put on for warmth.

The other boats left the dock earlier. Their boat was the only one in the vicinity. The sailboat was motored over to the largest dock and their lines were secured.

The captain proceeded to hand the bags of yellow polyester rain gear to his teams.

"Half of you aren't properly dressed. We always include raincoats for everyone. You may take them home with or without our logo. Foul weather is a given on the Great Lakes. Rain, sleet, and snow are common. I've been on the water when she decides to dump sheets of the fluffy white stuff."

A large pot of dehydrated eggs and instant mashed potatoes were placed on the galley stove. Cold slices of ham were wrapped in foil and put in the oven. The men cooked the breakfast, filled their own plates, and left the galley to the others.

The coffee was ready, and the fresh fruit was waiting. Paper plates were passed around and the rest helped themselves to the food. They all ate in silence. The weather dampened their spirits.

The captain was the only one in a good mood.

"Why don't we stay inside the boat this morning until the weather clears. We can talk about nautical terms and meanings, learn to read waterway signs, and develop our knot skills," said the captain.

Nick and Nancy were the first to agree. The two young lovers weren't fond of the rain. Seth and Dell nodded. The Erickson people didn't mind. Duane looked bored and mentioned that he was going to explore the island because he already knew this morning's subjects. Emily nodded her head.

The captain assured his crew the light mist would disappear. They listened to the captain's lecture and he gave them some paper tests to complete.

While they took the exam, the captain decided to go for a walk. In an hour, the students were finished and put their papers in a pile.

It was lunchtime. Emily brought out the bags of salad and dressing. Lucy and Mic helped make sandwiches. The students ate their lunch and wrapped some sandwiches for the captain and Duane.

Nick, Nancy, Seth, and Dell decided to search for Duane and the captain. The sky showed wisps of blue. In fifteen minutes, the captain returned to the boat and ate his lunch. Another hour passed. He grew angry that Duane hadn't yet returned, and the others went looking for him.

"Blast, we're going to miss docking while under sail if they don't hurry back."

Emily saw the direction the four people went.

"I can run the length of the beach to see if I can catch up with them."

"No, there's too many people gone; we'll wait," said the captain.

In an hour Nancy and Dell returned. They were out of breath.

Nancy tried to speak, and Dell blurted out, "We found Duane. He must have fallen and has a head cut. The men are helping him back to the boat."

"Good Lord, I better get my first aid kit. You ladies help the men as best you can. Bring Duane down to the galley where we can check his wound. He may need sutures. Emily, get some clean towels."

The captain and Emily went to retrieve their supplies. There was shuffling on the upper deck and the men brought Duane down the stairs. They sat him down in a chair and brought him a bottle of water.

The captain appeared and looked at the gash.

"Nasty cut to the head. At least the bleeding has stopped."

He looked Duane in the eyes.

"Can you talk?"

Duane blinked. "I need some aspirin. My head hurts. I can't remember a thing. I was walking and fell."

"No aspirin until we clean your wound and put some tape on your left skull. The tape should hold nicely but you will have a small scar."

After the captain was done, they wrapped Duane's head in gauze. He looked like a zombie. His eye was showing a dark bruise.

The captain went to his personal cabinet and found some medicine to reduce swelling.

"Take these pills. They will work better than aspirin."

Duane gulped the pills down.

"We can go back to shore and call for an ambulance to get you to a doctor or we can continue with our class."

The rest of the crew looked surprised by Duane's response.

"I'll stay. This afternoon's class will be skipped by me. I don't want the others to miss out on their trip lessons because of my stumble. Emily and I can stay on the dock to help with the ropes. First, I need to use the head or restroom."

There was the noise of dissent from the others about continuing class. The captain held up his hands.

"All right. Our guest has spoken. We'll do a shortened class, one attempt per team regarding docking a boat. I'll be Emily's partner in the last group. Then we stay here for the night. There is frozen lasagna we can microwave using the generator power," said the captain.

Emily frowned.

"Do we really think Duane tripped? Maybe there's someone else on the island."

"I saw no one nor any other boats."

The captain looked at the others. They shook their heads. They saw no one.

"We can always go back to Bayfield Shores Marina tomorrow morning if Duane gets worse."

Emily looked scared. Duane took her hand.

"I'll be okay, Emily. I'm made of tough stuff."

Duane leaned over and whispered in her ear, "No one is going to scare me off, especially the captain."

Emily's eyes grew wide.

"Let's get started. The daylight will be gone soon enough," said Duane

The others laughed, stood up, and patted Duane on the shoulder. They liked his attitude.

The rest of the day was spent docking under sail. Supper was filling and noisy. Emily let the others clean the kitchen. She and Duane went to the top of the boat to look at the stars.

"How's your head?"

"I feel fine and then I feel off."

"Should we take you to the marina tonight? Maybe x-rays or something would be a good idea."

"No, let's wait. I still wonder how I could have fallen. I don't ever fall, especially on clean sand. There were no rocks in front of me."

"You remember clean sand. How odd there were no rocks? If there were no rocks, where did you get the head gash?"

"A seagull squawked as if there was someone behind me. As I turned, there was blinding pain and whiteness."

Emily's eyes darkened.

"Are you saying we are unsafe here?"

"I'm not sure what I'm saying. Maybe I'm creating monsters where there are none. I don't know. Maybe I'm sick. Either case, just watch yourself, Emily."

"I will."

Duane took her hand and squeezed tight. She squeezed back. They were friends on a sailboat in a space in time. There was trust currently between them. Emily would recall their conversation.

Little did anyone realize; Duane would become ill before the trip's end. His illness would have nothing to do with the blow to his head. Emily was correct about the danger ahead.

6 Scuba Accident

Duane's head was unwrapped the next morning. His left eye swelling went down. The wound looked better.

"Well folks, it looks like wonder boy is better. How do you feel?" said the captain.

Duane asked for a mirror. He looked at his wound.

"Handsomer than ever. Virile strength shows in this manly smile."

"Give me that mirror. You are being absurd. We stop the feel-good drugs. You are too ebullient for my taste."

"Thank you, captain, for your stash."

Emily rolled her eyes.

The captain took over, directing the others toward their tasks so they could learn to sail the rest of their day. They would stop at a windier place, the last one in the chain called Outer Island.

"We will sail real waves. This will prepare you for our journey. If some of you decide to get off the sailboat, you will need to let me know. Seasickness can happen."

The brochure information included their route. The boat would travel the rocky shores to their next stop.

The boat would stay in the smaller marina for a day while the Erickson's snorkeled and the boat travelers did their sightseeing in the small town. The sightseers were given the address of a fish market to bring home supper. The selection of fish and salad was left to the boat travelers.

The two single women started making a list of fish and walked to the market. Duane stayed around the marina with Emily selecting fresh vegetables from the tents of the farmer market people. The other two single men went to a local bar.

"This romaine lettuce looks good," mentioned Duane.

Emily looked at the long stalks. "I think the Boston lettuce is fresher and makes little cups. We can chop tomato, cucumber, scallions, and cooked corn for a slaw to put inside the leaves. Sprinkle a little lime rind on top and we would have a perfect summer salad with fish."

"My mom made her own tartar sauce. It's too bad we can't buy mayonnaise here."

Emily looked in the pantry. There weren't any jars of the white stuff.

"I bet the cook makes his own mayonnaise. I don't see a recipe in this book. He may know the recipe by heart. Why don't we ask the local market people? They can point us into a direction or know a delivery person who will bring a few jars to the boat."

"Sweet relish, too. We need a jar of the pickles, dill seed, and horseradish."

"Not a fan of the horseradish," said Emily.

"There might be fresh. We need to use sparingly because the root is strong."

"Oh, we have a chef in the house?"

"My second hobby is taking culinary classes. I can whip up really good homemade pasta if the boat has Seminole flour."

Emily opened the cupboard and waved the bag.

The two of them searched for the pasta maker.

"Electric pasta maker and two hand cranks. This is a well-prepared galley."

The two went ashore. Emily left Duane to purchase lettuce, tomatoes, cucumber, and corn. She used the marina telephone to order the jarred mayo stuff and spice from a local grocery store. They delivered to the marina all the time.

Duane met her at the dock, waived the horseradish root, and she helped him carry the vegetables onto the boat. When they went down below to the galley, there was no one around.

"Wow, I wouldn't have thought the captain would leave this valuable boat untended."

50

Duane knocked on the captain's bedroom door and tried to open the door.

"His stuff is locked. The captain assumed we took our valuables with us or figured the insurance would cover our loss. How convenient? Or else he's been here many times before and knows where the security cameras are positioned."

"Maybe something happened."

Duane rubbed his sore eye.

"Let's make our salad and then we can relax."

The two quickly cooked and mixed the other ingredients together. The lettuce was washed and cleaned and put in plastic bags. They refrigerated their veggies. Duane was looking for the pasta recipe. Emily sat down on the upper deck.

The girls, Nancy and Dell, returned with their fish and deposited the food in the refrigerator. They brought their refreshments topside and waited with Emily. Eventually, Nick and Seth returned from the bar.

"Best pints of brown ale we ever drank," slurred Nick.

Seth held up one finger to let them know he was fine. He knew better to save his money for more important things. He bent over and kissed Dell who smiled.

Duane appeared and whispered to Emily, "Found a cookbook recipe for pasta and a great tomato sauce using canned tomato juice. There's parmesan Reggiano cheese in the freezer.

"Good."

A man in official garb hurried toward their sailboat with the captain. All the members on the sailboat stood up.

The captain was breathing heavily and let the young coast guard man talk.

The crew was thinking there might have been a fire in the marina. They looked at each other. No one called the coast guard.

"The Erickson's have been involved in an accident. Mr. Erickson's oxygen tank, which is Mic, ran out of oxygen somehow. The gauge appeared off or registered wrong. Fortunately, his wife was able to bring him to the surface and he is in the hospital recovering. We have submitted their gear to the police. The wife, Lucy, has decided to terminate their sailing trip. They will not be returning. Your captain asked that I come here to explain the problem with the circumstances his guests encountered while scuba diving."

Having done his duty, the officer left. Their captain remained standing as the others sat down.

"At least the man didn't drown. We should all be glad his wife was smart and level-headed in an emergency," said the captain.

Duane looked at his teammates who were locked in worried facial positions.

"I've used tanks before. A person must be careful and recheck everything before going under the water. They might not have been so thorough being on vacation and all."

"Aye, that was my thinking."

The captain rubbed his hands together to dispel the heavy atmosphere.

"The marina has an area for the boaters to barbeque and tables to sit. We might want to get started on our supper. Tomorrow we leave at eight o'clock."

The captain disappeared below to his quarters. The others dispersed to handle their part of the meal. They knew the drill and where the charcoal, coolers, etc. were kept. In an hour, fresh fish with homemade tartar sauce, lettuce cup salads, and French toasted garlic bread were ready to eat.

The teammates talked quietly among themselves. The captain made himself a plate and went back to his boat. He knew the crew would need to make their decisions regarding the continuance of their journey. He hoped they would stay. Filing the police report and a report to the boat owner for a refund was his reason for returning to the boat. He would request a full refund for the Erickson's.

The six players huddled around the fire. All the food was gone.

"Do we stay, or do we go?" asked Duane.

Emily was undecided. The two accidents creeped her out. The four single people argued. The men wanted to stay, and the girls wanted to leave.

Duane stood up. "Look, I don't blame you for wanting to go. I'm sticking the cruise out. This trip is important to me. I need to feel the wind and freedom from the boring everyday world. For the first time in my life, I feel strong. I can't let someone else's poor behavior change my forward motion."

Emily understood the need for the moving forward motion. "I'm in."

Nick spoke, "I have to finish the sailing classes and receive my certification." He looked at Nancy. The three young people agreed to stay. They cleaned their area and took the items back to the boat. Duane stored the coolers away.

The crew turned in for the evening. Emily noticed the captain's light was still on when she went to her bunk. She felt sorry for the man. He appeared visibly upset by the Erickson's misfortune. She wondered if his job would be in jeopardy for guests leaving, or if there was some other reason.

7 Captain's Record

The sailing couldn't have been more perfect. The travelers turned the boat into the wind. The captain showed them the danger of too much sail. He lowered sails for safety.

"I'll demonstrate a bad move and a correct move."

He turned to a lee helm.

"Instead of the boat turning in a circle into the wind, the boat turns away from the wind putting stress on the rudder and pulling the boat in the opposite direction on the sails."

He told them this was a bad move. The person at the helm and the boat were basically out of control.

"Putting the boat and passengers in danger of an overboard situation is never a good idea."

The captain showed them how to quickly get the helm back in control. He did a correct turn.

The crew members began to relax with their added knowledge.

They moored for the evening in another cove. This time the cliffs were higher. The trees looked etched against the sky. The rocks seemed to hold the sun's glow.

Emily thought of molten lava.

Tonight, was salad night with rotisserie chicken which was thawed from the freezer. Frozen yogurt was for desert with cookies and coffee.

Duane followed Emily to the front of the boat. They liked to sit on the bow with their feet dangling over the sides.

"The captain showed me his quarters this afternoon when I went looking for my headache medicine. His room is nicer than ours and very nautical. There were two twin beds, a great computer system, and a wonderful collection of photographs."

He paused.

Emily glanced his way. The man was not going to divulge what was in the photographs.

"Pictures of his family and this boat is what I imagine would be on our captain's walls."

"There was a picture of his son, Shane when he was younger. A few of his wife, but mostly racing boats in Australia with our missing cook. I'm talking professional, top-notch, turn the corner like a dolphin racing. The captain has the pictures of his metals with the famous racer, Don DiMarco. I can't believe the captain raced on DiMarco's boat.

If only my dream would come true? I would have killed to be on the boat in the picture, not to mention at the race. Nowadays the boats are sleeker, longer, and carry more sails. Still, the captain has me beat."

Emily frowned, "Great, our leader's as fast as a dolphin and as good as the DiMarco racing guy. That's excellent to know. We don't need to worry about our captain's skills. Wait a minute. There are no dolphins here. You must mean a sturgeon. I wonder why he has only shown you his room. None of us were allowed."

"Hey, don't get your short sail twisted. He showed me his room because it's logical. We are two of a kind. The love of sailing puts us in a special class, that and our intelligence. I've raced, but never anything like the captain. This kind of racing takes guts, stamina, and strength. Let's not mention the entire basket of knowledge and precision thinking required to stay ahead in a publicized, highly stressful race. The tension and excitement in a race of that caliber. Oh, my gosh, I'm talking awesome. I believe he felt I would understand his passion more than the rest of the crew. Maybe he also is guarded about letting the crew know his abilities. I'm glad the captain and I talked today. I wanted to share my information with you. He's the best. We can trust and count on him. I believe the captain could sail this boat blindfolded in a hurricane."

"Wow, hurricane, really?"

"Ha, I got you there. I meant gale, not a hurricane. Wow is too tame. Fantastic is a better word."

"Still, he should have shared some of his stories with us. We would have enjoyed the experience."

Duane knew she missed the blindfolded comment. Their captain had an instinct about water and weather pressure systems. He used all the senses when sailing. He saw the captain look at the computer and the wind meter. Then he wet his index finger and closed his eyes. The man could feel the wind. Duane tried it one day and gave up. There would be no correcting the captain from now on. The man walked on water as far as Duane was concerned. Hero came to mind.

"No, when you have all the right stuff in your arsenal, there's no need to brag. Speaking of the arsenal, he owns some antique pistols and a sword from a king. The sword is very old and probably worth more than the pistols."

"I would never have guessed. Guns, swords, and racing boats are a man's best assets."

Duane looked at her.

"Why are you so cranky?"

"I'm not cranky. I thought he might have hit you on the head.

"No, way!"

Emily sighed. She wasted her time trying to find information regarding their captain.

"I bet he knows how to shoot the guns."

"Most men do. You never know when weapons might come in handy. Now me, I carry a small pistol."

"You have a gun on this boat? I wouldn't have figured to bring a weapon. Nor did I think you were a gun person."

"See, looks can be deceiving. My gun is more a good luck charm and probably wouldn't stop a person in their tracks."

Emily looked at the dinghy fastened to the upper deck. She suddenly worried about a bullet hitting the rubber. She shook herself. She remembered the anxiety pills skipped for the day. Maybe she shouldn't have.

Duane shifted to look at Emily.

"He asked if I knew who attacked me."

"What did you say?"

Duane rubbed his head.

"I told him I didn't know. There might have been someone, but maybe there wasn't. He told me to be careful and to lock my meds. I'm to let him know if I see anything strange or peculiar. He emphasized the word peculiar. The captain is worried we might have someone on board who might want to mess with us. He also thought the equipment failure on the scuba gear a little too odd and convenient for the removal of two people from our numbers."

"Oh, my. You, too, were chatty. Now I am scared. The captain thinks we have someone unstable on board. Why would anyone want to harm us?"

Duane nodded.

"There are freaks everywhere. Let's hope we don't have a person go off the deep end or a nut job in our midst."

The two friendly crew members were quiet. The others were on the bridge out of hearing drinking more than coffee. Emily looked worried again.

The water glimmered in the night and quietly lapped against their sailboat. Five minutes passed. Duane debated about telling her the last part of the captain's conversation. The captain warned Duane about the affairs of the heart. The captain was experienced in the romance category and knew the male moves. Duane thought he was careful. The captain saw right through him.

"He also told me to back off."

"Back off from what?" said Emily.

"He reminded me that I am a married man and you are a very pretty single woman more intelligent than most. He said the way you rolled your brown eyes gave you away. I agreed with him."

Emily laughed. Her laughter echoed in the cove.

"Seriously, we are friends only. I'm not going down any other road with you. It's nice to have a friend when a person is on an adventure. The days have passed quickly."

Duane pondered her message. The woman couldn't be much clearer. He decided to go along with her comments. His feelings were mixed. This trip was important to him. He must remain focused. There was an important decision he needed to make in the future. He took her hand and lightly kissed her fingers.

"The days have flown. We're friends to the end. You can't control who loves you. I'm going to get some sleep. The captain told me the weather may be turning. We'll be awakened earlier than usual to get a head start from the rain that is approaching. Enjoy the red sky this evening. We might not see the hue for some time."

Emily sat holding her knees to her chest. Finally, she turned in for the evening.

The rest of the crew stayed topside until the early hours.

She awakened during the night and thought she heard someone arguing. Then there was quiet. She went back to sleep. Emily wanted to be bright-eyed and ready to tackle the next day.

8 Rain and Nancy's Exit

The sailboat caught the wind. The sails billowed to their maximum as an onslaught of air caught them. The men were sailing, and the women quickly made eggs and sausage rollups. They wrapped them in parchment paper and brought them topside with thermos cups brimming with hot coffee.

Emily went below to wash the pans and utensils. She grabbed her windbreaker and hat before going back to the upper deck.

The seagulls were eating their breakfast and eventually, disappeared. They flew toward the tall trees to hide.

The crew saw the sheets of rain ahead of them. There was time for them to get ready. Unlike the birds, there was no cover for them.

The crew grabbed the raincoats. The captain let Duane steer the boat while he went below to get his boots and gear. The mainsail was lowered, and the front sail totally furled tight around its pole. The items that were on the top side of the boat were secured. They would have to go slower through the rainstorm.

"Captain, how far are we to our next marina?"

The captain looked at the computer and adjusted the wheel to a new heading.

"We're going to try to maneuver around the first bout of rain. We'll head into that area to the left and try to catch some speed by using the wind and waves to our advantage. If we can't we'll try something else. From the looks of things on the computer, we have spots and a large mass. We want to avoid the center of the mass."

Duane looked at the computer.

"There will be shifts in the wind between everything. Everyone needs to hold on. We don't have the time to mess with a man overboard. Do whatever the captain tells you."

The crew looked where the captain pointed. The area was in deeper water. The boat was headed further into the lake.

Emily swallowed and looked at Duane. He spoke.

"I see the break between the spot. Very good, captain. If anyone is scared, they can go below or wear their harness brace."

Emily sat crouched and held onto the railing near the hatch. The two women went below. They would let the men tough things out. Emily watched as Duane brought the harness brace lines closer in case they were needed. Running the waves meant water cascading over the boat. At the last minute,

Emily, too, went down below to pray and go to the bathroom.

The three women sat below and could feel the boat rise, race, and fall. The rainwater covered the windows. Emily peeked outside the hatch window and saw the two men wearing their harness braces over the yellow raincoats. The captain gave them waterproof pants to slip over their jeans. The captain was dressed in a more expensive rain outfit. He and Duane were holding tight to the steering wheel with their all-weather gloves.

The rain slowly abated, and the wind kept driving the sailboat, making her lean as she was tossed about. After two hours, the boat appeared to be running in calmer waters.

She looked out the hatch window and the men were removing their braces and tethers. Duane removed his hat and checked the wind direction on the sails. The captain was wiping the computer screen.

"Stress and cold make people hungry."

Emily jumped up and busied herself with activity. She found the carrots, celery, apples, and cheese. Putting pieces in large cups, the women brought them with bottled water to the male crew members. The captain excused himself and went below as did Duane.

LINDA MCKOWN

Duane mouthed the words to Emily, "Thank you. I'm really beat."

Nick and Seth were at the wheel arguing about the heading and setting. It seemed that the two men argued a lot lately. Nancy rolled her eyes, threw up her hands, and went below. Nick saw her and pounded his fist on the wheel. Seth shoved the man aside and took over.

Emily was surprised by the anger in the first man's eyes. Nick stormed below almost knocking Duane back inside the galley. The captain came back to the upper deck and talked with Seth.

Dell sat next to Emily and whispered, "I think Nancy is going to leave the boat when we dock at the marina. I heard her talking to someone and a motorcycle was mentioned. Nick won't be happy. He's a real control-freak."

"Oh, god, you mentioned the word freak. Is Nick dangerous?"

Dell looked at Emily, "How would I know? We only met them at a party a couple of times. They suggested we do this sailboat cruise. Seth thought we should go play with them. You know, expand our horizons, and make new friends. Nick is handsome and she was witty. I said, why not? But, trust me, we haven't enjoyed their company. All they do is argue. I think the fire has gone out if you know what I mean? I don't think we'll be seeing Nancy or Nick after this trip."

The rest of the journey that day was calmer. Anyway, the water was better for sailing. The explosion of two unhappy crew members would surface fifteen minutes after they reached the shore.

The captain already knew about Nancy's departure and made a point of showing Nick the local marina store for purchasing fishing lures while Nancy hopped on her friend's bike and took off. Nick went running after the bike and threw his bag of groceries at them.

Duane and the captain helped Nick pick up the items which were needed for their sausage and gravy supper. The English muffins had a little bit of sand in them. No one seemed to mind. The fishing lures were placed on a shelf.

Nick kept using his cell phone to call Nancy while the others cooked. His efforts were to no avail. The woman was gone for good. No amount of love or money could fix the two of them. This might be where someone usually flips out. The heart can only take so much before it breaks apart. Nick didn't flip out at all. He became deadly quiet. Finally, he put his cell phone away.

Seth and Dell tried to get Nick to talk and was ignored. There was another storm brewing and it wasn't on the lake. They didn't know Nick was harboring a grudge against their captain and Duane. But first, there was Seth to torture.

The crew kept their distance busying themselves by rechecking their supplies. They purchased a few more items and bottled water before the crew left the marina.

Their next journey would be four days of sailing before they saw another marina and safety.

The captain let the others sail the boat after discussing their location and how he wanted sails trimmed. He charted their turn points into the computer to make things easier. The captain planned an education class on coastal navigation but thought better of it. The mood on the boat wasn't conducive to learning. People's attention spans were short at best.

The skies were gray and gloomy which matched one person's dark mood. Then the man brightened and started bantering back and forth with Dell about her career choice and college sorority. This didn't sit too well with Seth. A rift would develop, and a rivalry would push Dell away from Seth.

Emily decided Nick might be the one to watch. His moves were cold and calculated. Yet, she felt drawn to him. He exuded arrogance and a devil-may-care attitude. She kept her thoughts to herself. Her anxiety medicine was forgotten. She wanted to be wide awake and fully functional. Something was clicking inside Nick's brain. The show was just beginning.

9 Nick in a Mood

The crew sailed the first day with no problems. They moored for the evening close to a visitor park. There was a small clearing where other small boats lined the shore.

A few sailboats were attached to a large round red fender anchored to the bottom. A small sailboat could grab the short line and clip onto the fender. They were provided by the park service. Their boat stayed away from the buoys marking the shallow area. They dropped their anchor.

Dell, Seth, Nick, Emily, and Duane went ashore with a small cooler filled with beef shish kabobs, chips, and liquid refreshments. The captain would only allow one drink per person. That way he would be assured the dinghy would return to the sailboat before midnight. They were instructed by the captain to not stay on the shore. His company couldn't be responsible for them.

The people onshore seemed friendly enough. They cooked their food and ate hungrily until they were full. Emily looked at her watch and the time was ten in the evening.

"We should return to our cruise."

Dell confirmed that she was tired and needed some Aloe gel for her windblown face. Her face was red, and blisters were forming. Emily told her a bigger hat brim would help. She offered hers. Every one of the crew started packing to return to their boat except Nick.

Nick adamantly refused to get in the dinghy. He wanted to stay on land and party. Duane and Seth argued with him. Finally, Duane told Nick they would return for him at seven o'clock in the morning. If he wasn't there waiting on the shore, Duane would recommend to the captain that they leave Nick behind. Nick didn't seem to care one way or the other. His answer was he could find another boat to finish his cruise. Other people would be glad to take his money.

Duane and the others returned to their sailboat cruise and stored the dinghy.

"I'll go explain to the captain what has occurred. You might want to turn in for the evening."

Emily and the others said their goodnights.

The captain, of course, was livid.

"I have a good mind to move the boat right now and dump the nasty little deserter."

"The sky is dark, and the others have turned in for the evening. We should wait until daylight. Then you will have a good reason to leave Nick behind."

"Aye, you are right. I have run into this type of occurrence before. The cook and I have purchased a device for anyone trying to sneak on the ship after dark. Why don't I get the blasted thing out of the hold? You can help me run the power cord back to the generator."

Duane was curious about the device. They threw a net over the side of the boat to make it easy for someone to climb aboard. They strung the aluminum lights and horns with rope back and forth on the cleats.

"Are you sure this will work. These items are amazing. Your cook is brilliant."

The captain laughed. "The whole campground will be awakened for sure."

"What if our good sleepy crew already on the sailboat stumble out here tonight?"

The captain held up the wooden box. On the backside were the words, *Don't Enter, Dangerous Material per Captain.*

About five o'clock in the morning, the captain thought he heard a footstep outside his door. He opened his door and saw a frightened Emily.

"There's a box by the hatch."

"I know because Duane and I put it there in case Nick snuck aboard. We've set a trap."

"Oh, are we trying to catch Nick?"

73

Duane came out of his bunk, putting his shirt on.

"What's all the commotion?"

At that moment they heard a thud on the upper deck, the horns started blaring, and the bright revolving lights filled the sky. Emily, Duane, and the captain peered out to see Nick with a strange woman on the deck. The woman was screaming, and Nick was trying to keep her quiet.

They could hear the campers yelling from shore.

"I think I better pull the plug, or those boaters will get mutinous and make us walk the plank."

"We don't have a plank, sir," said Emily.

"Mutineers will make one with their long johns. They'll be red for sure."

Duane and the captain started laughing at Emily's horrified expression. She caught on quick.

"Aye, captain, the visuals of the underwear scared me the most."

Duane went back and disconnected the alarms while the captain went topside.

Emily went back to her bunk to get dressed and grabbed her shoes. Rather than go outside, she started the coffee. Duane went up the steps to give their captain reinforcement, not that he needed any. The boat was his to manage.

Nick had broken a major rule. The crew members were to follow orders onshore and offshore for the duration of the cruise.

The captain and Nick were discussing his options when Duane approached.

"This woman is not coming with us on the cruise. We haven't checked her background properly. The company is strict."

Nick became surly, "She's an okay person and I'll pay her way. You can call the owner for approval. His name is Shane."

Duane intervened.

"You heard the captain, Nick. He is in total charge of this ship while the boat is under sail, at anchor, or moored."

"No, he should allow Mara to be on this boat."

"You're not in charge, Nick, give up your argument."

The strange woman put her legs over the side. She had seen enough. She jumped down into the small motorboat next to Mike. She knew when she wasn't wanted on a rich person's property. Nick told her the sailboat was his own. He lied.

"Mara, come back, I'll buy you a sailboat."

Mara raised her hand in the air and gave Nick the finger. She told Mike to drive away from the sailboat. The motorboat sped toward shore.

The captain stared at Nick.

"Are you staying or leaving?"

Nick watched the motorboat reach the shore.

"She wasn't worth it anyway."

He went down below to get coffee and pieces of bacon that were frying.

Emily looked at Nick while she stirred the pancakes. Dell was setting out the orange juice. No one spoke.

Dell didn't chat anymore with Nick. His ability to select a woman at a moment's notice made her realize he was the fool. Dell took two bottles of juice and went to see if Seth was dressed.

The people in the cove quieted down after the captain picked up his bullhorn.

"Thank you, everyone, for your patience. We were testing a new alarm system. Somehow, the device went off earlier than planned. We might have bought a lemon."

The people on the shore grumbled about the lemon electronics they purchased last year and forgot about the sailboat.

"Well, Duane, we can start to box this stuff and eat our breakfast. Wasn't this a fun morning?"

Duane grinned. "Eventful and noisy. The only items missing were the fireworks."

"Blast, I'll put that on the list for next time."

The captain was whistling a familiar Yankee Dixie tune as he undid the horns.

10 Coastal Navigation

Duane commandeered the helm the next morning while the captain talked about coastal navigation.

Emily paid attention to the captain's remarks about keeping the boat at minimum twenty-five to thirty feet from shore and to never steer directly toward shore. Unless you wanted to hit the bottom of the earth with your keel and pay a hefty repair job, his recommendation should be followed. The repair bill was high due to the manual labor involved with fiberglass. The only time to head towards shore was when the boat was in the middle of the lake and a person could see tankers fifty feet off the bow.

"Rocks are the enemy to a keel and the bottom of a boat. We have almost thirty-two thousand square miles of water on Lake Superior and the lake is over a thousand feet in spots. However, the shores can be shallow. Trust me, I've come close to running the boat over the top beds of the hard rock. I know this area. The stone layers are filled with granitic or granite-like material containing lots of quartz. Quartz can cut glass and scrape a hull. There are iron ore and copper. Throw the limestone in the mix. Some of the rocks are a billion or more years old. There are other minerals. My favorite is agates."

He took a large red agate out of his pocket. The rock was larger than his fist.

"I found this one along the shore. She's a beauty. See the delicate lines."

The others handled the rock and returned the specimen to the captain. Dell asked the question all of them wanted to ask.

"Where else have you sailed, Captain?"

"We need to break for our lunch sandwiches. I see Nick is still asleep. This might be a good time to tell a story while we eat our sandwiches," said the captain.

The crew hurriedly made their sandwiches and iced tea. They carried their lunch plates topside. The captain ate half his sandwich and started talking.

"I once crewed with a racing team in Australia."

Dell asked him, "With whom?"

The captain looked flustered and Duane nodded.

"You probably don't know the man. He has passed away. His name was DiMarco."

Seth stopped eating his sandwich and ran down to the galley to get an ink pen. He came topside and handed his paper plate to the captain with the pen.

"Autograph, please."

The captain complied and started to hand the paper plate back to Seth, "You're not going to sell my signature?"

Seth replied, "Not on your life."

"Good. I can continue my story."

His assembled team nodded their heads.

"There is this one race. My cook was with me on the racing boat and DiMarco's team. We were in the lead and there was a point where we needed to turn around a buoy. Another boat cut in front of us. We were inches and we got caught in their dirty air. We were fine with that except a line broke on our forefront sail which slowed us considerably. Boats flew around us."

Duane tethered the helm. "What did you do?"

The captain took a drink of his water and a bite of his sandwich.

"My friend grabbed a line and crawled up the forefront cables and started feeding the new line. He was done attaching the new line and was on his way down when the wind switched just like that. We saw the forefront boats hesitate and yank down their forefront sail. We dropped our forefront sail lickety-split and hoisted our spinnaker. We caught the full force of the wind and instead of last, we came in third place. DiMarco was delighted to have placed and win a smaller trophy. He liked our skills. The next year, we were guaranteed a spot on his racing boat."

Duane said, "I have to get back to the helm so we can come about. Team, get to your stations."

The others complied and the captain finished his meal. When the boat was on the changed course, they all gathered around the captain.

"The next year was filled with racing. There was no other life. All we did was work. In the end, we won."

His audience was in awe. Duane knew which year. He saw the captain's framed pictures of the trophies. He tightened the sail a notch so they could get a little closer to their destination.

A sleepy Nick stumbled on the top deck and saw the captain with his crew members.

"What are you doing?"

The captain stood up with his empty plate and water bottle.

"We're taking a break from a coastal navigation class. We hope you will join us."

Nick quickly went below to grab his sandwich that Emily placed in the refrigerator with his name attached. He selected an apple juice and went back to his bunk with his lunch.

The captain went below for a few minutes to make sure Nick was contained. Then he went topside to relieve Duane. He didn't need to bother. Dell and Seth were handling the helm.

The captain sat down next to Emily as Duane went below to eat.

"Did you enjoy the coastal class?"

"Yes, Captain, I didn't know the shore could be so treacherous."

The captain knew Emily worried, but he thought it was important for her to understand the dangers.

"There have been many a small boat that has lost their ship and gear on these shores. They are usually the twenty-four-foot jobs with inexperienced captains. The water here changes each year depending on rain and the tide. No, I forget, the Great Lakes is non-tidal. However, the waves can create a wave that oscillates. They call this wave a seiche. In other words, the water level can fluctuate much like a tide. The smaller boats are deceived. They believe they are in deep water. The smaller boats hug the shore unknowing about this wave structure. We are fortunate that our length gives us more strength and aerodynamics. Therefore, we use our length to stay away, and have no need to travel close."

"Thank you for explaining. I will remember to avoid shoreline. I also loved your racing story."

The captain laughed.

"Good girl. My friend, the cook, is a monkey. He can climb anything. I would never have done what he did that day. I know my limitations."

Emily's eyes twinkled. The captain was satisfied.

"I think I'll take a short nap. The boat is in good hands. If I don't come topside in an hour, have Duane wake me.

"Will do."

Emily watched the captain go through the hatch and disappear. Duane came through the doorway with two cups of hot chocolate.

"Hey, beautiful, how about some sweet drink just for the heck of it. Today was great."

Emily smiled. The day was a good one. She took the chocolate. The sailboat was becoming more comfortable. She didn't think about her old job or her lost life. She wondered if there was a future waiting for her that was meant to be. Her skin was certainly getting tanned and she could feel muscles in her arms and legs.

"I stirred the pasta batter. The dough is resting in small mounds. The sauce is on the stove simmering."

Duane disappeared to make noodles.

"I hope there's only good in store for my future. Who knows, there might be someone special around the corner."

Nick relieved Seth at the helm.

Emily felt Duane was on her list in the special category. She went below to help make the noodles. Dell and Seth were cranking another batch. Their teamwork showed Emily they were experienced at pasta making. Noodles hung on the wooden rods.

Duane handed Emily the crank pasta maker. He wanted her to feel the elasticity of his dough. She expertly ran the dough through twice, changed the thickness, ran the dough again, changed the thickness, and gracefully handed him a long strip for cutting with the electric machine.

He pulled the noodle strips from the machine.

"Fantastic."

11 Spinnaker Lesson

Emily's turn at the helm was in the early morning. Nick was given the task of doing breakfast dishes. Duane was to scout the front of the sailboat for any wind.

"Turn the engine on, Emily. We are drifting too fast toward shore," said the captain.

Emily did as she was told and steered the boat gently away from shore until they were three hundred yards away from their original point.

"Okay, turn the engine off. This should be fine. The sails are luffing. You need to set your course."

The captain turned off the computer. Emily looked at the device on the mast. She couldn't tell the wind. She started to turn the wheel and the captain's hand quickly stopped her.

"Wrong."

Emily turned the wheel in the other direction. The captain stopped her again. Frustrated, she licked her finger and held it up. Still, she had no understanding of the wind direction.

The captain handed her a device.

"This looks like a lighter?"

"A very special cigarette lighter that floats and has a small LED inside."

The captain lit the lighter and held the flame in front of her.

"Walk all the way around the flame and then tell me where the wind is coming from. Be careful. You don't want to grab your first thought. Study the flame."

Emily did as she was told.

"There is a slight wind behind us."

"Yes. What do we do when the wind is blowing up our backside? I'm being polite because there are ladies in my presence. We could turn around, but we would be going the wrong way."

Seth and Dell looked at each other. They knew the answer. Emily knew the answer.

"We need to put up the Spinnaker."

The captain nodded.

"I'll go below to check the weather report. We don't want the gigantic sail if the wind is going to rip her off in an hour. You keep steering the course a few degrees away from the coast. I'll get Nick to help Duane with the spinnaker. Seth, you get the bag from storage. We bring the spinnaker outside through the front escape hatch."

Emily jumped up in delight. The spinnakers always looked pretty. This one was red, black, and white. She would need to get a few pictures to send her parents.

Nick noticed her and yelled, "Wild Woman."

Dell went below to help Seth.

Duane said to Nick, "Give her up man. She's not in your class."

The men lowered the main and rolled the jib sail manually. Duane tied down the mainsail. The captain stuffed the huge spinnaker through the front hatch for Nick to start attaching. The captain handed him the spinnaker poles.

Once the spinnaker filled with air, the sailboat lifted, and they were moving across the water.

Nick and Duane stayed near the front of the boat in case they needed to release the poles quickly and haul in the spinnaker. The captain came back to make sure Emily kept the boat away from the shore. Seth and Dell sat near the helm to watch and learn.

"We have approximately an hour of pure pleasure. There's a large turn in the coastal land. That's where we need to take the spinnaker down. Anyway, I hope we make it that far before the weather descends."

Emily frowned.

She gripped the wheel. The captain sat down to enjoy the ride and kept silent. She trusted Duane would know what to do when the time was right.

After an hour, the captain went below to check the radio. He came quickly outside and went to the front of the sailboat. She could hear the men talking and pointing. Emily couldn't see the object ahead of them.

Duane and Nick immediately removed the spinnaker poles and the three men took down the spinnaker and began stuffing the fabric down the hatch. She wondered why they didn't try to fold the sail first. A folded sail was easier to store in the bag. Seth went below to pull the sail inside.

The captain hurried toward Emily and turned on the computer. He quickly took over the helm and raised their mainsail. Emily sat next to Dell. The women held on. A gust of wind rocked the boat and she saw Duane and Nick grab the metal railing. That's when Emily saw the huge tanker sitting directly in their path with anchors out.

Dell gasped.

When the two men jumped down the hatch and closed the window. The captain raised the main and let the computer unfurl the jib. He turned the wheel to catch the wind. Their sailboat was racing on the water to avoid a collision.

Emily could see the men on the freighter waving their hands and shouting. The three men came topside.

The sixty-five-foot sailboat looked small against the rusted hull. Obviously, the tanker developed engine problems and parked their ship in the most unsuspecting place.

Duane and Nick watched to see if the captain needed their help. The captain motioned them to sit on the high side of the boat. He was adjusting the sails to find the best aerodynamics of keel and sail to push them deeper into the lake. They ran into waves that tried to slow them down. Emily saw the tanker get closer. Her knuckles were now gripping the railing with raw fear.

"Man, this is going to be close. The captain must turn this direction, or we would have beached," said Duane.

"I wish you hadn't told us those facts. At least we would be closer to shore and could have swum to safety. Should I say my prayers?"

Nick's eyes were transfixed on the tanker. Emily saw an odd smile on his face. He looked stoked. It was almost as if he wished they would collide into an explosion of boom and busted sails.

The sailboat heeled more. The crew held on. The sleek white and black boat cleared the back of the ship by twenty feet. The captain again tacked and turned the sailboat."

"Geesh, everyone, move to the other side."

The crew did as they were told. The boat arched around and missed the back-anchor line by three feet. The crew saw the heavy chain as their captain tacked again. He spun the wheel as the main and front sail changed positions. The crew members held on. The boat was racing again. The sails were loosened, and the boat slowed.

Duane was the first to leave his seat and stand by the captain as they continued to maneuver the sailboat in the newly found wind. The tanker captain honked his horn to acknowledge their boat was clear. The sailboat honked their horn

"Fancy sailing captain."

"Don't thank me yet, Duane, we are a half-day away from our stop for the evening. With the storm I heard on the radio, we might get slowed down. I want you to keep this heading until you can't stand the waves, then turn inward."

"Are we in for trouble?"

"The anchored tanker was a minor intrusion. The storm looks nasty. My arthritis is talking to me very loudly not to mention, we're in a gale warning."

Duane took the wheel as the captain went below to recheck the radio messages regarding the weather.

"Shit, I hate gales. I'll need my sea-sick pills for sure."

12 Loose Cable

The sailboat caught the edge of the bed weather. They were lucky to encounter wind, waves, and some light rain. Their sailboat handled the situation with ease with an experienced captain at the helm. After three hours, they were out of the weather and searching for their next stop for the evening.

The captain knew the cliffs and saw a familiar landmark.

"The grouping of green pines is where we will anchor for the night. I'll try to find a spot where we have larger rocks. The little ones catch our anchor."

Emily looked at the shoreline. There appeared to be pine trees running along the top for the last three miles. She didn't see anything special about this area for the captain to choose it. He saw her confusion.

"One tree stands out at about nine o'clock."

"I see it."

The boat dropped anchor. They ate a frozen meal that evening of Cornish hen, mashed potatoes, and carrots. Emily turned in early. Nick followed her.

"Emily?"

"Yes, Nick, what do you want?"

"I just thought you were terrific today."

"Can the compliments, Nick, I'm not interested."

She slammed her bedroom door in his face.

"Predictable."

Nick went to his bunk and tried calling Nancy a few more times. There was no response. He threw his phone on the floor in disgust.

Duane stayed topside for another hour before turning in for the evening.

"Emily must be all right or she would have called out."

He saw the way Nick looked at her during supper. He would need to be on the vigil and protect her if he could. His headaches were starting again. The medicine wasn't helping.

Duane wondered if yoga exercises would work. He thought he'd ask Emily if she wanted to do some together the next day. Duane felt better and went to bed.

Dell and Seth stayed topside talking about the incident.

Usually, every morning the crew checked the equipment topside. The task was something the captain insisted upon unless they were in imminent danger and needed to get underway. Having traveled through a storm made the captain extra suspicious. The inspection was slower and more thorough than previously.

Nick saw the fray in the wire at the T-bar and pointed out the problem to Duane. Duane shouted at the captain. He used his binoculars to see the wire.

"Take a look. The storm did take its toll on our boat. I'll go get the replacement wire, some shackles, and pins. Duane, the tools are in the back deck holding bin. Have you ever done this type of repair before?"

Duane shook his head in the affirmative. He had done the same type of repair on smaller boats.

"The removal and replacement system are the same. Nick, you stay and give Duane a hand if he needs help. I'll help Emily get breakfast ready. Holler if Seth should be there."

After an hour, Duane came into the galley holding the frayed wire. The captain looked at the fray and threw the item in the trash.

"After breakfast, we'll check the sails for any worn spots. We should be all right. These sails are two years old and appeared fine the last time we checked. However, you never know what could blow into a sail in a powerful wind," said the captain.

When they inspected the mainsail, there was one frayed area. The captain checked the spot.

"We should be fine. I'll put a patch over the spot as a marker for the boat repair boys to sew a patch when we have completed our cruise."

They went over and used the computer to hoist the dinghy.

Nick commented, "The dinghy looks very sound and expensive."

"Yes, the small watercraft is one of the best on the market. The small compartments inside have all the safety equipment to survive a few days if our sailboat should fail. There's dehydrated food, water, and a special tent enclosure that snugs over the craft. The tent can be used as a sail with the ends of the two paddles."

Duane remembered a boat show he went to one time.

"I've seen this watercraft. It's very sophisticated and sturdy. The boat show kept a demo video running of the craft being set up for a lifesaving situation."

Nick seemed really interested in the video and wanted to know which boat show and the name of the company that made the craft."

Duane showed him the tag on the back with the company's name, the serial number of the craft, and the year she was made.

The captain beamed, "My son, Shane, buys only the best for this sailboat. Everything on this boat has a useful purpose. Let's check the lines."

The men each took one half of the boat to examine the heavy black nylon ropes. They showed average wear and tear. The captain was checking the computer. Emily appeared.

"The galley is all tucked and locked tight. We can start sailing whenever you are ready, Captain."

Nick and Duane went to the front of the boat to watch the anchor.

"Whoa, stop, we're caught in a rock," yelled Duane.

The captain brought the mainsail down and partially unfurled the jib. He started the engine, pulled forward, stopped, and put the boat in reverse. The anchor wouldn't release. He let Emily take the wheel.

"Aye, we can see her crystal clear with one tip in a crevasse. We need to turn the boat ninety degrees and try to rock her. If we can't get her loose, we'll have to leave the thing here to rust and rot with the rest of them."

"Wasn't this anchor an expensive one? Maybe I can swim down and try to dislodge the tip?" said Seth.

"No, I won't recommend doing that. We're in twenty feet of water. You could get stuck in the crevasse. It's cheaper to let the iron go."

Nick smirked, "I don't know. I'd bet on the anchor over him any day of the week."

Duane answered, "We should let the dim wit go down and see if he can remember starboard from the port."

Nick picked up a hand crank from the winch and the captain gave them both a look.

"I'll not have any fights on my boat."

Nick replaced the crank.

"He called me a name."

The captain looked at Nick contemplating his next move.

"I'll be turning to starboard to try to loosen the angle on the anchor. Try not getting knocked in the drink by the jib."

Nick looked panicky. He couldn't remember which way was starboard. Duane ignored his crewmate who never seemed to learn even though they were on the boat for two weeks.

Duane relented and decided to give Nick a hint. "Left is a four-letter word."

Nick still didn't understand.

Seth said, "Port is a four-letter word."

"Oh, right, the captain's turning the sailboat to the right."

"No, he's turning starboard."

The captain gave the signal and the two men grabbed onto the railing. The captain turned and went slowly. The line loosened.

The water clouded and cleared.

"I think the anchor is free from the ground captain. I'd still go slow and start the lifting mechanism."

The men could hear the chain lifting and disappear inside the casing. The anchor came out of the water and the men cheered. They made sure the anchor was secure and came to the back of their boat.

The sails were already raising, snaring wind, and pushing the boat over. The crew took their stations. The captain liked to sail the first hour or two.

"Fifteen knots appear to be our comfort spot this morning. We should be making better time."

The early morning tiff seemed to have vaporized in the air. Nick went below and found a black marker pen. He put a letter P inside the bottom of his shoe leather and pocketed the marker. He returned to the topside.

After two hours Duane took over while the captain went below to file his reports. Emily went below to write in her journal. Duane had time to think about Nick. The man irritated him. There was something about Nick that seemed fake.

"Maybe money does that to a person. They never have to learn because someone else helps them figure things out. Anyway, this guy is stupid."

Duane tacked the boat and watched some seagulls swarm the area he left.

"Maybe I can try to catch some fish this evening. A good bass or sturgeon would be fun. Maybe the captain will let me use his rod and reel. We won't let Nick near any of the hooks. He can handle the net. On second thought, he might drop the net in the water. It won't matter there's a long pole attached. The seagulls are smarter than he was, and they didn't need a pole to capture the fish."

Duane laughed at the sight in his mind. Nick falling overboard with the net. The seagulls waiting for him to swim back to the boat.

"A cold swim might cool his desire for Emily down a notch."

Seth and Dell were taking a nap.

Nick came topside for his turn at the helm.

"What did you say about Emily?"

Duane showed Nick the heading they were supposed to sail.

"I wondered if we might get to take a swim when we are done with the cruise. The surface of the water is usually warm. Count on only about nine inches of warm."

Nick took the helm and Duane went to the front of the boat to make sure the sails looked tight with air. He motioned one degree with his finger. Nick turned too far, and Duane signaled back two degrees.

"Close enough."

Nick sat in the chair at the helm and relaxed. He was bored and started daydreaming.

The computer alarm sounded when Emily came up from the galley. Nick quickly tacked the sailboat to get the rig back on track. She handed him a cola.

"I can steer for fifteen minutes if you need a break."

Nick let Emily have the helm and disappeared. He was gone for half an hour.

"Finally. Did you have lunch on your break?"

"No, I didn't know where they kept the sandwich meat."

Emily looked at him.

"The second bin in the refrigerator. The sandwich meat is there because I seem to be the only one getting the meat out of the freezer lately."

"Ouch, I suppose I shouldn't ask you to make me a sandwich?"

"No."

Emily sat down. Today was a make-it-yourself lunch day and clearly marked on the small chalkboard. Emily decided Nick never read the board.

"Tuna and deviled eggs."

"What?" asked Nick.

"I made tuna salad, deviled eggs. There are lettuce and pickles in the other plastic bins. The other foodstuff is on the top shelf of the refrigerator. Bread and chips are already out on the table."

Nick didn't know where the paper plates were stored. One look at Emily and he decided not to ask. She was in a mood. He figured Duane put her there. He couldn't figure out if they were having sex or not.

Emily's turn for taking the helm came too quickly. She was enjoying the view of the coastline. She sailed for three hours and Duane came to her rescue. He sailed her last hour. Seth took the helm. The captain came to the helm and pointed on the computer.

"There's old man Murray's dilapidated dock about here. We'll anchor a good one hundred fifty yards from the last set of old pilings in the water. There's probably nothing left of the top boards on the end. I hear he's in a nursing home now. His daughter won't mind us staying or stepping on her property. She usually has her gardener bring down some firewood for us. They place the wood next to an old fence. We'll have to look for the fence. There are probably tall weeds hiding the gray boards from the beach. The fence is about fifty feet from the end of the dock on the left. A tiny stream spills out occasionally and creates a nice sand dune. Inside is warm water. So, you might want to change in swim trunks."

"Are there any fish in the stream?"

"No, but you can cast offshore. I'll show you my gear later. If you catch anything, I'll bring the grill top out. We can clean the fish onshore and make our supper."

Duane looked at his gauges and where the captain had shown him.

"Don't worry, we'll see the pilings. Go past them and come back. Then we'll drop anchor, release the dinghy, and get Nick to take you to shore. Seth goes with you. Whoever catches the biggest fish doesn't have to cook tomorrow."

"That sounds fair. However, I'm not sure Nick knows how to open a can of beans much less cook a hamburger."

The captain laughed. "Do you think he now knows starboard?"

Duane rolled his eyes, "Nope."

LINDA MCKOWN

13 Fish Contest

The sailboat anchor dropped silently to the bottom hard surface and dug in the sand.

Their captain released the back anchor which would be a secondary hold, so the sailboat didn't drift. The wind dropped to a gentle breeze as the sails were wound down into their casings.

The sky was still light. Nick, Duane, and Seth took the rods, reels, and gear to shore. Emily and Dell watched with the captain as they reached the shore and secured their small craft.

After an hour, there was a shout from Nick, he caught a small bass about fourteen inches long.

The captain waved.

"I forgot to tell the lads there's one lure in the bunch that will catch a bigger fish. There's a white stripe on silver that intrigues the fish. The lure wiggles more than most. The shape is a new design. The lure packaging is interesting. There's a mermaid on the top. I'll have to buy another one. Two is always better than one. We'll see who has the little gem on their rod. At least, two of us will eat tonight."

Emily couldn't help, but smile. The fishing was rigged. The three men on shore were in a fierce competition to obtain their evening meal.

She finally went below to make a canned pea and cheese salad with cooked macaroni. At the last minute, she opened the chunked pineapple. The bamboo skewers were floating in a tray of water. Grabbing skewers, she and Dell alternated the pineapple with jarred red peppers and peaches. The balsamic vinegar and olive oil were lightly sprinkled on top.

"Too bad we don't have a couple of coconuts. Hunks of coconut are always good."

Dell scoured the pantry and found the canned coconut milk. Taking the frozen cream from the freezer, she melted the mix of cream and coconut in a small pan. Throwing in a piece of dried lemongrass and ground pepper, she tasted the mixture.

"Now that's perfection for any fish cooked on a grill."

Emily dug out the metal plates she saw in the cupboard, assembled the knives, and forks, and put her items in a heavy duck cloth basket. The cooler was filled with drinks, the salad, and fruit mixture. Putting the lid on the sauce, she grabbed the rope and tied the lid through the handles. She threw in napkins, hot pads, and garbage bags. She stared at the items.

"I forgot the board and fish filet knife. Plus, we need a pan and salt."

Hastily, she added the rest of her menagerie for supper.

The captain came below and was beaming.

"Duane caught a catfish weighing eleven pounds."

"Ow, I don't care for catfish."

"That's not the best part. He caught a twenty-pound sturgeon. You should see the fish. It's too beautiful to eat."

Emily went outside and hollered at Duane. She saw him turn and hold up the large fish. The grin on his face was wide. Then she looked at Nick. He was kicking sand into a newly built fire. There appeared to be a sulky expression on his face.

She waved and called out to Nick.

"Nick, come get us. We need a ride. There's plenty of salad to go with your great catch."

Nick seemed to brighten and moved toward the dinghy. Duane put the fish on a weathered log and added more firewood to their cook box. Large stones were placed around the area. The rocks appeared to have been there forever.

At the last minute, Emily brought out the aluminum blankets they could use for sitting in the sand. Super large marshmallows were added to the bag. The dinghy was overloaded. The captain didn't seem to mind a little water splashing in the craft.

The captain showed the men how he filleted fish. The scraps were thrown into the water a distance from their location. The seagulls and other birds would also have a feast.

Looking at Emily's scornful look, the captain said, "I know, I know. Today we are tourists. Next time, I'll bury the remains. May they rest in peace."

Dell smiled.

The captain placed the wire grate between two rocks over the fire. The fish was seasoned and wrapped in foil. The bamboo kabobs were laid on layers of foil. Emily untied the small rope and placed the saucepan with the cream sauce to the side of the fire to gently warm the broth.

As soon as the fish was cooked, the salad was brought out with the refreshments. Everyone filled their metal plates and moaned.

"Emily and Dell, this meal is the best."

"Thank you. The fish are superb. I can't decide which one I like better. If there's

106

any left, we might make fish sandwiches for lunch."

Dell nodded in agreement while drizzling more sauce on her fish.

Duane grabbed another helping of fish.

"No way, this is too good for leftovers. Let's do the salads for lunch."

Emily was having a good time. The men and the rest of the crew seemed to be doing the same.

"We can have Nick make bologna sandwiches. The leftover salads will go nicely."

Nick beamed. "I lost, but I do know how to make bologna sandwiches with jalapenos, black olives, mustard, and mayo."

The other two men nodded. The male species knew how to put together that sandwich. The bologna meat was the first one to turn to when a person was out of eggs and bacon. Salami was a running third.

When they were done, the garbage was collected with the dishes. Leftovers were placed in the cooler. The men used the cooler lid to pour water on the fire logs. The crew made two trips to the sailboat. The dinghy was secured. Emily brought out hot chocolate and used the large marshmallows.

Everyone was pleased and looking forward to the next day. They would practice overboard-drills for an hour before sailing to the next small marina. The captain didn't tell them a crew member was returning to the sailboat.

14 Man Overboard

The morning was slightly overcast as Emily put on her black one-piece swimsuit. She looked at herself in the bathroom mirror. The swimsuit covered her small frame nicely. She put the life jacket on and felt better. The jacket hid the curves. Emily wasn't on this boat for sex. She wanted to learn to sail. The certificate was important to show herself she was good at something.

The other men were waiting for her. They drew straws and Emily lost the challenge. She would be the first one in the water. Nick was next and then Duane. The captain would man the helm. The four would rotate positions. The only ones not going in the water were the captain, Seth, and Dell. They weren't interested in receiving a certificate and decided to watch the show.

Emily jumped in the water and screamed, "The water is cold on the bottom. Hurry up, I have goosebumps on the tips of my toes."

The captain quickly brought the boat around, dropping the sails early so the sailboat would slow. He started the engine and made the boat come to a standstill. His ability to judge space and timing parked the boat within four feet of Emily.

Duane threw her the yellow twenty-four-inch float and she grabbed onto the life preserver. She was back on board in a matter of minutes.

Seth and Dell clapped their hands and whistled.

Nick's turn was next. The captain let Emily handle the helm. She took off her wet life jacket and put on a windbreaker. Nick noticed her curves.

She put the sails up and tacked to return closer to shore. The captain gave the signal and Nick jumped into the water. Duane shouted, "Man overboard".

Emily repeated what the captain did previously. She tried to remember all the steps necessary. Her return wasn't as graceful.

She was twenty feet from Nick. He swam toward the life preserver and missed grabbing onto the yellow fabric. Duane yanked the life preserver in. The captain motioned for Emily to put the engine in reverse and stop. Duane threw the preserver a second time.

Nick grabbed the yellow preserver and Duane helped him on board.

"Women drivers are nuts. You need a hundred-foot rope at the end of the device. Fifty feet is too short. I bet you parallel park the same way."

They let Nick stomp around the boat.

"This isn't a car Emily," complained Nick.

"Okay, okay, give your brain a rest. She at least might save your life in the future. Twenty feet isn't so bad. I've seen much worse. Trust me. This is her second drill and I'm impressed. Besides, it's been my experience to always keep a woman in your good graces. You have a mother and know what I'm talking about. If you make her mad, who knows what could happen," warned the captain.

Emily smiled and held her fingers on her head for horns. Fortunately, only Duane saw her. Then, she quickly felt remorse or guilt.

"The captain is correct. I did really try. Sorry about the distance. I do park my car a little too fast. You're lucky."

Seth and Dell looked at Nick.

"Why am I lucky?"

"I didn't steer a mile past or run you over."

Nick looked sideways at Emily. He was almost calmed down. She decided to throw a parting shot.

"I see you are winded. Maybe you should give up smoking."

Seth slapped his knee and was having difficulty refraining himself from a case of laughter. Dell smirked.

Duane decided not to irritate Nick any further. He kept his thoughts to himself. His turn was the next one, and Nick would be steering the sailboat.

The captain stepped below for a moment when Duane moved over to the railing. He positioned his body better for the jump. He was on the outside of the railing watching the water. Emily was beside him on the inside.

For some reason, Nick decided to tack, and the white boom came swinging around. Emily saw the boom and ducked. Duane took a direct hit and went into the water.

Nick quickly realized his mistake and got the boat under control.

Emily shouted, "Man overboard." She raced to the front of the sailboat to watch Duane. He didn't appear to be moving.

"Hurry, Duane's not moving in the water."

The captain immediately jumped the stairs and shoved Nick out of the way.

"Get ready for pick up. Jump in the water, Nick, to help him."

Seth and Dell watched in alarm.

As soon as the boat slowed. Emily threw the life preserver. The boat hadn't even stopped, and she instinctively jumped in. Quickly she swam over to Duane. He appeared to be unconscious. She shook him. When he didn't respond, Emily dragged him while swimming toward the preserver.

She grabbed the yellow fabric and Nick pulled them toward the boat. He threw the netting down so they could get a foothold. They heard the captain drop the anchor and turn off the engine.

They couldn't lift him.

"Bring him to the back of the sailboat. The steps might be easier. We'll use a harness to bring him forward."

The captain attached the harness to a special lift device. The men got Duane aboard and the captain started CPR.

Duane quickly came to and threw up water.

"Man, oh, man, I'm wet. Did I go swimming? The water was freezing. Who are all of you people?"

Emily looked with alarm at the captain. The captain had a strange look on his face. Emily frowned.

"You're joking, right?"

Duane laughed and tried to sit up.

"Ouch, my head hurts. I think I'm done for the day. Emily, can you get me a beer and some aspirin."

Nick went below to get out of his wet trunks. The captain helped Duane down below.

"Emily, watch for any drift until we get back. Good call jumping in the water to help a person in trouble."

She went to the front and looked at the anchor. The boat appeared fine. She looked at the water and wondered what made Nick turn the boat. He told them there was a gust of wind. Emily didn't feel any wind.

"*Evil. Even veritable ignoramuses lie.*"

Emily shook herself and wondered about her thoughts.

"What motive would Nick have for hurting Duane?"

She couldn't think of any reason. Glad that Duane appeared to have survived the accidental dunk in the water, she went to the bridge and unlocked the harness from the lift.

"This gear worked."

All four men came back to the bridge. Duane was drinking orange juice and Nick was drinking flavored water. Emily went below to change and make sandwiches. The time was almost their lunch hour. They would be sailing soon enough. Their map showed another small marina.

Duane came below.

"At least we passed our second man overboard drill. I'm glad you jumped in the water to save me. Thank you."

He lightly kissed her hair, grabbed his hat, and went back through the hatch to sit on the deck.

She touched her wet hair. Her fast reaction in an emergency was important. There was no fear when she jumped into the water a second time. However, the drama was a little too much today. Emily would be glad to take a short break at the next stop. Their crew was staying a day to replenish supplies.

Emily wondered about their surprise visitor. She overheard the captain talking to someone while he was in his bedroom. The door was slightly ajar.

Nick saw her and turned around. His aloofness was unsettling.

Dell told Emily that they would permanently be leaving the sailboat cruise. They received another call. Their friend's health worsened. There was a real emergency awaiting them at home. Emily hugged them. She would miss the two young people.

15 Reunion and Trouble

The large sailboat cruised into the harbor and the crew tied the lines to the dock cleats. Seth and Dell departed. Before leaving, a final picture was taken of the group by a dock worker using Dell's phone. She promised to send Emily a copy.

A man and woman slowly approached the boat. The captain was smiling. The man jumped onto the boat and the two men hugged.

"All the stars in heaven couldn't make me happier. I'm glad to see you are finally walking better."

"The doctor told me I could come sailing with you. I've only brought a few of my things with me."

"Everyone, meet Cyrus Allen, our sailboat cook."

The others introduced themselves. The woman came on board and there were more introductions.

"My coolers are in Clara's truck. Will you boys help her bring them down to the dock. There are a folding table and a small grill. We are having lobster and very large shrimp for supper. The salad is already made and there'll be huge homemade brownies. If anyone's allergic to chocolate, we have rice crispy bars over an inch thick."

The crew cheered. Emily and Clara went to the galley to get the plates, utensils, and drinks. The captain sat talking to his old friend.

"I'm glad you have arrived. We seem to have run into some bad karma this trip. Things accidentally happen to my crew. I'm not liking the vibrations."

"When you called, I figured there was an urgent need for my services. The second pair of hands and eyes are always a good thing to have on a sailboat."

The captain nodded. The two women were assembling items on the dock and the men returned with a large cart full of the cook's wares.

"We'll talk later this evening."

The crew assembled on the dock and ate a grand meal.

Nick disappeared. Emily and Duane went for a walk. The captain and cook were cleaning the dock and galley. A boy from the small store was helping Clara put the items onto the cart. The boy would help Clara to her vehicle.

Duane and Emily stopped at the store for ice cream.

"You are awfully quiet. My ice cream is good. How's yours?"

"I don't know," grunted Duane.

"Your face is really pale. Are you feeling all right?"

Duane put his cone in the garbage.

"I haven't felt good since I went into the water. My headache medicine is not working. I'm going to have to leave the cruise."

"I'll call the captain."

Emily dialed and the captain immediately answered.

"I think Duane needs to see a doctor as soon as possible. Who do I call?"

"Let me make the emergency call. Where are the two of you located?"

"We're in front of the little store."

"Can Duane walk back to the boat?"

She talked to Duane.

"He told me he couldn't and needs to sit down. Duane, oh, no!"

Emily dropped her phone to catch Duane as he fainted. She slid with him to the boardwalk. Emily picked up her phone.

"I think he passed out."

"Keep him still. Cyrus has called for a helicopter. The medics should be here shortly. I'll grab Duane's duffel bag and gear. We'll be over in a few minutes."

Emily, Cyrus, and the captain waited with Duane until the emergency team arrived. He was wrapped in blankets and they rolled

118

him onto the stretcher. The stretcher was taken to the awaiting helicopter and they flew to the hospital.

"We should contact his wife."

The captain nodded to Cyrus who went back to the sailboat.

"We'll alert Duane's wife. She will be with him soon. Can I get you anything?"

Emily looked at her cone in the dirt. She wanted to cry but couldn't.

"Let's get back to the sailboat. We probably won't hear anything until morning."

Emily knew the captain was responsible for his guests.

"I wish I could have done more."

"Duane is strong and is in good hands. They will get him to the hospital."

They walked back to the boat. Clara gave Emily a hug and stayed another hour. Finally, she left, and Emily excused herself. She needed to rest. The boat felt empty without Duane's voice. Sleep was slow in coming.

16 Dean Needs Money

Dean Peters saw the large sailboat at the boat docks in the marina. He couldn't investigate because he was meeting some bikers at the marina store. He saw the two people in a truck and frowned. They weren't riding their motorcycles.

Susie Ortiz went around the other side, opened the door and helped the man on crutches out of the vehicle. She pointed to the furthest outside table. Dean went over to shake hands with Henri.

Henri Ortiz looked at the biker.

"Can't you see my hands are holding these metal stilts?"

"Well, Henri, I'm not blind. I know they are crutches. What in the world happened?"

Susie said, "He broke his leg swatting some hornets."

"Did he get bit by the buggers?"

"No, asshole, I broke my leg."

Dean saw the leg brace and quickly sat down. He briefly thought of a rocket man. Put a second brace on the other leg, a small motor, and a person would disappear in a puff of smoke. Dean wanted to become a tiny dot high in the air. On second thought, Henri could become the dot.

"You're rocket man with the crutches and everything. You probably don't get my joke?"

Henri glared at the biker in ripped jeans. Susie intervened.

"Settle down, Henri. I get the joke. You do look like a rocket dressed in red, white, and blue."

Henri stomped on a large ant with his good foot.

Dean jumped.

"There's no need to bite my head off. Stop with the killing ants. The floorboards shook underneath me."

Henri said, "Trains shake my floorboards. They are much heavier than I am. I'm heavy enough for taking a man down."

Dean felt the sweat on his collar.

"Why did you want to meet me? I'm busy."

Susie snorted.

"You haven't worked in three years. Mara lets you live on the porch for free in the summer and the attic in the winter. Busy is not in your curriculum. That's why we are here. Henri can't work and I've got to visit my sister."

Dean thought about what she told him.

"I can't babysit your husband."

Dean knew the minute his words were spoken; he was in the wrong in a big way.

Henri grabbed Dean by the collar and pulled him out of his chair.

"I don't need a babysitter. We want the money you owe us. Paying ten dollars when we see you don't cut it anymore, smartass."

Dean unlocked the burly man's hands from his shirt.

"How much more do I owe you?"

Susie took out her notebook.

"The fee for burning the garage was five thousand dollars. The figure decreased to three thousand seven hundred fifty dollars."

"I didn't realize the amount was so high. Are you sure about the amount?"

Susie took her phone out of her pocket.

"The interest rate pushed the number. The amount now is six thousand two hundred dollars."

Dean swallowed. He remembered them telling him about interest. He was going to ask if the new figure was correct until he saw the look on Henri's face.

"I promise you that we'll have the money. A friend of ours has pulled into the marina. I'm positive he will want to help."

Susie slapped Dean on the back.

"Good, we'll be back. We decided to be nice. One week or the interest rate doubles and continues until payment is received.

They left Dean Jesse Peters to himself and rode away. There was no way he could find the money. He thought about fleeing the area but looked at his motorcycle tires.

Taking a quarter out of his pocket, he held the coin on the tread. There wasn't much left.

"The tires won't work another year. Therein lies a problem."

He left the marina to find Mara. Her small house was not very far. He saw her hanging the laundry on the line. Getting off his bike, he approached her.

"Susie and Henri drove by, honked, and waved. They were in a truck."

"I know. We talked. They want their money and then some. You need to lend me the money."

"How much?"

He told her.

"I don't have the money. If I did, I would buy a new dryer."

Dean looked her in the eye.

"Nick is in the marina. You need to ask him. He likes you and as a woman; you can force him to pay."

"You want me to blackmail Nick Kent?"

"Yes, you had sex with him."

Mara took her basket of clean clothes and put them inside her home. Dean tried to follow. She slammed the screen door in his face. He walked into the house.

"Mara, you owe me."

She stomped her feet and tried to kick him. Dean jumped aside.

"Get out of my house and don't come back."

Mara came outside with Dean following. She threw his clean clothes in the dirt, went back inside, slammed her door, and hit the lock.

Dean tucked the clothes into a plastic bag from the box by the garbage cans. He put the bundle on his bike and drove into town. Buying a six-pack of beer, he tried to think of a way to find some money.

In the morning, a plan was developing. He remembered Mara telling him about an insurance policy. He didn't know if she changed the policy recently. He hoped not.

"If she doesn't get the money from rich Kent, then I'll think about a different way. Or maybe leave and pray the tires will hold. Okay, so I haven't been to a church in thirty years."

He drove to the park and took out the small nylon tent. He kept the tent close to the trees so no one would notice. The tent was dark brown and was barely noticeable. No one bothered him.

Later he went to the marina and watched the boats. When the others were off their boats, he went down to the docks and stole. He took items that could easily be removed and sold to bikers or took them to the pawnshop. Dean was good at stealing. The stolen items were free for the taking.

He stopped to look at the boats at the marina docks. Most of the boats contained masts and sails. There were a few smaller cruisers.

"Why didn't these people purchase large motorboats? I could drive a big boat with an engine. There's room enough to live aboard. If there was a decent motorboat here, I could steal the dang thing and go to Duluth. From Duluth, I could join a freighter to get money to pay for my gas. Freighters are always looking for crew members to work small jobs."

Dean thought awhile.

"Nope, I'd have to really work. I hate hard labor. The small jobs might require me to lift heavy stuff. We're not going to Duluth."

He scanned the docks again and saw the empty dock.

"There should be a houseboat parked on the very spot. I could catch fish and live on the water. My bike would fit. I wouldn't need but a small amount of gas."

He smelled hamburgers and French fries coming from the café. Dean left his spot near the boats and drove to the pawnshop. The sign read closed for the rest of the day. He drove to the park and stashed the items and went back to the marina. Positioning himself away from the shop, he held out his hat to some people walking on the pier. A man from a cruiser gave him five dollars.

"Thank you kindly, sir."

Dean bought his dinner for the evening and stashed the remainder of his money in the worn wallet.

"I need money. Mara, you better deliver."

Dean rode his motorcycle down the highway to get cool before he turned in for the evening. The next day would be when he would move. He was glad his clothes were clean. He hated doing his own laundry.

Mara was angry about Dean's visit. She told him not to hire Susie and Henri. He didn't listen. Now she would need to bail him out of trouble. Her savings contained four thousand dollars.

She looked at her tiny diamond necklace. The pawnshop might give her a thousand more. She looked out her window. She didn't want to give up the necklace. Nick bought the jewelry for her at an antique store across the road from where she first met him. She touched the diamond. He used his credit card. He stayed with her until morning. She wanted to see Nick again.

The attic contained an old chest. Mara took the cardboard coin holders out of the trunk. She counted ten holders. She opened one of the boards which contained the mercury dimes. Her father showed her the wing-headed lady. He said they contained ninety percent silver.

"The coins should be valuable. Maybe I can keep my necklace and talk Susie into accepting four thousand plus the coins."

Mara took her phone and took pictures of the coin books. Pulling the images into an email, she sent herself a note describing the coins her father left in his will.

Next, she opened the leather pouch. Her father told her the 1897 o Morgan Silver dollar was rare. There were twenty coins. She opened the old newspaper article dated ten years ago. The value was approximately five to six hundred dollars. She knew the coin must be more valuable today. She placed the dollar coins on the floor and took another photo. She sent herself a second email. Mara wanted to try a coin shop before approaching Susie.

She saw Mike Nichols pull into her driveway from the attic vent. Mike made a lot of money each year fixing boats. She went out with him a few times and rode in his small motorboat. Mara groaned. She didn't have time for him today. She put the coins in the trunk and came downstairs. Mike was sitting on her kitchen table.

"What's in your attic, Mara?"

"Nothing."

"Why are you up there? Seems to me there might be something valuable. We should go look."

He touched the chain around her neck and pulled the gold tight.

Mara moved away. Since she broke off with him, he scared her.

"I'm cleaning out the attic. I might rent the space. I'm driving to the marina to buy some cleaning supplies and a new lockable doorknob. There's dust everywhere in the attic."

"Dean likes the attic. Why should you clean the space?"

Mara frowned.

"I kicked him out of my home. He won't be staying here."

"Well, well, pour Dean. There's nothing happening at the marina. I checked and will pass going back with you."

Mara never asked him to accompany her to the marina. Mike was another person she needed to have gone from her house. She grabbed her bag and went out the door. He hopped on his red motorcycle.

"I'll see you tonight," said Mike.

Mara didn't want to see him. She would tell him they were done for a second time. A better class of people was what she wanted.

17 Engine Repair

The next morning the captain tried to start the engines. One of the engines wouldn't turn over. Cyrus talked the shop owner's son into driving him to a marine parts store eighty miles away. The captain made the decision to stay another day while Cyrus repaired the engine.

Emily went to the marina store to purchase more shorts and tops. Nick disappeared. Emily heard the bikers approach the marina and she was surprised to see Mara.

"Hello, Mara, do you live around here?"

"You're the girl from the fancy-pants sailboat?"

"Yes, I'm Emily Erin. This year, I selected a cruise to learn how to sail."

Mara extended her hand. Emily shook Mara's dry hand.

"The dryer broke. My hands aren't normally so coarse. My last name is Peters. I have a small place close to the park. I'm out of food and cleaner so I came to get more. Is Nick Kent around?"

"Nick is still with the cruise. Most of the others have dropped out of the sailing journey. We will be leaving in the morning.

The captain and Cyrus are repairing one of our engines."

"There's only four of you on that large boat? That's a real shame. Nick tried to get me a ride. We could have bunked together."

"Yes, your visit would have made life interesting. Do you sail?"

"No. I also can't swim."

Emily looked surprised.

"I see your disbelief what with my living close to the lake and all. There was no one to teach me."

Mara wasn't sure she should mention her information about Nick but changed her mind.

"I did some digging on my computer. Nick's daddy is rich. Nick is no longer a student in college in Chicago. He was kicked out due to a fight over a young woman. I think her name was Nancy or Nan."

"Interesting."

Emily found a white pair of shorts and a navy top. She carried them to the counter and came back.

"I'm not surprised. Nick has mentioned his father a few times. He hasn't talked about college or his major. I'm surprised he went to college. He doesn't appear to like classes or learning. Even on the sailboat, he forgets important things. Nancy was on the boat but left early."

"I didn't know she was on the boat originally. My, my, there's a man who keeps secrets. I assumed he was alone on the sailboat. He told me this cruise was his father's idea. Nick must finish or else his dad won't give him any more money. I guess Nick has dropped out of too many things. Was she pretty?"

Emily found a gold-orange top and green shorts.

"Yes. She seemed angry. I shouldn't talk about her. We didn't really connect as friends. Excuse me, I need to pay for the clothes. It was nice seeing you again."

"Same here, have a safe trip."

Emily walked out of the small shop and bumped into Nick.

"Whoa, Em, what's the rush?"

She sidestepped out of his way and Nick went into the shop.

Later in the day, she could hear Cyrus and the captain tinkering on the engine. Emily washed some of her clothes earlier and they were drying on the upper railing. Her bras and panties were a little wet because they were under the tops. She started folding her clothes and sat down until her underwear was dry.

The day was more than pretty with pale blue skies and a few wispy clouds.

"Mare's tails. Those clouds probably mean the weather is coming our way."

After an hour, she put away her clothes. Emily read the recipe on the counter in the galley. She agreed to make the evening dinner of beef soup and cheese sandwiches.

The two men finally were done, and she could hear both engines start. They washed their dirty hands and sat down to their supper. There was no sight of Nick on the dock or boat.

Emily did the dishes and put the soup in freezer containers. The captain and Cyrus were playing chess into the evening hours. Emily was reading a magazine she purchased at the store.

She worried about Nick. They were leaving at eight o'clock in the morning. She turned in for the evening and the two men did the same.

About four in the morning, Emily awakened. She thought she heard a thud. She went topside and saw a cart was on the smaller dock which was across from their boat. There didn't appear to be anyone on the dock. She didn't hear any more sounds. Emily went below to her bunk. After an hour and a half of trying to get some sleep, she gave up and went to make some hot tea.

She was sitting near the helm when a very wet Nick scared her.

"Nick, please don't make me jump like I was shot out of a cannon. I thought you were a sea monster. What on earth were you doing?"

"I took a swim and now I'm going to sleep. I'm so glad we are done with our classes and received our certificates. Now my old man will put money into my account."

"Yes, I'm glad we are done and passed the exam. Did you see anyone on the small dock?"

"No."

"Someone was there with a cart."

Emily saw blood dripping off his arm.

"Your jeans are dirty, and the right arm is bleeding!"

"A simple wound. I'll need a band-aid."

"I would put antiseptic on the cut. It looks deep. Maybe you need stitches. You also have scratches on your arms. Were you in a fight?"

Nick wiped the blood on his jeans.

"Stupid bikers. They got a little weird last night. I'll take care of the cut. I don't need a doctor. Good morning, Emily."

"Okay."

Emily frowned and looked at the small dock. The cart was no longer on the dock. Someone pushed the object into the shallow end of the water. Emily took her tea and walked toward the small dock. She was halfway there when the captain called her.

"Emily, we're having crepes with fresh blueberries for breakfast. Cyrus made homemade hot syrup. Hurry back."

She looked one last time at the dock and cart. A strange feeling of dread hit her. There was something wrong, but she didn't know what.

"I feel like a black cat walked over my grave. Now, Emily, cool your jets, that's nuts. You like furry cats. I'm getting those anxiety attacks again. Kids probably pushed the cart around and into the drink."

After breakfast, they motored out and put up the sails. The captain and Cyrus sailed the rest of the day. Emily watched them move together in perfect harmony. Nick didn't appear until three in the afternoon.

Emily noticed he wore a long sleeve shirt to hide his cut and scratches. She thought his attire was odd. The air was still warm. They dropped anchor in the evening.

During dinner, Nick seemed to be overly talkative and amazingly cheerful. Emily wondered about the change as did the captain.

Finally, Cyrus said, "Are you always this cheerful?"

Both Emily and the captain answered, "No."

Nick laughed. "I have money. My dad put two-hundred-fifty-thousand dollars in my account. I called my bank. The money is there. Finally, I can leave this boat at our next marina."

The captain was impressed. "Are you returning to college? Your application showed that you were a senior."

Nick stopped with his fork in the air.

"I might, but I doubt it. I'm not sure a degree is important. I'll be working for my dad eventually."

"What do you plan on doing with your life in the interim?"

"Travel. I want to go back to Europe or maybe Africa."

Emily said, "A European holiday was my favorite. I went once. You should have fun. Africa, I'm not sure. I think of wild things."

"That's my motto from now on. *Choose wild things*."

He looked intently at Emily.

"I'm not wild."

Nick looked at the other men. They looked at the ceiling.

"You could have fooled me," said Nick.

The captain put his plate in the sink.

136

"One of our black ropes has been cut. We are missing about twenty-five feet of rope. The line is an extra one and was on the starboard side."

Nick turned away.

"I thought I heard a thud about four. I wonder if they cut the line then."

"Thank you, Emily, I'll call the local authorities to report the theft. We usually never have a problem with this marina. This rope is strong and not too expensive to replace. Still, boaters don't like their stuff stolen. This marina might need to upgrade their security with cameras on the docks."

Cyrus nodded. "There is a lack of cameras. I saw two around the store, one inside and outside."

"I remember the camera inside at the checkout counter. The locals used the second door where there's no camera," said Emily.

She recalled using the second door and bumping into Nick. Nick avoided the camera.

Emily didn't look at Nick. She avoided his penetrating eyes and watched the waves on the water.

18 Nick's Wish

The captain and Cyrus were at the helm sailing their vessel. Nick and Emily were sitting forward of the jib sail. The wind was gentle, and they were moving slowly through the water.

"This is perfectly fine. I'm glad the boat has slowed. I need to talk to you."

Emily turned to look at a serious version of Nick.

"My father has been correct about me. I've squandered my time in college. His plans are for me to join his company and work for him. I've been reluctant until this cruise."

"You don't appear to like your father."

Nick thought about her response.

"We've had our differences. Most of the time he's been generous."

Emily thought about her parents. They did pay for her college and help whenever she needed them. She remained silent.

"I wish we met a couple of years ago. I know we would have been good friends. You're different from the other women that I date. There's also been some type of spark between us. I've never quite felt this tug on my chest. I'm glad there was an opening on this cruise; otherwise, we wouldn't have met."

She didn't know what to say.

"I was allowed on this adventure, too, when someone canceled. How odd?"

"See, fate wanted us to become friends."

Emily ignored his remarks about tug on the chest. She thought he meant heart. Nick flirted with all the women on the sailboat. He was a good talker when he wanted to enhance his image. She was the only female left on the cruise. The male in front of her, without a doubt, would have naturally drifted her way.

"Yes, I think we might be friends."

Nick was encouraged by her comment.

"Do you like children?"

Emily wasn't sure. She was an only child.

"I don't know. The subject never arose while I was dating."

"I like kids. Maybe I can have a baseball team of boys."

"Cross off ninety percent of women from your dating book."

Nick watched a bird swoop into the water, catch a fish, and fly toward land. The woman was at least honest.

"I'm thinking about buying a boat. I was wondering if you would like to join me for a week of sailing in California?"

Emily was stunned. She wasn't sure how to respond. There was some feeling happening. Her heartbeat faster whenever Nick was close. To go sailing with him for a week sounded interesting. She was certainly old enough to make her own decisions about men.

"This cruise was important to me for many reasons. The brochure of the scenery was key to my signing onboard. Also, I needed some fun time in my life. A little adventure into the unknown was required. Granted, sailing on Lake Superior isn't as exciting as traveling to the moon. Yet, there was something pulling me. After this cruise, I'm visiting my parents and then looking for a job. Your sailing trip sounds exciting. I wouldn't mind being a member of your crew. Unfortunately, I'm going to decline due to the items I previously mentioned."

Nick knew she missed the fact that there would have only been the two of them sailing. They would be the entire crew.

"I like California and sailing in the area. Maybe I can visit you afterward. They say the area is an adventure waiting to happen. Grapes growing for the wineries, the sun dazzling the eyes, and the water, let's not forget the glistening ocean at sunset."

Emily saw the picture he painted.

"Throw in a few cows and sheep among the trees and the picture is complete. The state has charm. I'd like a house close to the ocean someday."

"A house close to the ocean is a nice dream. We'll be dropping anchor soon. The sun is slowly dropping," said Nick.

Emily watched the bright ball. Nick spoke in a low voice.

> *The sun drops silently*
> *spewing her splendor,*
> *weaving the azure sky*
> *in silk bands golden bent,*
> *and soft clouds shimmer*
> *a scarlet-rimmed goodbye.*

Emily couldn't believe his words.

"The poem is lovely and powerful. I like the colorful images and the repetitive *S's*. Who's the author?"

"Pick a letter from the alphabet."

Emily felt the challenge.

"I pick the letter E*.*"

Nick wasn't used to creating more poems on the fly. He thought about Emily's side that appealed to him. Words formulated.

> *The evening light exists*
> *in a person's heart*
> *but more so in Emily.*
> *She keeps a list*

ever long which is an art
of past loves and ecstasy.

Nick shouldn't have enticed her to play. Now he would need to explain.

"I write poetry on occasion. I have a book at home filled with similar wordplays."

Emily touched his arm. He saw her look of awe.

Their shoulders touched. He turned. She turned and Emily spontaneously gave him a quick hug.

"Thank you. I will remember your poems whenever I see a sunset and think of the evening. Speaking of goodbyes, as soon as our trip ends, we will go our separate ways. The world is filled with some very beautiful women. You should find one and keep writing your poems."

"Em?"

"*Yes, maybe.*"

Emily left Nick and went into the galley to find some fruit.

Nick sat watching the ripples ahead. The sailboat turned and followed the ripples. The wind lifted the bow and the boat heeled over. He braced himself. Nick was disappointed that Emily turned down his date request.

"Make that two requests and I get a maybe."

He thought about their talk and her hug. The hug was like his grandmother used to give him. Evidently, her impression of him even after the poem was not matching his desires.

"You are one of those beautiful and sexy women. Although my head is mixed up, I'm not blind to a very lovely female. I'm trying to get my life straight but somehow keep moving backward. Emily, you might be correct. My feelings might change once we are off the boat and I run into other females. They won't come close. You're way ahead in the race."

Nick sat for a long time thinking about the future and his plans. His wish was for Emily to be in them. He didn't know how to convince her.

"I messed up my chance. I caught Emily off guard. The wrong move reminded her of the past. Time is what I need."

Nick went below and prepared himself a sandwich. He called his father to let him know he would take the job in Africa. He required his own money to build a house. There was a massive change required to catch the woman of his dreams. His turn at the helm was next.

Emily was writing in her journal.

He could imagine her writing next to his name, "Writer of poems. Is Nick real?"

His demeanor was moody again when she saw him. Their intimate talk was parked in a box and nailed shut by Emily. Nick got too close.

Cyrus and the captain looked at each other. They saw this behavior before on their boat cruises. Two people were struggling to avoid the heat between them. The men would be stumped by the future turn of events.

Cyrus commented, "I am reminded of masks."

The captain looked at the sun setting in the huge lake. The sky turned a brilliant orange hue.

"Never saw two people struggle so much with their feelings."

Cyrus nodded, "Fate is an awesome force."

"Aye."

19 Stolen Boat

They moored for the evening. There was a small strip of beach and they needed firewood. Nick purchased a second phone at the marina to use as a hot spot so he could check the news on his cell phone while they were at anchor. A woman's body was found under the small dock at the marina. He heard the name of the dead woman. Nick believed that he was the last person to see her alive.

"Let's do supper on the beach," said Nick.

The captain looked at Cyrus.

"We can pack our coolers with steak. Potatoes, carrots, onions, butter, and foil will make a fine meal. I'll throw in the oatmeal cookies."

At the last minute, Cyrus put apples, oranges, and lemons on his pile on the table. He liked to cook them in foil. The citrus made his mouth feel clean.

"Emily put lots of ice in the two coolers that I will place on the deck Also, there are spare foil blankets we can use for sitting on the sand."

The four crew members busied themselves placing the items in the dinghy. They made two trips to the shore. Nick told them he forgot the seasoning and steak sauce.

"Bring the cinnamon and sugar packets," said Cyrus.

Nick jumped in the small craft, started the engine, and went back to the sailboat. They saw him lightly fasten the dinghy to the side and disappear into the galley.

The captain and Cyrus were collecting firewood. Emily was unrolling the silver blankets and securing them down with the coolers.

The sound she heard was an anchor chain. Emily saw Nick at the helm. He started both engines and steered the boat away from the beach.

The captain and Cyrus came running. They were hollering at Nick to stop. Emily stood there in a daze and couldn't move. The mainsail lifted, and the sailboat disappeared.

"The bastard is in our boat. Blast, I should have seen this one coming."

Cyrus shook his head. "The man is crazy to think he can getaway. The coast guard will find him."

The captain checked his phone. They were away from the sailboat and in an area with no service.

"Shane will know what to do when he doesn't get my nightly report. We might want to walk the shore to find the dinghy. I saw the line go in the water. The fool knows we don't have enough gas to reach the marina, but at

146

least we could use the craft for cover. There are water and dehydrated food we'll need later in the dinghy."

"How long do you think it will take Shane to find us?"

"I'm hoping two days, three, or four at the most."

Cyrus pointed. There is a spot. Let's follow the shoreline. The two men started walking. The captain stopped. Emily was staring at the water.

"I'll talk to her for a minute. You watch the craft. I'll bring our life jackets. We may need to take a swim."

Emily looked at the captain.

"We have to get the small craft. You will be safe here. There are only the seagulls."

Emily looked at the birds hovering in the air.

"I'll wait for supper until you get back."

"Eat an apple if you get hungry. But first, collect the firewood."

He handed her his lighter.

"When it gets dark, keep the fire lit so we can see the light. Here's my knife if you need something to cut the dry grass for a starter."

"Okay, I can follow orders. Why do you think Nick took the sailboat?"

The captain debated about telling Emily about the call he received from the local sheriff. He noticed she didn't say Nick stole the boat.

"Mara Peters was found dead under a dock close to our boat at the marina. Her body was hidden by someone who stole our rope. The police want to question Nick and me. I kept quiet for everyone's safety."

Emily couldn't see Cyrus anywhere.

"You must go and help find the craft."

"Aye.

The captain jogged along the waterline. He finally saw Cyrus swimming. The captain breathed a sigh of relief when Cyrus climbed inside. He quickly put the plastic oars together and started rowing.

When Cyrus reached the shore, they took turns walking the craft in the water. By the time they reached Emily, it was dark. The small fire was burning, and they shouted to her. "Get those steaks on the fire. We're famished."

Emily took out the foil packets and placed them on the grill grate. The steak would go on the grill in about ten minutes.

Both men secured the dinghy away from the fire. They sat on the silver blankets and were winded. The men drank a bottle of water. Cyrus peeled an orange.

Emily started talking.

"I saw Nick in the morning. He was in the water swimming. There was a cut on his arm and scratches. I should have told you. We both saw Mara in the marina store. I wish somehow I could retrace my steps."

"We don't know what happened to the woman or if Nick was in any way involved. I personally won't jump to conclusions in a murder. We do know he is in a heap of trouble for taking a sailboat. The judges in this state own boats. They won't think kindly of a young man with money borrowing or hijacking another man's craft."

Cyrus put the steaks on the fire and moved the foil packets away from the hot spot.

"Was Nick that good of a navigator?"

The captain scratched his head and removed his hat.

"He knows the important stuff. My theory is that he checked the map for our area. He needs a safe spot to get off the boat."

Cyrus removed the utensils from the cooler.

"He'll pick the highway."

"That's my thinking, too," said the captain.

"The water is deep in the one spot close to shore. We've anchored in the place before. Let's hope he drops anchor and swims to shore."

149

"Aye, I would hate to lose her on the beach."

They ate their hot steaks in silence. The cookies were saved for breakfast.

The men created a large hole in the sand and let some lake water drain into the hole. The coolers were placed inside. The packages of food and extra water jugs were taken out of the small craft. They dragged logs to build a one-sided barrier. Then the three flipped the dinghy on top to build a strange-looking type of teepee. The men used the line to secure the craft and the small tent structure.

The silver blankets were brought inside. They talked about the tasks they needed to do in the morning. Fishing was number one on the list. The box of lures was inside a pocket of the dinghy. The captain was glad he asked Nick the night before to put the box inside the compartment. Making hats out of reeds was next. Both Cyrus and Emily would need headgear.

The men took turns guarding their campsite. They weren't sure if Nick would return in the night. Cyrus and the captain worried about Emily. Nick seemed a little too enamored with her before he stole the sailboat.

Both men saw the look in his eyes. They knew the fireworks were only beginning. Nick would see her again. No one told Emily.

20 Shane's Work

Work kept Shane busy for two days. Finally, his office was contacted by the sheriff. The sailboat didn't reach her destination. The police were waiting on the docks to take Nick and the captain to their department for questioning.

"Let me call you back, sheriff. I'm flying right now and should land in thirty minutes."

Shane returned the call from his office.

"Mr. Hanigan. The police talked with your father regarding a client on your sailboat. We want to talk to Nick Kent regarding a young woman named, Mara Peters. We believe she was murdered. The autopsy should prove our theory."

Shane sat up in his chair. He dialed his father's number. There was no answer.

"Let me try Cyrus. There's no answer on his cell phone either. My father turns in a nightly report."

Shane read the date and time of the last report. Quickly reading the information, his father revealed some misgivings about Nick. There wasn't anything incriminatory in the report.

"There's no report for two days and my sailboat has not arrived at the marina. I called my friend there. I have two employees and an Emily Erin on the sailboat with Mr. Kent. I need to file a report with you and the coast guard. The last location from the report was at these coordinates."

Shane gave the sheriff the information. He contacted the coast guard. They would dispatch a helicopter right away. There were cutters in the search area.

"Let me know if you find anything."

Shane alerted his secretary and contacted one of his pilots to return to the company's home base. Shane would also engage his plane in the search grid. He quickly looked at the map charts.

"Where are you? You're probably running with my boat. Let's hope my people are safe or I'll track you down until I die. Mr. Kent, you picked the wrong sailboat to commandeer."

The next morning, Shane and another pilot were flying in the area. They started at the northernmost point, working their way south.

"There she sits in the water, sir."

They flew overhead and contacted the coast guard.

"Do you want to land, Shane?"

"I'm not sure. There isn't anyone on the deck. Let's buzz the boat."

They flew low. No one appeared.

"We've got to return and get fuel."

Shane looked at his fuel gauge.

The coast guard called Shane back. They were an hour away from the location.

"Let's set ourselves down. I need to go on my boat. I'm responsible."

"Okay. I'll get my gun. I know you don't like us to carry them. This time is different."

His crewman handed Shane the loaded weapon. The floatplane came close to the back of the anchored sailboat. A rope was tied to a back railing. Shane scrambled onto the wing and walked toward the sailboat. He jumped and grabbed the rail.

Pulling himself forward, he crawled along the port side of the boat. The hatch door was open.

Shane debated about entering with the gun or calling for anyone inside to appear. He went inside with the gun in his hand. His eyes adjusted to the inside of the sailboat. Slowly he checked the rooms. There was no one. He saw Emily's washed clothes, Cyrus's large bag, and his father's room.

"The computer is missing, of course."

He checked in the hold. There was no one there. Shane came out to his floatplane.

"We're empty of all occupants. I've started the generator. The refrigerator is warm, but the freezer is still frozen. Whoever was here hasn't been gone long."

His crewman asked, "Do the engines start?"

Shane started each engine separately and checked the tanks. He turned the helm computer on.

"Things seem to be working." He turned the engines off.

Shane went to the lines. They looked secure. He walked the boat and checked the outside.

"No scratches and no leaks below the decks. The insurance company will be happy. They'll want a thorough inspection."

The coast guard cutter appeared. Shane waved at them. He knew the driver. His sailboat was boarded.

"Hi, Shane, anyone else here?"

"No, just us."

"That's what I was afraid of. We haven't found your father or anyone. Tell me you didn't touch anything important."

"I did. I needed to verify whether I can sail her to a port. I don't want to drag her. Let me look at the map again. They must be between these two points."

The coast guard man disappeared to radio the helicopter. There was only an hour of daylight.

"I'll leave you to your job of handling this beast alone. I'm sure you've done it before. Just sign my report."

After the coast guard left. Shane untied the floatplane. The plane coasted away from the sailboat. Shane raised anchor and then the jib. The sail appeared to be intact. He raised the mainsail halfway. The sailboat heeled over and moved. He waved the floatplane off.

Once the sailboat appeared to be doing fine, he tethered the wheel. Walking the upper deck, he looked at each sail. The wind was a nice breeze and pushed the boat.

Shane looked at a map of the area and selected a place where he would stop for the evening. Using the computer, he raised the main to the top. Settling in his seat, he singlehandedly sailed his boat.

"Your performance is a superb old girl. We'll find them. They must be on the shore. Anyway, we hope the thief wasn't a psychopath."

He suddenly remembered Emily's underwear on her bed.

"Nice lace underwear."

21 Day 3 of Survival

The captain was the first one awake. He hoped to see Shane by now in his floatplane or maybe the return of his son's sailboat. Digging the map out of the dinghy, he went to the campfire and spread the laminated paper on the wood. He laid twigs on the map and looked at the triangles.

Cyrus walked down the beach to do his business and came back.

"Twigs work. I would have used blades of grass."

The captain pointed. Cyrus looked at the position.

"I don't know. The water is rough around the turn. If there were just the two of us, I wouldn't care. We've got Emily and at least one cooler to haul."

Walking over to the craft, the captain tested the outside and came back.

"We have to move one way or the other. I'm getting tired of eating fish. There's very little freshwater left."

"We can try cooking water."

The captain frowned.

"The coolers are plastic, man."

Cyrus handed him his hat.

"The reeds swell, and we have the aluminum foil."

"If we were in Tahiti, we could use coconuts," said the captain.

Cyrus looked at the trees.

"We have seagulls."

"Their skin is too thin. Besides, Emily would have a fit. She likes the damn things."

Both men stared at the map with twigs. Emily approached. She tried to figure out if they were inventing a new game. She picked up a small seashell and placed the item on the map.

Both men looked at the spot.

"Northwest, we head in that direction. It's further to go, but much safer. We walk as far as we can and then camp for the night."

Emily and the men ate the last of the fruit and drank some water. They put the cooler, blankets, and gear inside the special compartments on the craft, Pulling the dinghy, they walked the shoreline, stopping in the shade when they could.

The sun was low when they stopped.

"We need to keep a fire burning at night. When we leave tomorrow, we add more wood to create smoke. Someone should see the smoke."

They ate fish again and cooked their water. Once the water-cooled, they poured it inside the cooler. Emily found some wild raspberries.

The three survivors gathered around the fire. Cyrus disappeared and came back with a short empty log and a short thick branch. The captain took the wood and branch. Emily looked at the two men questioning the two pieces.

The captain took the stick and pounded out a few beats.

"Sounds good enough. We need to entertain our guests. We planned this song for our cruise guests on a night at the beach. Together we decided to continue with the program. We know where we are in this universe and our beach camping trip has been extended a few days longer than planned. Although we've lost our recorded music, Cyrus does have a beautiful voice. He sings in the church choir. We decided all he needed was a beat to make the sound a success."

Now Emily was intrigued. She wondered what song was chosen. She was thinking of a gospel song. Cyrus began humming. Emily knew the melody. She clapped her hands.

"Hawaii or heavenly other places close to an island?"

Cyrus said, "We were thinking Tahiti and selected Hawaii. I'm glad you recognized the melody. Sit back and have fun."

The captain dragged out branches of leaves.

"We need to pretend they are palm leaves."

The captain began the familiar drum beat and Cyrus sang the words. Emily was entranced. Cyrus beckoned her. He hummed the rest of the music and twirled her around. Their feet were dancing in the sand.

Emily hugged Cyrus and the captain. The end of their day was filled full of life and music. She no longer was afraid. The men would help see her to safety. Their faith in believing was beyond anything she witnessed before. The three rested their third night on the shore. The dinghy was positioned to keep out the cold and any possible predators.

Before the music and dance, Emily talked about her parent's home in California. Cyrus talked about his wife. The captain refrained from talking about Shane. Shane would worry about the sailboat first.

They let Emily fall asleep. The men moved back to the fire and talked. The captain was worried his son was taking too long. They tried to keep the daily routine from the cruise program just like the music arrangement to entertain Emily. They wanted her to feel safe as if they were close to the sailboat.

"Do you think Emily has forgotten Nick?"

The captain filled his pipe with dried seaweed.

"Nope."

"Will Nick return our sailboat?"

"Another no. He'll park her in a good spot."

Cyrus looked at the moon.

"I stole my old man's sportscar once."

The captain grinned.

"Mine was my old man's highly prized and restored pickup. He called the machine, *The Dream*."

"Was she?"

"Oh, yeah!"

Cyrus thought about his next comment.

"Stealing from family usually evolves into forgiveness."

The captain kicked his foot in the sand.

"Shane won't consider Emily or Nick as family."

"Too bad."

Cyrus noticed the captain was slightly more offbeat than usual. He stumbled putting the log and branch in the fire. He noticed his friend, the captain, rubbing his chest more than once. The captain confessed to having some health issues. His medication was on the sailboat. They discussed their next day's options.

In the early morning, Emily was surprised by the happiness of the two men's faces. The captain spoke.

"The wind has shifted. She's coming from the Southeast. We can try to sail. Also, Cyrus has found a cairn about two hundred seventy-five feet in the direction we're headed."

"What is a cairn?"

The captain looked at Cyrus.

"Stacked stones done by the human hand mean we are close to civilization and possibly the road. People stack stones to mark a trail or to sit and meditate."

The captain said, "People might stack them near a vortex which I doubt happened in this place. Usually, the vortex groupies are in Sedona."

Emily wandered to the pile of rocks and saw different colors. The stones were flat and large. She tried to move the top stone. The white rock was heavy.

"There must have been more than one person who created the cairn. Very artistic."

She returned to see the two men attaching ropes to the silver blankets. There were large eyelets on the end of each blanket.

"How far is civilization," asked Emily.

"If we were on the sailboat, one day's ride would reach the spot where we'd see a view of the road. Walking would be two days or a little more."

Emily looked crestfallen.

Cyrus said, "The cairn folks might know a different shortcut through the trees. We should watch for more markers along the beach."

Emily looked down the beach as far as she could see. They were like stragglers on a deserted island using whatever gear and tools they could find. She could live onshore for two more days. Emily put out their breakfast campfire.

They dragged a pole over and placed the unused cooler lid in the center of the boat. The wood pole fitted neatly into the cup holder. The captain tied some twine he made from stripping a tree. He wound the twine around the wooden pole. Later he would strap the pole to the handle grips on each side of the dinghy.

Cyrus held the boat while they stored their gear and climbed into the craft. The two oars were taped together with duct tape to form a crude keel. He pushed the craft into deeper water and pulled himself inside. They placed the tent over themselves and the gear. Cyrus tied the tent in a few places. He showed Emily and the captain so they would know where to exit the craft if she turned over. The tent would help keep out the water from any waves.

The captain took hold of the keel and nodded to Emily. She let go of the silver fabric. The wind filled inside, and their small craft was moving through the water. They watched the waves and tacked quickly. Cyrus kept an eye on the shoreline. They didn't want to be too close or too far from land. The ride was bouncy and fun. Their reed hats were secured on their heads with shoelaces. Emily couldn't help but laugh. If anyone saw them, they would think they were a bunch of zombies.

Their faces and bodies were overly tanned. The clothing was faded and torn. Emily's orange shirt was a soft peach color. Their hair was either gray or dyed bleach blonde from the sun. She wished her phone worked so she could take a picture.

After sailing four hours, they steered toward shore. A restroom break was required. They needed to drink some water. The men disappeared in the trees after securing their craft. Emily stared at the horizon. She looked Northwest.

"Seagulls don't fly that far from shore."

The image was getting closer. Emily rubbed her eyes.

LINDA MCKOWN

"The white spot in the distance was boat sails. I can't believe the glorious picture in front of me."

She started jumping up and down. She was hollering. The men came running. Cyrus saw the boat.

Both men began dragging the driftwood on the beach. Emily saw the letter "S".

"SOS, extreme duress, of course.

She began dragging logs to form the second letter. A splinter caught her hand. She ignored the pain. There was an ointment on the sailboat.

22 Boat in the Distance

Shane let the sails luff. He looked at the shoreline with the high-powered binoculars. He was glad he could travel swiftly and make a faster time compared to the previous night. That area was one where the coast guard searched before. He was in another new grid.

"This grid needs to be checked for survivors."

He went below to grab the cold roast beef sandwich he made before going to bed. Slathering the bread with barbeque sauce, he spoke into the wind.

"I feel guilty about eating this sandwich. I wonder if they have food. At least my meat came from a freezer. The menu on the board shows ham with scalloped potatoes and pineapple crisp. The writing looks like Cyrus."

He went below and took the casseroles out of the freezer to thaw. As soon as he could cut a few slices, he'd put the rest of the dinners back. Peeling the foil backward, he smelled the cold dish.

"Cyrus loves tarragon. This dish is one of his recipes. Would you look at the cherries in the pineapple crisp? Oh, man, he used the yellow Bing-type cherries from

Washington state. I saw the bill. He flew them into the marina. I bet he would like a slice."

Shane left the food on a rubber mat on the counter and went outside. Turning the sailboat, he trimmed the sails after placing a marker on his map. Shane put his hat back on and let the boat glide across the water. When he reached the next point, he noted the time.

"One thirty in the afternoon. If they are out there, they might be taking a break."

Again, and again, he turned the boat to look at the shore. There was a bright blip of light. Shane turned the boat toward where he saw something shine. He held the binoculars while continuing to sail. He saw the aluminum blankets blowing on the beach. Next, he saw the wooden letters. Turning left, there were three people on the beach waving their hands.

The sailboat inched closer. Shane monitored his depth. The sailboat was getting in shallower water. He tacked.

Emily cried, "No, we can't have this happening to us. The boat is turning away."

The captain looked at their map.

"The water gets shallow here. Let's see what the sailboat does. I would turn around and come back to a good place to anchor."

They waited in suspense on the shore.

Emily's voice and throat were suddenly dry.

"Aiden, you're correct. The boat is turning. Now his sails have luffed. He's taking them down. The anchor must be dropped."

Cyrus saw the light.

"A spotlight blinking is coming from the boat. He's using Morse code. It's Shane. He has our sailboat. Nick parked her."

The captain grinned.

"Good boy, after all. Shane wants us to try to use our dinghy."

"Why doesn't he use the extra inflatable one which is below deck."

"Maybe Nick used the other craft to reach the shore. Swimming was too much work. The small motor was stored next to the foot pump and bag. He probably saw the items when our guests toured the boat."

The two men threw the cooler in the dinghy and grabbed the sail. They were holding the small craft. Emily wasn't moving.

"Well, Emily, we don't have all day. The sooner you get in the craft, the sooner you can take a soapy shower."

Emily hurriedly splashed into the water. She wanted to feel warm shower water and sweet-smelling soap on her skin. She wanted to eat food, real food. The sailboat contained food and a clean foam mattress. There would be no more very cold sand. She could almost smell the coffee.

It took them a little longer than they thought to manipulate the tiny sail. Shane put the netting over the side to make the entry onto the boat easier. As soon as they were alongside, they let Emily go first. She quickly climbed the netting. Shane held out his hand to pull her over the railing.

"You must be Emily Erin. We talked on the phone before the start of the cruise."

Emily nodded and hugged Shane. She was so happy to be on the big boat; she didn't care how he felt. The pressure of her warm body filled Shane with relief.

"I've got to help my father. We can hug later."

Emily let him go.

Cyrus looked at Aiden and motioned for him to go aboard. Everyone helped push and pull the captain forward.

"Hello, son, nice to see you. What took you so long? We need to buy a homing beacon for our dinghy."

The two men briefly hugged and turned to grab the dinghy ropes from Cyrus before he climbed aboard. Emily went down below and found a cold bottle of water. She took two sips and dug out two more bottles.

The men were slapping each other on the back. She handed the water to the captain and Cyrus. They drank and talked at once.

"Wait, let's talk about your survival experience this evening. I need to get this small craft back in its place and contact the coast guard. I'd like the two of you to then rest while I get you some food."

"Make mine a grilled cheese sandwich. We can do supper around six. I believe there are scalloped potatoes on the menu," said Cyrus.

Shane knew the men were okay. He reached them in time. The small craft was secured, the cooler emptied of the water and the blankets stored. The wooden mast was left to float away.

Emily went below to attend to her splinter and join the survivors in the galley. They ate their sandwiches. There would be a good dinner for their next meal. They were glad it wasn't fish.

Emily took her shower and put clean clothes on. Cyrus and the captain did the same.

Shane saw her bandaged hand.

She told him there was a stubborn piece of wood that she eventually dugout.

He was relieved.

Finally, the coast guard cutter arrived. The three people told their side of the story.

Emily, the captain, and Cyrus downplayed the experience. The captain didn't like the tone in his son's voice when he kept referring to them as survivors.

Nick Kent became a wanted fugitive for theft. The police would be contacting his father. The coast guard people disappeared.

Shane and his father made the decision to put the second anchor out. They would stay where they were for the night. A decision would be made in the morning of which direction they would travel.

Emily was sure Nick's father would freeze his son's account. She wondered how much of the two hundred and fifty thousand dollars were already spent. She shook herself.

"I shouldn't worry about Nick. I just camped my way through a challenging experience, one that he put me in. If I never see him again, I will be blessed. I'm glad we are all safe."

Emily dialed her parent's phone number to let them know she was back on the sailboat. She didn't go into too much detail. There was no need to scare them.

The men were talking to Shane. Emily decided to write in her journal. After some time, she went on the top side of the boat.

"I've heated the casserole. We can eat. Aiden and Cyrus, there's even dessert with wonderful cherries. Yum, I ate the top on one piece. Will anyone of you know if I eat all the cherries?"

The captain and Cyrus scrambled below. They weren't going to trust Emily with homemade food.

"We're coming. Don't eat mine," shouted Cyrus.

Shane shook his head. The two men pushed each other in their effort to be the first person through the open door.

After their meal, Cyrus and the captain offered to clean the galley. Emily was happy the food was mostly gone. She thought the cook should write a cookbook. She would buy one.

Emily went above the deck and sat on the outside seats. The captain stuck his head through the doorway.

"We must handle our affairs and go to bed. Don't stay up too late."

Shane went below and returned. He poured some evening cocktails for the two of them.

"We need to talk and celebrate."

Emily complied. She appeared to be left alone with Shane. He probably had questions about her experience. She was surprised they didn't talk about her last four days.

"I've read your initial contract. You decided to sail with us. There was mention of a break in your career. Are you currently looking for a job? If you are, I would like to hire you. My company can use someone with your experience."

Emily really looked at Shane. He was an attractive man and appeared to be very polished and intelligent.

"How did you manage to sail this large boat by yourself?"

Shane impressed most people. He was glad she noticed.

"I guess we'll talk about your skills in the future. I have been sailing since the age of three. This sailboat is as familiar as driving a large RV."

"Three years old. Now, I am impressed. You sail, fly, and run your own business. My career seems to have come to a halt. This trip has been fun until four days ago. Your father and Cyrus are good people. I'd like to continue with the cruise on its return to your home port. Then I can take a bus from there to Chicago and fly to my parent's home in LA. Your job offer is much appreciated. If you can wait, I'd like to take three more weeks to decide."

Shane smiled, "I think that is fair. We will more than likely need to talk with the police. I also have some insurance issues to settle. My job takes me to California on occasion. I could take you out to dinner. Only if you can accept my apology for a very rude client that my company allowed on my boat."

"Yes, I'd like dinner. I don't want to talk too much about Nick."

"I'm glad you want to do dinner. Now tell me what you like to do when you aren't looking for a job or sailing."

Emily and Shane talked until midnight. They immediately liked each other's company. Emily yawned.

"I need to turn in for the evening. I'm glad we talked."

Shane took her hand. "I'm glad to have found and met you also. I'll suggest we continue with the cruise. We should be in our home port in three and a half to four days depending on the wind. I'll make sure you get a ride to Chicago. I know some people who have a limousine service."

"Thank you and goodnight."

"Goodnight, Emily."

Shane sat at the helm for another hour. He took a tour of the sailboat to make sure the anchors were holding. He touched the place where the cut rope was located. His floatplane carried the rope to the police as evidence. One last look at the shoreline and sky told him the weather looked stable until morning.

"There might be a light mist. We'll be ready. A little mist doesn't bother us."

He went below to send a text to his secretary before going to bed. The alarm was set for two hours. He would recheck the boat anchor.

Previously Shane changed the passwords on the sailboat computer. The new software alarm was installed on the computer at the helm.

His father and Cyrus were given the new codes. If anyone tried to use the device, they would be sorry. The handgun his friend owned was placed where all three men could find it. Anyone trying to steal the boat would be shot in the future.

Shane wasn't going to go through another experience like this again nor have any of his crew in danger.

He thought about Emily before falling asleep.

Shane didn't want to tell her about Duane Ramsey yet. There would be time after they arrived in port. His father and Cyrus knew Duane passed away during brain surgery. Shane, somehow, wanted to believe Nick was partly responsible. However, Duane's wife told him there was an aneurysm.

He knew Emily would take his death hard. His father told him they became good friends. Shane could understand why. Emily was a very nice person.

"There, I've said *nice* twice now. Perhaps bright and pretty should be added. I want to know her. I hope she's interested. My father did warn me. A woman would come along and she would rearrange my life."

Shane smiled.

"Life became more interesting today."

23 Emily with Shane

During the days sailing to the company's home port, Emily created a website with Cyrus's help. They were inputting his recipes into a special file. She showed him how he could share the recipe for the day with any fans. They began taking pictures of the food, his cooking in the galley, and the beautiful sailboat. There were pictures of the shoreline, birds, the water, sails filled with wind, and sunsets.

Emily went topside to talk to Shane. She looked toward shore and saw rocks. Unbuckling the binoculars, she looked and shouted.

"Captain and Cyrus, come quickly."

She handed the men the binoculars. Shane slowed the sailboat.

"Another cairn with variegated stones."

The captain looked and scanned the trees.

"Look toward one o'clock on the top of the ridge. There is another pile and what looks to be a pathway."

Emily grinned at her two friends.

"You were right."

They sailed another two hours and saw the road through the trees. Emily knew she was never lost. The men's experience was beyond the normal person.

"Awesome, we were this close."

The captain relieved Shane at the helm.

"What is awesome?"

"The cairns were leading us to the road."

"Interesting viewpoint," said Shane.

Shane became involved in the new website.

"We can hook the old website to this one. This will give our clients a better glimpse of the cruise and what we have to offer for excitement. People love gourmet meals. That's why they go on huge ship cruises."

Emily said, "This will definitely be better than the bland brochure. Food, scenery, and sailing are the main topics."

The captain also saw the beauty in the layout when Cyrus relieved him at the helm.

"I agree. Good food, sunshine, and romantic nights should be our focus. Sailing outlines can be in the background. We use the sailboat as a subliminal impact. You've even prepared some fancy beverage drinks. People will want to sail with our company in the future."

Cyrus was pleased with the time-tested menus he created for the cruises. The ordering of supplies was made easier. There were extra food items in the pantry if the external fishing excursions didn't work.

The large grouper fish and frozen papaya with red chili peppers were sitting on the counter. The meal was to be a Caribbean affair with couscous, mushrooms, and fresh herbs.

The last stop sold fresh plants and Cyrus purchased most of the items in the cart. There was a tiny lemon tree with a few small lemons growing on the side. In the morning, he would put the clay pots in a plastic basket, water them, and leave them in the sun for at least four hours.

Emily sat the pots on the front of the ship, laid down, and took pictures of the fresh herbs. She used basil and a closeup of the lemons for their opening website page. The last page was a tiny purple lavender flower.

In the evening the captain and Cyrus drank espresso and played chess in the galley. For the next three nights, Emily and Shane disappeared to the upper deck. They watched the moon move across the sky and pointed out the star patterns that they knew.

Shane figured there wasn't Duane on the boat to entertain her and he was delighted. He didn't mind getting close to her. His life was too busy in the past to find a permanent girlfriend. Most of the serious ones moved down the road after a year. The disappearance of his employees and a client brought his busy day job to a screeching halt. He realized the opportunity of a lifetime was right in front of him. He decided to savor every moment. Shane believed Emily felt the same.

One evening, he helped her to the bridge. Their hands touched. He took the moment to lightly kiss her hand, Emily hesitated and gave him a quick kiss. Shane knew the light kiss was important. Emily didn't randomly kiss people. From then on, the two of them were seen holding hands. Emily would stand close to Shane when they were sailing. One time he put his arm around her.

The captain didn't miss anything on the sailboat. He was impressed with how Emily and Shane were bonding. The two old men talked in the evening about young people.

"I bet you a hundred dollars we see a wedding in a year," said Cyrus.

"How I wish you were correct? Shane has dragged his feet when it comes to women. They usually get impatient with him and leave. My wife, when she was alive, told me to let her boy figure things out. I think he needs a good shove in the right direction. Emily fits my bill for a daughter-in-law just fine. I'm on for the bet."

Both men took out their wallets and put money into a plastic coffee mug. Cyrus wrote in black magic marker, *don't touch per captain's orders.*

"Independence can be a handicap."

"You're speaking about my son?"

Cyrus contemplated his answer. He put the cup in the cupboard.

"Both of them have a determined streak inside. Emily appears weak, but she's proved her metal in our beach campout drill."

"Had we known the fool was going to steal our boat, I would have packed a lot more food and water. Drill! Heck, I've been in military exercises that were easier."

Cyrus agreed with his friend.

"We have seen the young boys fall out of military training."

"I believe she would have walked to the moon with the dinghy in tow."

Cyrus chuckled.

"There was no way she was going to leave either one of us old farts behind."

The captain smiled.

"She has become a good friend. Never once did she disparage Nick."

There was no more to be said. The men called the game a draw. Cyrus carefully put the hand-carved wood figures in the mahogany wood box. The finish was worn off in spots on the pawns. A brass metal counter and pen fit neatly into the side of the box. The brass locks were closed. The captain stored the box in his cabin. The two men retired for the evening.

They heard the young people retiring as well. The two men listened. Emily went to her room and Shane went to a different room. The captain shook his head.

"Moving too slow for my taste."

Cyrus said, "Must come from the other side of the family. When we raced, we were in the competition to win."

24 Funerals

The sailboat was neatly moored at her permanent slip in the harbor across from Bayfield on Madeline Island. The men tied the lines, threw out the floats, and ensured the outside was secured. The men stayed with the sailboat watching the cleaning crew take out the garbage, wash, shine, vacuum the marine carpet, clean the galley, and bathrooms. The sheets and blankets were replaced with clean items. The additional bathroom supplies were put in the hold. Another set of people was there to inspect the dinghy.

Shane walked with Emily to buy their tickets for the ferry. He made hotel arrangements for two rooms. He would stay with Emily until the limousine driver arrived in the morning.

"Shane, you don't need to be so extravagant by staying with me. I will be just fine."

"No, you are my responsibility. Also, don't forget Nick is still out there. I'm amazed he has avoided getting caught by the police. Besides, there are some things we need to talk about that can't wait."

"I'm going to think hard about your job offer while I'm at my parent's house in

Los Angeles. Nick is only wanted for questioning."

"I wish you wouldn't defend Nick. There must be right and wrong. I'll await your decision regarding the job."

He looked at his watch. The noon ferry wouldn't arrive for an hour.

"I must tell you sad news. There's been a funeral. I believe they held the small ceremony yesterday. The body was cremated."

"I imagine the police have released Mara's body."

"I don't know about Mara's funeral. Duane Ramsey's surgery was successful. However, he passed away a few days ago. They thought he was all right, but then there was a blood clot."

Emily sat still and turned gray. Shane tried to take her hand and she moved away. She walked over to the coin-operated metal scope. She put a quarter inside and looked through the viewfinder. Emily could see across the water a great distance. Then she looked at the same view without the scope.

Shane casually came to her side.

"Everything looks so small and inconsequential without the scope lens. Then I look through the lens and can see people going about their daily lives. They are unaware that a good soul has been lost to this

184

world forever. Duane, you weren't indestructible."

"His wife told me the sailboat cruise was his best and most wonderful of adventures. Duane wanted to sign up for the next one. We are booked for the rest of the season. However, we would have welcomed him on the boat as a crew member. His knowledge of the water and a ship was a match for my company."

They saw the ferry dock. Emily started running.

"We have time, about twenty minutes to be exact."

"I want to get a bouquet of flowers."

She disappeared into a shop. Duane picked up their gear and followed.

Once on the ferry, they sat in the seats on the second deck. When the ferry was halfway across, she released the small wildflower bouquet. The stems separated and the petals drifted a short distance before disappearing. The water was so clear, there were a few flowers visible when she glanced back"

Emily felt better.

"He was the best. Duane told me once that he loved me. I told him that I felt the same. He respected my feelings about his marriage and kept a safe distance. There were times when I wish he hadn't."

Shane made another attempt to hold Emily's hand. She let him and leaned on his shoulder for the rest of their ride.

The next morning, he tucked her into the limousine.

"I'll call you later this evening."

Emily waved as the vehicle moved away. She would see him again. He told her she wasn't going to escape a proper dinner. Their meal at the hotel didn't count.

XXXXXX

There were thirty motorcycles at the tiny cemetery for Mara's funeral. The chrome on the bikes was clean and polished. Dean's bike showed aluminum tape over the rust. The men and women from the motorcycle club wore their best leather gear. They wanted to pay respect to one of their own. Huge arrangements of flowers adorned her gravesite.

The mourners waited for the minister to speak his final words. They stepped aside as the grave helpers lowered the casket, filled the space with dirt, and placed the arrangements on top.

The biker people stood in a small circle a short distance away. Mike Nichols stepped aside to let Dean move forward. Mara's brother stepped in the center to speak.

"My sister's death took us all by surprise. She was robbed of her youth and life by some rich kid's son. The police want Nick for questioning. We want more than a few words with him. We saw Nick with her the night before she died. We may look scruffy and stupid. We aren't."

The crowd shouted. "We'll give him a slice of hell."

Another person chanted, "Kill him, kill him."

The police car stopped, and two officers approached the noisy group. The older officer talked.

"Is everything okay here? The cemetery company called us. You should be moving along."

A heavyset biker shouted, "Why are you hassling us when there's a killer loose. Shouldn't you be looking for him?"

"Look, folks, I know you are upset. The woman appeared to be one of our town's good citizens. She was only arrested a few times. We'll keep searching for the person who took her life."

"Her name was Mara Peters and my name is Dean Jesse Peters. The man you are trying to find is Nick Kent."

The bikers shouted profanities at the mention of the man's name.

The younger policeman looked at the other officer. They both thought about crowd mentality.

"Now, we are aware of the names. There's no need to get excited. This should be a quiet time to show respect to Ms. Peters. If a few of you need to stay, we can understand. The rest of you should disburse. I hear Tommy's Shack is having half price hamburgers and hotdogs in her honor. I know Mara used to like eating there."

Dean wiped his brow and put his kerchief on his head.

"The officer is maybe trying to help us in our grief. We do need food to decide on an action plan going forward. I'll buy the first beer for everyone."

The officers watched as the bikers took off on their motorcycles. The other officer noticed one of the bikes had expired tags and made a comment. The older officer held up his hand.

"We don't arrest the biker today. That would be suicide unless you don't want to eat dinner this evening."

"I didn't see the tag."

"Good. I would hate to be Nick Kent. Right now, he has over sixty enemies from this group. Who knows how many other friends or relatives couldn't make her funeral?"

The two officers slowly drove by Tommy's Shack. The second officer was glad to see people eating quietly at the outside picnic tables. A few people were adding some firewood to the fire pit. A metal farm bin was dragged outside and filled with ice. Cans of beer were dumped and tucked into the cold mix. The other officer looked worried.

"Why are you looking strange? Tommy's place always drags out the bin for parties."

"What we are seeing is no party."

"A bereavement celebration. See, there's a girl bringing a vase of flowers."

"The flowers aren't roses shipped in for the occasion. The green stuff is seaweed from the water."

"Why would they choose seaweed?"

The lead officer shook his head. The younger guy didn't know very much.

"There's a saying my mother used to tell me. Don't go near the water. It looks calm today, but tomorrow is where things fall apart. The storm rips the rocks and trees from the hillside. If a person looks again, the entire beach has disappeared. The water is dangerous. Those bikers are like the storm, loaded and ready. Mara was found in the water. That's where they plan on putting

189

Nick if they find him. Let's hope we get him first."

The younger officer swallowed. He wasn't pulling any biker over in this neck of the woods for six months.

"No, sir. I mean yes, sir."

25 Pickup for Sale

Nick saw the truck by the roadside. The sign read, *For Sale*. He felt confident in approaching the farmhouse that was set back in the trees. The large yard looked newly mowed and the fence freshly painted white color. Knocking on the door, an elderly man opened the screen door.

"You must be here about the truck. She runs just fine and has forty thousand miles. Well, maybe a little more on the mileage. I've bought myself a new truck with the money I received from a church raffle."

Nick looked around.

"Do you live alone? I didn't see anyone other than a large garden."

"No, there's only me that lives here. I sell the vegetables at the market in town. In about two weeks, the foodstuff should be ready. Maybe a little longer. My son used to help but is gone. I have a grandson in college."

"The garden is impressive. The cherry trees are full. What price do you want for the blue truck?"

"Eight thousand dollars and not a penny less."

Nick thought the price was a little high except he needed transportation.

"How about seven thousand five hundred dollars. I can put five hundred dollars down today and give you the rest tomorrow."

"No, I just bought the license tabs. I'll do the deal for seven thousand eight hundred dollars."

"All right. Here's the five hundred as a down payment. I need a receipt."

The old man wrote out the receipt and started to hand the yellow paper to Nick. Wait a minute, I didn't get your name."

Nick hesitated. "Nick Kent."

"Well, Nick, see you tomorrow. What time do you think you will stop?"

"Lunchtime, probably around noon."

The two men departed ways. Nick went back to the empty garage he saw a mile down the road. He selected a couple of apples from the old man's trees.

Exactly noon the next day he returned with his gear and money. The bills were counted and folded into a roll. Nick noticed the truck was missing from the road. He wasn't worried. The old man probably put the vehicle in his garage. The garage door was down. Nick knocked at the door. The old man let him inside.

"Here's your five hundred dollars back. Another man bought the truck for eight thousand five hundred dollars. He gave me a check. I already deposited the money in my checking account."

Nick's mouth fell open. He was mad but took the money and placed the bills inside his gear. His knife was in the knapsack. He placed the knife in his palm.

"I would have paid you more if you only waited."

"I won't argue with you."

The old man didn't see the knife. He turned his back on Nick. Walking toward the door to escort his visitor outside, the old man's hand touched the screen.

"I might want to sell the white truck. The vehicle is too short on the bed. I need something longer. Come back tomorrow with money. I'll make you a fair deal."

Nick really wanted a truck and handed the five hundred dollars back to the man.

"Sure, I'm thinking around thirty thousand?"

The old man nodded and pocketed the money. Nick was delighted. He would have transportation.

"Oh, you need to change the receipt from the blue truck to the white one and the price."

The old man corrected the figures and initialed the receipt.

The next morning, Nick drove to the old man's place. He opened the back door and hollered. There was no response.

"You must be out for the day. I'll make myself at home."

He sank into the living room chair and turned on the news. He was upset the police were still after him. He thought if he waited a while, the old man might appear. He fell asleep.

Upon awakening, Nick went back into the kitchen. There was no one in the house. He looked out the windows. Not one single person was on the property.

He stopped and saw the car keys on the wall on a metal hook. A look of relief spread across his face.

"This might be a good place to crash for a few days. The old man is probably off selling vegetables."

Nick opened the refrigerator and the freezer. He saw hamburgers and TV dinners. There was a whole duck and some pork chops. On a whim, he went to the garage to look at the new white truck.

"This truck is better. There's even a full tank of gas."

He searched the garage and found there was a back door to the garage. Stepping outside, he saw the tractor under the metal awning with the blade on the front. The keys were in the ignition. There was a small potato garden in the shade. He thought the placement of the garden was odd.

"Potatoes need sun. However, the truck fits the bill perfectly."

Nick drove the tractor back and forth in the driveway. This was the first time he drove a tractor. He was easily entertained.

There were some potato plants under a grow light in the garage. Half the potato plants were gone. Nick didn't think anything about the plants. There seemed to be a watering system that turned on in the evening.

A week went past and Nick was ready to leave. Not realizing his fingerprints were all over the house, he dropped paper bills on the kitchen counter.

"Thirty thousand dollars should be enough for the white truck. He left a note with the money, *As agreed.*

He saw a paper on the floor. He read the note, *went fishing.*

A map was spread on the kitchen table. He marked the county roads he would take to reach the freeway. He would head South and turn West on the second interstate. He took the address out of his backpack. The address was Emily Erin's family home in Los Angeles, California.

He used the old man's computer for finding a leasing company. Using his credit card, he leased a twenty-four-foot sailboat for three months from a dock in Oakland.

Right before he left, there were pills in the medicine cabinet.

"Sleeping pills. They might come in useful."

Nick pocketed the bottle. He took the truck keys and left in the white truck.

26 Her Parent's House

Emily yawned while waiting for her rental car. She called Shane.

"I'm at the rental agency. I've talked to my parents. Tomorrow they leave for a three-week boat cruise to Mexico. It looks like I will have the run of the house and the use of a vehicle. They want me to rent a car and they'll have our gardener return the rental."

Shane was glad Emily was no longer in the area.

"Sorry about your parents leaving. They seem to travel more than when you were younger. I thought they owned a dog."

Emily laughed.

"The dog is visiting his favorite posh kennel."

"I wish I could take some vacation. We could have more fun together. The insurance company wants to see the dinghy. The bottom is scraped."

"We might have been tired on occasion in pulling the small craft along."

"I'm not too concerned. They get paid handsomely for my company. We will insist on complete repair or replacement."

"I've got to run; my car number has popped up on the rental board."

Shane reluctantly ended the call. She would text him before going to bed. He ordered flowers for her. She would get them in the morning after her parents left.

He didn't want to tell her that his company's lawyer received a call from Nick Kent's father. Mr. Andrew Kent's lawyer would be suing Shane's firm for negligence. The father didn't believe Nick stole the sailboat. The father also thought Shane's company was responsible for his son's disappearance. The death of Mara wasn't mentioned at all.

Shane would need Emily's testimony to clear his firm. She would make a good witness if they went to court.

Emily was happy with the flowers. A week of calm sunshine days helped to lift her spirits and phone calls with Shane.

One of her old college friends was home for the summer. Emily decided to visit her for five days. They went shopping, got their hair done, played golf, and hung out in the pool.

"I need to see if the house is okay. When I talked to the landscaper yesterday, he saw a window open. I might have not closed the latch properly."

She talked a little bit about her sailing experience, particularly about meeting Shane. Emily said goodbye to her friend Cari

Higgins. They assured each other that next time, they would try to get together sooner.

Arriving home with bags of fresh vegetables and fruit, Emily called her parents. They were having fun. She agreed to call them in three days.

Making a salad and chopping the ham, she looked at her parent's pool. The water was crystal clear. Emily thought about going for a swim later. Instead, she decided to get a book and read.

Shane called.

"Hi. Where are you?"

"I'm in my room at my parent's home. My wardrobe has been replenished."

"I have a question for you. My lawyer has some papers which we need you to review. Your signature is important to explain the events that occurred with Nick Kent. I'd like to fly to LA. We can do a special dinner."

"I would be very pleased to see you. I thought the police report would be enough."

"I know. My lawyer wants the facts nailed tightly down. How about Thursday?"

"Two days is good for me. I can pick you up at the airport."

Shane laughed.

"No need, I'll need a car to do some company business. I was thinking about a convertible."

"Get a red one, but only if you want to drive slow."

"I'll get the silver one. This time I feel things will be going faster with a special someone."

"Ooh, now I'm intrigued. I can hardly wait."

Emily disconnected from the call. She decided to check the temperature on the pool and cut some yellow roses for the kitchen table. She usually locked the patio door but forgot this time.

At ten o'clock, she was getting sleepy and decided to take a shower. She was undoing her ponytail when she heard a noise. Emily crept down the hall and turned on the light.

There was a man with a small growth of mustache and beard standing in her living room.

"Hi, Em, nice pad."

"Nick? How did you get into my parent's home?"

He pointed to the patio door. She saw a white pickup in the driveway. Emily looked at Nick suspiciously.

"I paid thirty thousand dollars cash for the truck. This old man and I agreed on the price. However, he wasn't there when I came back. I didn't steal the truck."

Emily wasn't sure if she should believe him.

"The police are looking for you. Mara was found dead at the marina."

Nick opened the refrigerator, opened a cola, and sat down at the kitchen table. Emily remembered her cell phone was in the bathroom on the counter. She didn't know if she should run or stay.

"Obviously, you found my parent's address in my book. I wondered why my bag was moved on the sailboat."

"Yes, I knew you were visiting them. On a lark, I wrote the address on a piece of paper. I planned on seeing you again. We had such fun together."

Emily wasn't sure why Nick wanted to see her. She never encouraged his advances. Or did she? She remembered her hug. Then, there was his ill-timed stealing of the sailboat.

"You need to leave. I won't be an accessory to your misdeeds with the law. I'm very pissed you left us ashore. I did like staying on the beach except for the comfort of a sailboat offshore was missing. Taking the sailboat was stupid."

"I only borrowed the sailboat. I overheard the captain talking to the police. The police scare me. That's why I left the cruise. Don't be mad. I'm here now. I came to California because you were the only person who was nice."

"Nick, you are in big trouble."

"I know. You must listen. I don't think I'm going to leave here unless you come with me."

Emily jumped out of her chair. Nick caught her arm.

"No, we can't have you talking to people about me. I'm desperate. You must come with me."

Emily shook her head. Nick became angry.

"We'll walk to your bedroom where you can pack some clothes. No fancy stuff; pick useful. We'll be on a twenty-four-foot sailboat. I've leased her for some time."

"No."

"Yes."

Emily looked at the stranger in front of her. She walked into her bedroom and threw some clothes in a bag. Nick saw inside one of her dresser drawers. He opened the drawer and selected the red bikini swimsuit.

"This one will look nicer."

He handed her the bikini and his cola can.

"Drink."

Emily knew there must be drugs in the cola.

"Nick, please. Don't do this."

202

He looked at her with softness. Now she was worried. Emily could feel a panic attack coming.

"I promise I won't hurt you. I can't hurt you."

Emily took the can and drank. Slowly, Nick's face disappeared. She didn't talk. There was no need to speak Shane's name. She didn't want Shane anywhere near this man. Emily wasn't sure how long her captor would keep her alive. She would try to stay alive. There were people she needed to love. Her final thoughts.

"A lifetime's worth of loving is what I would miss."

27 The Cabin

Emily awakened. There was tape over her mouth. She could see daylight. Now she required bathroom facilities. Fully expecting to hear the lap of ocean water against a hull, all she could hear were birds. The room was pinewood like a cabin. She was confused. Suddenly, Emily remembered.

"Nick."

At that moment, he chose to appear with a load of firewood.

"We might want to have a fire. I tried the stove and the pilot won't light. My matches are too short. I did drive into town to get a box. We are in luck. I bought their last box with the stripe on the side."

Nick disappeared. Emily tried to make a noise with her throat. He turned around.

"Oh, you might need a bathroom break. I've removed any tool you might use."

He untied her and took the tape off her mouth. Leading her into the bathroom, she noticed the bathroom rods, toilet lid, and mirror were missing. The window was boarded shut. There was a chain holding the tank lid. Shutting the door partially, she did her business and used the thin toilet paper.

After five minutes, he led her to a chair and tied her hands in the front. He put a chain on her feet. She could only take steps.

He unwrapped a sandwich and placed the paper and bread in front of her.

"Turkey was on the special menu today. You should be full until supper. We have soup, crackers, and cheese."

Emily ate hungrily and drank from the bottle of water. When she was done, she hobbled to the lumpy couch.

"Where's the sailboat?"

"*Change of plans*. The sailboat is in the harbor. The item will be used as a decoy. At the last minute, I used my old man's credit card he gave me to rent the boat. The police will eventually surround the harbor. I thought we could watch the news."

"Why did you take the white pickup and why me?"

Nick looked at the ceiling.

"Now the truck is a sore point. I really wanted to purchase the older blue one. Again, I needed to change my plans. Why you? I told you."

Nick disappeared to light the water heater. Emily looked outside. She couldn't remember what Nick told her. All she could see now were trees. She tried the door. The knob wouldn't turn. She looked through the keyhole. There was only the main room, a bathroom, and possibly a bedroom.

"We should have hot water by morning."

Emily was grateful. She missed her cell phone. Nick was holding an object. She gasped.

"Tell me about Shane Hanigan. He's the big shot owner of the sailboat."

Emily looked at the refrigerator.

"Did you buy any apples?"

He went to the refrigerator, selected an apple, and threw her the fruit. She almost fell over trying to catch the red sphere.

"Shane found his sailboat where you left it after you stole the boat. We became friends on a short trip to port. Plus, there was a police report, the insurance company, etc. I must sign documents. Mr. Hanigan's lawyer has already prepared them."

"I didn't steal Mr. Hanigan's boat. I only borrowed the boat. He was flying here to take you to dinner."

Emily couldn't remember how much information was in her texts.

"The papers he wanted me to sign were regarding the stolen boat."

"Did he specifically tell you those facts?"

"Well, no."

"Then the papers could have been about something else."

Emily frowned. She didn't know what she was meant to sign.

"The dinner, Emily, tell me about this date."

"It wasn't a date. I agreed to an expensive dinner. The dinner was Shane's way of thanking me for not suing his firm. I was placed in a survivor position by one of their crazy clients."

"Crazy. I suppose what I did was unwise. Mr. Hanigan might pursue legal action. There's even more reason for me to disappear."

Nick paced and put her phone in the sink. He filled the sink with water. Emily's spirits deflated. She should have purchased the more expensive waterproof phone. Now there was no way for the police to find her.

"The flowers, Emily. Tell me why he bought you flowers and was going to rent a silver convertible."

Emily bit her lower lip.

"Duane Ramsey died after brain surgery. Shane knew I was still upset. His funeral was about a week ago. The flowers were nice. The convertible would be a rental because he does have business interests in LA."

Nick wondered if Emily was lying.

"Duane is really gone?"

Emily shook her head.

"Duane took the sailboat cruise even though he knew about the brain aneurysm. Per his wife, he was delaying the surgery."

Nick wasn't sorry Duane was gone. The man hovered over Emily the entire sailboat cruise. This made Nick jealous.

"The man appeared fit other than headaches."

He wondered if the hit by the white boom harmed Duane even more. Nick hoped that he wasn't in trouble over the incident. The crew thought the hit by the boom was an accident. Nick knew otherwise.

"Yes, we heard Duane comment frequently about his head hurting."

Emily was quiet. She missed Duane's voice. If he were here, Duane would help her. She was relieved to have steered the conversation away from Shane.

Nick tied her to the bedroom railing while he went into the main room.

He refused to answer her questions. She could hear him listen to the television. He was flipping the channels.

She tried to see out the dirty curtain. The yard looked weedy. Emily would need to wait and see what else was coming. Evidently, Nick's plans flowed and switched faster than the wind. His logic was not there.

208

The person she knew on the sailboat cruise was different from the person in front of her. Emily wondered if she could convince Nick to turn himself into the police. There were no experiences in her past to have prepared her for Nick. She never met anyone like him. Was there a chance his demeanor would change?

"Does water flow uphill? There's your answer. Fat chance."

28 Reading Book

Day 2 of her captivity started early. Nick disappeared and returned with an egg burrito, delicatessen coffee, yogurt with fruit, and a paperback book. The address label was ripped off the book package. He must have ordered the book before they arrived.

"Preplanning."

Nick heard her.

"What did you say?"

"My burrito is a little cold. I plan to heat it in the pan. There's no microwave. Next time, get one."

Nick wasn't sure how to take Emily's jibe. He watched her heat the burrito.

Emily took a napkin and picked the burrito with her hands. She almost dropped the hot food on the floor.

Nick was not talkative this morning. He let her use the bathroom, tied her in the bedroom with the book and left.

"This book is about *Sailing a Catamaran*. Why would I want to read this book? Of course, Nick is getting a catamaran to escape to either Canada or Mexico. I guess it doesn't matter the direction."

Emily started reading. At this point in the game, more knowledge couldn't hurt.

After three hours, she stopped reading. Her captor was not on the property.

She wiggled her handcuffs. They were tightly secured to the iron headboard. Noticing the chain, her legs were starting to get red and sore. She knew the chains must be removed or infection would set in. There was no medicine cabinet in the cabin.

"Shane probably has arrived in LA. He will be upset when he finds that I'm not home. He'll contact my friend and the police next. My parents will be called. They will believe the worst. They will think Nick or someone kidnapped me. I know Nick's fingerprints are on the patio door and glass. By tomorrow, my face should be on the news as a missing person. I didn't really want the notoriety."

Emily tried to exercise on the bed. Her muscles were getting flabby. Strength was important if she was going to sail a catamaran or escape.

Nick returned and turned the television news channels on. The volume was turned low so she couldn't hear.

Coming into the bedroom, he released her, and she was given a bathroom break.

"Why have you kidnapped me?"

Nick looked at her suspiciously.

"I haven't."

Emily held her hands out in front of her.

"These cuffs and chains say otherwise. My legs are turning to raw flesh from the chains."

For the first time, he noticed her legs and bruising skin.

"You are hurt. I shouldn't have used the chains. I'm sorry."

Quickly he released her chains and handcuffs. Walking to the door, he unlocked the device.

"You're free to go. Don't think too unkindly about me."

Emily believed Nick was lying about letting her go. Somehow, he was going to trick her. She wondered if the news was what triggered her release.

Slowly, she walked through the wooden door and saw the rutted drive filled with weeds. Although her legs hurt, she was determined.

"One step, one more, keep going. Don't look back. He's probably watching."

Emily reached the open gate and saw a large field of hay. Through the edge of the field, she saw water.

"We're close to the ocean. I can walk along the shore. People have beach houses and cell phones. Help is steps away. Maybe no one is home. Someone must be home. If

212

not, break a window, and find a weapon. Freedom awaits. Run, Emily, run!"

She tore through the tall hay and was a third of the way across when she heard an engine turn over. Glancing over her shoulder, the truck was coming. The white truck's front looked menacing.

Emily groaned.

"No, no, he's coming after me."

The ground was uneven, and she stepped into a gopher hole and fell headlong into the hay. The white truck drove round and round her, flattening the hay. Emily stood watching Nick open the door. He was ten feet away and blocking her path to the water. Emily thought she saw a seagull.

"*Change of plans*. You can't go yet. We haven't talked. You still think I'm guilty. I'm not."

There was a glimmer of hope in her heart when he said the last sentence.

Bravely she told him, "Take off my chains and locks. I'll travel with you to the border. We will be two strangers on a trip like before. No funny stuff. After we've talked, then we will part. You will let me go. That's my deal."

Nick looked at the sky. He knew she would keep trying to escape. He needed to get to the border. The moored catamaran was a distance from a close-by rickety dock. He shouldn't leave the boat there too long. It might float away. There were groceries and water to purchase.

Emily waited and swatted at a fly.

"Okay. I will get supplies this afternoon. You can help me select the food. You know how to cook better. We'll leave early in the morning. Once on the catamaran, no locks. If you try to leave me before we are at the border, I will stop you."

Emily knew there was a possibility to escape in her future if she played Nick. She would need to be careful.

"We buy some antibiotic cream and band aches or gauze wrap so I can take care of my legs."

He agreed.

Emily went to him. He moved out of her way and she climbed into the truck.

In the evening, they ate the last frozen meal in silence. Emily went to the small bedroom, closed the door, and read more of the pages in the book.

Fitfully she tossed and turned. Her dreams were filled with white foam and waves crashing into rocky ledges which made for a fitful night. In the morning, she was exhausted.

Nick packed their meager bundles of clothes. She was surprised they left the white truck.

"This way, Emily, there's a path for almost half a mile."

Walking through the woods, she saw rocks strewn in the dirt and a few broken arrow signs. She had no clue where they were but knew they were more than likely in California. There was a steep hill before the land dipped.

She saw the thirty-two or thirty-five-foot catamaran.

Nick saw her look at the boat.

"She's forty feet."

"Expensive?"

"A woman is always expensive. This one cost me about two hundred thousand dollars."

Emily wanted to ask him where he found the boat. She decided the question would need to wait for later. Now she understood where his money from his father went.

The wood on the dock was warped and filled with holes. She watched her step.

He tossed their bags into the small dinghy and rowed to the catamaran. He helped her onto the first hull, and she stepped over the railing. Nick pulled her close to him.

Emily ducked her head and went below. She looked around and was amazed at how clean the boat was inside. Sticking her head out of the hatch, she said, "This will do. Is there computerized navigation?"

Nick tucked the bags into the two beds and moved to the galley.

"We have some electronics that will be useful. The computer is not as sophisticated as the sailboat on our cruise. I'll show you later how to work the system, the sails, anchor, and other controls. We need to watch the sails. The boat can speed fast on the water and lift. I'm not used to that much tilt. You aren't either."

"Duly noted."

Nick secured the dinghy onto their vessel, undid the lines from the buoy, and turned the engine over. They cruised out a distance. The sail was raised, and they were sailing. The engine was turned off. Emily took the helm.

Nick found the life preservers.

"We need to wear these while sailing."

Emily buckled her vest and smelled the salty air. She was almost free.

29 Catamaran

Nick and Emily took turns learning the wind capacity on the sails, the light touch of the steering wheel and reading the charts on the navigation system.

They alternated sailing the coastline. She wondered if they were North of Los Angeles. The land was not familiar to her.

Emily watched the boom swing when she turned, the wind speed, and the waves on the water. The position of the boat was important. There was a turn that seemed to be faster. The boom swung more rapidly. She counted the seconds required for the white boom to swing.

If there was ever a plan to escape, Emily was formulating one. She memorized everything in her brain. The timing was crucial to her future survival.

Nick noticed Emily's concentration.

"You are quite the sailor. I see you concentrating. Is this catamaran too difficult?"

Emily tacked smoothly and tightened the sail.

"Impressive. My partner knows how to sail. You read the book that I gave you. Wonderful. I'm taking over the helm. We have a destination close by. The water will be a challenge. I am lowering our sails and motoring the rest of our path."

Emily sat down as she saw some distant island.

"Where are we?"

Nick was pleased. She was in the dark. He remembered the pathway on the water into where the houseboat resided.

Emily saw the red bridge. We are in San Francisco. I love this town. It is so beautiful."

"Emily, hold on. We have cross currents. I put in a larger motor to get into the harbor."

Emily watched Nick. The man knew this area. Familiarity was evident. Suddenly, she felt happy, almost euphoric. The sea air was exhilarating. Being close to Nick was bringing feeling into her lithe body that she'd packed away.

"We're almost past the current," said Nick.

She saw the lights of a harbor. They were going to dock the boat.

The catamaran rocked and Emily held on.

"She's handled the cross-waves superbly."

The catamaran took some more turns and they pulled into a dock. Nick refueled.

Emily knew where they were stopped.

"Grab your things. I've hooked into the electrical system at the dock."

She did as she was told. They went out of the harbor and into another area. There were restaurants with amazing smells. Emily was wondering when they would eat. The food on the boat was bland and boring.

"I want to eat out tonight."

Nick didn't respond. Emily walked beside him. People were mingling between them. For a moment, Emily wanted to disappear in the crowd. They came around a small building. Nick grabbed her by the throat. She struggled. He pressed his body close to her and blocked any escape. His brown hair and dark eyes scanned her face for some emotion.

"Don't even think you can disappear."

He slowly touched the outline of her lips. His finger traveled down her neck and stopped where he toyed with her collar.

Emily didn't move. Her body tingled with a mixture of senses. Nick's body was hard and strong. Feeling a man's heartbeat close to her made Emily want to be loved again. She wanted his company and pleasure. He was waiting for her reaction. So many barriers she had erected around her heart came crashing down with the surf. This made her upset.

"Em?"

"Our emotions are frayed."

"Speak for yourself," said Nick.

Steeling her resolve, she finally looked at him with brave belligerence in her eyes.

He released his pressure and stepped away from her soft body. Emily took a breath. His eyes seemed darker. Nick was having trouble staying in control. The flicker of fire between them ignited and was easily extinguished for the moment. She heard the people in the street. They were oblivious to the young couple. Emily knew she was in the calm before the storm.

"We have a deal. I know the plan. You need to settle down. No more thinking wild thoughts or hurting me. Try this move again and I will disappear."

Nick gently took her by the arm, not quite trusting Emily. He didn't talk.

He let hold of her to punch a code of numbers into the waterfront gate. Emily was confused until she saw the houseboats or houses on water tethered to the very secure and wide dock system.

"I was wrong; we're in Sausalito?"

They were standing in front of a houseboat on the water. Nick keyed in another code, opened the door, and lightly shoved Emily inside when she didn't move.

She looked at him questioningly.

"My father owns many companies and others. There are properties all over the world. I know where every one of them is located. My father hired nannies to watch me or sent me to rich boarding schools. When I was older, he gave me the codes and the keys. I could always choose my destination and my credit card. This one has an electric fireplace. Not very romantic, but we won't turn the switch unless you are in the mood."

Emily was shocked. In front of her stood a young man who was given privilege beyond the normal. There was no need for past events to have happened.

Nick showed her to a tiny bedroom. He was on the phone. In twenty minutes, a delivery driver dropped off their meal.

She was pleased the dinner was oriental. There was shrimp, garlic beef, sweet and sour chicken, multiple entrees of appetizers, and rice. A bottle of white wine was included.

Emily and Nick stuffed themselves. Nick put the cartons in the refrigerator and poured the final glasses of wine.

"We needed different food. Also, there's cable here and good mattresses. If you want to take a shower, now is a good time.

I've set the recorder on the machine to the news channels. Most of them I've seen."

Emily wanted to watch the news but knew his comment was a command. She did as she was told.

Turning on the shower water, she tried to listen. The place was better built than most houseboats. This one contained sound insulation. She gave up because she couldn't hear.

Emily wrapped herself in a plush towel and took out new clothes to wear.

Nick came into her bedroom. His expression was unreadable. He came over to Emily and kissed her.

"No."

He was surprised by her response.

"We have a deal. You break it, I run."

He looked at her.

"Women want me, especially when they know I have money.

Emily sighed.

"Nick, drop the money thing. I'm just not interested. I broke up with someone before the sailboat cruise. I don't care who you are in this world. You could be a king. The king isn't on my dating list. Let me repeat myself; I'm super not available. Please understand."

"You have a dating list? Wow. What are the criteria? Meek and mild or wild and

222

sexy? Don't tell me. But this bloke, was he important?"

Emily sat on the cream-colored chair.

"We dated for four years. We talked about our future. One day, poof, he's gone. Four years of my life are down the toilet. I'm not looking to repeat the pattern."

Nick understood.

"I've lived through the poof mode myself. The only thing was the timing. Mine was two months."

Emily stopped talking. Nick was supposed to leave her bedroom.

"Earlier, you called the catamaran a she-person."

Emily stopped fidgeting with the trim on her chair. She didn't know what to say.

"Yes."

Emily moved from her chair and sat on the bed. Nick sat on the bed close to her.

"Do you know why a boat is a woman?"

Emily did not.

"Unpredictable. A woman changes with the wind. You might change."

She was tired of sailing and the riddles.

"I need to sleep. I'm so tired. My arms ache from holding the steering wheel."

Nick resigned himself to the fact that he was in the same boat. The waves were brutal.

"I've called a company in San Francisco who has a tether so we can tie the steering wheel in position. We'll have an easier time. We'll stay here for another day. You can come with me to the boat store."

Emily brightened.

"Can we eat lunch on the wharf in San Francisco?"

Nick couldn't believe Emily.

"All you think about is food."

She clapped her hands.

"The answer is a positive."

Nick chuckled, "Yes."

Emily laid down on her bed.

"Tomorrow is going to be food heaven."

Nick was delighted there was a change in attitude. Leaving Emily on the bed, he looked forward to the next day. This was something he was not used to doing, pursuing a woman who was oblivious to his charms. Emily was the bright spot in his life after he met her. He knew she was special toward the end of the sailboat cruise. Nick needed to convince her.

The next day they bought the special tether and stopped at a restaurant on the wharf. They were laughing and talking. Nick

224

touched Emily's hand. She didn't move away this time. A camera at the restaurant caught the two people. The waiter brought them more wine. He would remember the pair. They were tanned and happy.

The waiter said, "If you play together, you will remain the same as you are now."

Nick watched Emily blush.

30 Shane at the House

Walking through the house of Emily's parents with Cari Higgins, Shane commented, "She told me that I could take her out to dinner. We planned to go for a ride afterward. She hasn't answered my texts or phone calls. There is something wrong. Emily is in trouble. I've got to find her."

Cari checked through Emily's closet.

"The clothes she bought are here. Her bed is made. There's nothing missing that I can tell. Wait, her backpack is gone, a red swimsuit, and some sailing clothes we bought for her trip on Lake Superior. She carries her journal inside the backpack. Her cell phone isn't in the house. We tried to call and didn't hear any ring. Maybe she took off for a few days. Emily is unpredictable and very independent. She might be on the beach near a nice hotel."

"How long have you known her?"

"We went to high school. My parents moved to LA before my senior year. We also went to the same college where we were busy studying and going out on double dates. Next thing I know she has a boyfriend. Her boyfriend kept her busy. She moved away when she found her job."

226

"She didn't tell me about a boyfriend."

Cari looked at the pool through the patio doors. Brian was old news. They stopped dating. She told him about Brian Nelson.

"I think we should contact Mr. Nelson."

Cari dug out her phone and called a number. She talked briefly with the man and hung up.

"He hasn't heard from Emily for some time."

Frustrated, Shane sat on one of the bar stools. He looked at the furniture.

"I contacted her parents and they didn't seem worried. They asked that we make sure the doors are locked before we leave."

Cari wrote a note.

"If she returns to the house, I know Emily will call me."

Shane gave Cari his business card. He looked at the drooping roses. The water was almost gone in the vase.

"I'm sure Emily is fine," said Cari.

Looking at his watch, Shane told her that he must leave for a company meeting. He didn't like the fact that Emily wasn't home. She didn't appear to be the type of woman to stand someone up.

Shane contacted his father.

"If Emily calls you or Cyrus, please let me know."

His father assured him that Emily would appear.

"Emily might be with someone. Nick was infatuated with her on the sailboat. Maybe they are together. If so, he wouldn't intentionally harm her."

Shane was doubtful.

"I don't believe she would go with Nick willingly. The man stole my sailboat. He's not exactly reliable."

Shane wanted to go to the police. His father reminded him that there was no evidence. He disconnected the call from his father.

Still, Shane wouldn't give up his thoughts. He was afraid Emily was spirited away by Nick against her will. He couldn't prove his theory. He just knew Nick's type.

"What have you done with Emily? If you hurt her, I will come after you. Nick Kent is a piece of crap in my book."

Shane left to attend his meeting and flew back to Michigan.

After three weeks, there was no word from Emily. Eventually, her parents went to the police and filed a missing person's report.

31 Shark in the Water

They were North of San Diego when Emily decided to take a dip in the ocean. She stayed close to the boat.

Nick hurriedly called out.

"Swim to the boat now Emily. Make your legs move faster than a race car in the final turn."

Emily complied. He reached down to grab her hand and pulled her forward so fast they both stumbled and fell on the decking. A great white shark jumped out of the water and circled their craft.

"Oh, my god. Did you see how large his teeth were not to mention his size? Why didn't you let me know the man-eating fish was nearby? Most people yell *Shark* quite loudly or honk the horn."

"I knew you would freeze. I've seen you do that move before. I couldn't take the chance."

They watched the shark swim around their boat.

"We didn't throw any garbage into the ocean. He shouldn't stay this long."

Nick tried the catamaran's horn.

"His behavior seems off. There must be something under our catamaran that is holding the shark's attention. We'll need to stop at the marina in San Diego to get supplies, water, and gas. I'll check underneath the boat."

"Is there something dragging in the water?"

"There could be a line or piece of plastic caught. The ocean is full of junk."

The two went down below to get the boat secured for traveling. Upon reaching San Diego, Nick found the large sticker label and threw the item in the trash.

"We shouldn't be a magnet for the shark anymore."

"Where do we get supplies?"

Nick looked at Emily. They still hadn't talked very much about Mara. He needed to explain.

"You'll stay with the boat?"

Emily looked at the marina filled with vacationers. All she needed to do was yell help and someone would come to her rescue. Nick was waiting for her reply.

"I'll stay."

He went out of the marina gate. Emily didn't know what was wrong with her. She should run.

"The captive is off her rocker."

She saw the laundromat sign. There was a roll of quarters and soap on the catamaran. Grabbing her clothes, she stepped over the railing. Stopping herself, she went below and grabbed Nick's dirty clothes and put their items in separate plastic bags.

Nick returned to the boat with the supplies and couldn't find Emily on board. He panicked.

"She went to the police. I need to leave. He looked at the shops and saw her with a cart full of plastic bags. She punched the guest code on the gate and came to their mooring.

"Our laundry took me longer than I thought. Here's your load. I'll get mine."

She deposited the cart, came back, grabbed her clean laundry, and jumped onto the deck. Nick looked inside his bag. The clothes smelled clean. He went below to store the items. Emily did the same.

They cooked steak and vegetables for their evening meal. Emily washed the small pile of dishes while Nick cleaned the grates and put the grill away.

Emily made coffee and brought two cups topside.

"Tell me about Mara," said Emily.

Nick dreaded telling her. There were parts of the story that bothered him.

"I ran into Mara at the Marina store if you recall."

She nodded.

"Mara and I talked."

Nick began his side of the story. He knew someday the police would have to hear the same version.

"The other time we were together, I bought her a small diamond necklace. There was an antique store across the highway which sold jewelry. She said I was romantic. I had my ulterior motives. She grabbed my phone and took a selfie wearing the necklace. She seemed pleased with the present. I wanted her to feel special. When I saw her the second time, we went to the park with some beer. Her brother was there. He is not a real brother, but a distant cousin. Mara told me Dean Peters wasn't his original name. His last name is Jesse."

He took a long sip of his coffee, enjoying the flavor.

"Dean was in the park and we got into a fight. I made the mistake of taking my knife out. He got my knife away from me and took a swipe. You saw my arm."

"I did."

"Mara went nuts and climbed on his back. She pounded on him until he fell and let go of the knife. She told him to leave. Dean left the park angry. Mara was all cuddly and sincere about being my friend. I believed her. One thing led to another. We went to her small house or cottage and made love. I left her place. She was alive. Mara knew I would

232

continue the cruise which was leaving in the morning. She understood my drifter nature."

"Mara was alive? I don't understand. You ran. The word stupid comes to my mind."

"I don't know if I was stupid. My sperm was inside the woman. The police would naturally assume I was the killer. You saw me swimming in the water the next day by the dock. Your testimony wouldn't help. Then there's the black rope someone planted."

Emily remembered past events.

"Those are your reasons for kidnaping me?"

Nick paced the deck.

"I don't exactly call what I did a kidnapping. No, I have other reasons."

"You are absolutely wrong."

Emily dumped the contents of her coffee in the water and went below. She slammed the door on her bunk.

Nick finished his coffee.

"Now, there was a very predictable move by a woman. I knew she wouldn't believe me. Crap, I'm so screwed."

32 White Boom

They traveled for two more days and moored the catamaran.

Nick leaned over the front of the boat to watch the anchor.

"We're close to the border. The anchor is not holding. Crank her up. Emily, pull the sail up a little and come around. We'll save the gas."

Emily waited and tacked one direction. She realized the wind, sail, and boat were in perfect position. Nick was standing opposite the white boom. Without hesitation, she tacked again. The boom caught Nick off guard, and he went into the water. The engine was already running when she tightened the sail and the boat flew out of Nick's reach.

Emily slowed the motor and turned the catamaran to watch Nick swim to shore. In the distance, she noticed a movement.

"No, no. A shark fin. Make that two fins."

She turned the engine and boat toward Nick. She started yelling at him.

"Get in the boat now. We're at the raceway."

Nick stopped his swim toward shore and saw Emily coming toward him. He thought she was going to run him down.

Suddenly, she dropped the sail and reversed the engine and stopped. Throwing the life preserver, he took ahold. She pulled him in as fast as she could.

Nick finished the job by pulling himself over the side. Emily restarted the engine, turned the boat toward San Diego and raised the sail.

He moved out of the way of the boom. Emily pointed. Nick saw the two sharks and shook his head.

"Give me the helm. Why didn't you yell *Shark*? Raceway, unbelievable. Go sit down."

Emily was shaking. She almost killed Nick.

"I don't know what came over me."

"Be quiet, Em, for once in your life."

"Nick, I shouldn't have turned."

"Em, please, we can talk after we move to a better spot."

There was silence between them until they stopped for the evening. The anchor held.

"I'm taking a shower. I'll try to make this one quick. You should do the same. Your face is still white and stiff."

Nick went below. Emily looked at the sun sphere elongate and drop into the ocean. For a normal couple on vacation on a boat, this would have been a perfect romantic evening. Her whole life was never normal.

She thought about Mara and the story Nick told her. She wondered if he lied to her again.

"He bought Mara a necklace."

She started to cry. Emily hadn't cried since she was a child. She felt there was something missing in her life. No one bought her a diamond necklace.

"Maybe the sun was too much today or the sharks."

Nick was wet with a towel wrapped around him. He took Emily in his arms.

"Don't cry. The big bad fish didn't stand a chance with your sailing experience. I shouldn't have cranked at a scared person. If we ever get a chance, I'll take you to the car races. They drive fast on the track, but the curves are way cool. We'll have a good time watching other people try to kill themselves."

She couldn't help but laugh. He was trying to cheer her out of the tears.

"Nick, stop. I almost killed you. The track sounds great. Still, I'm so sorry."

He touched her face where the teardrops showed. She was coming out of her frozen mode. Nick was glad.

"No one has ever cried for me before."

"Not even Nancy?"

"Good grief, no. That woman doesn't know how to feel sympathetic. Her narcissism and negativism finally got to me. Was she why you avoided me on the sailboat?" asked Nick.

"You were enamored or seemed overwhelmed."

Nick said, "She was someone I knew in college. I thought we could rekindle the good stuff. She proved me wrong."

"Do you miss her?"

There was only one way to give her the answer.

He bent to kiss her mouth. Emily kissed back. There was a confused look on Nick's face. He moved back. There would be no pressure from him. Nick waited. Now was the moment she would blow him off. Emily pulled him close.

Nick held her and let her take her time. There was no rush. Her love was what he wanted. There was a wildness in her eyes he couldn't quite forget. A sparkle of light appeared when she tried to hide the glow.

Emily said, "In a past life, I think we met."

"Was I a pirate?"

"No, you were a lifeguard."

Nick held her close and kissed her neck.

"Lifeguards save people."

"I know and therein develops a hero-worship thing."

Nick stopped kissing her.

"I do worship you," said Nick. He touched her lips and cheek. Emily closed her eyes and kissed him as if he were the last man standing on the earth. Her tender sweet love rocked him faster than the incoming evening tide. The impact was fully felt. He should have braced himself.

"Nick, I'm ready."

He crushed her to him, kissed her with the same treasured love, and emptied his heart and soul.

"Hush, no more promises."

Nick nodded. He was putty in her hands. Emily brushed her lips evocatively and foolishly across his once more.

"You're sure?"

"Yes."

Nick wasn't going to ask why the word, *maybe,* disappeared. He reached for her after he went down the steps.

Her solitary isolation ended. Emily was no longer trapped in the deep. She felt excited and alive. She gave him her hand. Their future paths were moving beyond friends. Emily could feel the wind increase because she tempted fate. Throwing caution and self-control away, neither one could stop the powerful force.

The two people went below. Emily crawled in his bed. Nick welcomed and pulled her into his aching arms. They let their emotions take over. The two lovers kissed and moved through the night as most young people do when passion overtakes them. There was a beating of dual hearts.

The dawn might bring a different light. However, the night was theirs to hold captive. Time and the long night mattered. Emily wasn't disappointed. Nick was gentle and held her tight. The stars were dim compared to the warmth that existed between them.

Eventually, Nick went to the refrigerator and brought back a plate of strawberries.

"Even wild things need to eat."

"I'm not wild."

Nick disagreed. Emily's lips were red from eating the berry and the precious juice. Nick kissed her slower this time tasting her mouth. Their lovemaking was now familiar and more pleasurable. She fit her curves against his body. Again, the two made up for the lost time. Yesterday was forgotten. The waves gently rocked the boat in their safe and secretive world.

"This creature is pleased" sighed Emily, "and full." Finally, they fell asleep.

XXXXXX

In the morning, they talked and argued.

"Nick, turn yourself in to the police and stop this madness of running."

"I can't Emily. I'm used to drifting. There's the system which I don't trust. My dad and his lawyers will try to buy my way out; and if they can't, they will create chaos. Right now, I want some peace in my life. I want you."

Emily started to interrupt. Nick held up both hands.

"Freedom is what we agreed. You have your freedom. Since Sausalito, you could go. There was a moment between us that was memorable. Your body touching mine made me stop in my tracks. I didn't tell you because my need to be with you overpowered my thinking. Then you gave me hope. The look in your eyes yesterday told me yes. I'm glad we made love. I'd like to be able to see you when I can."

Emily knew Nick wasn't going to stop running.

"I'm glad we made love, too. The storm between us was brewing for a long time."

Nick now took notice.

"Even on the sailboat cruise?"

"Yes."

Nick shook his head, "Now I know I acted stupidly."

Emily wondered where their plans would have taken them. There were errors in judgment on both sides. They were paying the price.

As if reading her mind, Nick said, "We return to San Diego. You go home. I go to Mexico and drift some more. I need time to decide where to live. My dad will help."

Emily was quiet. There was no other choice. Separation and heartache would happen. She kissed him on the lips. She didn't want him to leave. The captive wanted to be with the captor. Nick saw her distress. He took her in his arms.

"I'll miss you."

Nick held her close and whispered.

"Wait for me."

Emily looked at Nick. She couldn't answer. His words triggered a memory. She tried to pull the vision in her brain.

Nick saw her hesitation. He misinterpreted her feelings. Bravery wasn't one of her strong points. Nick let her go and prepared the catamaran for their journey.

When they arrived at the San Diego dock, Nick was taken by the police for kidnapping Emily Erin.

Emily argued with the police at the station. The police captain intervened in the uproar.

She told the police that the two of them were traveling together on a vacation. Neither one had a job, so they decided to continue sailing. She voluntarily was on the catamaran. There was no pressure from Nick for her to stay on the boat. Emily mentioned their stop in San Francisco. There was a waiter at the wharf who could verify her statement. The two people were lovers enjoying a good time. She gave the police the name of the restaurant.

The catamaran was dry-docked, and Nick was taken into questioning about the Mara Peters murder while they checked with the San Francisco restaurant.

Emily called her parents. They came to the station and convinced the captain to relinquish their tired daughter. They informed him that their daughter was headstrong at times but sane.

Her parents took her home. After two months, she made the decision to leave. Nick gave her the address to the cabin. The Shane

A. Hanigan company refused to drop charges. The Mara murder was being investigated. Nick's father was attempting bail.

Before she could leave, Shane Hanigan appeared at her parent's door.

33 Meeting with Shane

Emily left her bags in the hall. He saw her luggage. Her sundress was empire-waist in a white batiste with tiny purple flowers. Her hairdo was upswept by white bobby pins with purple flowers.

She handed Shane an iced tea and sat barefooted in a soft white leather kitchen chair. Her parents stepped out to the pool area.

"Hi, Shane, you didn't need to stop here. Like I told your secretary, my parent's lawyer doesn't want me to sign any papers from your firm or anyone else's."

Shane shook his head.

"The legal papers were important to the insurance company. I can live without them. I have some business in Los Angeles and wanted to make sure you were all right."

"As you can see, I'm fine."

"I saw a news media story. The reporter mentioned you were lovers."

Emily didn't respond. Her relationship with Nick was private.

Shane took another tact.

"My father, Cyrus, and I were worried that Nick Kent kidnapped you. We believed he coerced you into claiming otherwise. His actions on the cruise made us

244

suspicious. We never trusted the man. You didn't seem to trust him."

"I believe your father and Cyrus were worried. I don't believe they would think Nick kidnaped me."

"Okay, I included them in my kidnaping statement. You've heard of the Stockholm syndrome?"

Emily went to the refrigerator and sliced some lemon. She brought the slices to the table and offered him some. He declined. She dropped two pieces in her drink.

"Don't even go there. I'm not ill nor do I require a psychiatrist to help examine my feelings. I do miss my two old friends. Thank them for worrying. Like I told the police, I went willingly with Nick. There was no hostage and captor situation. End of story."

Shane rubbed his brow. He tried one more tact.

"Emily, your heart is soft, and I could see how Nick's manipulation of the situation would appear to you as confusion. Nick tricked you into making illogical statements."

"I took psychology courses. Drop your theories because you weren't there. I was on Nick's catamaran and my mind was not confused. Nor is my brain fuzzy or sentimentally off.

He knew she would clam up if he pressed further. Emily was a private person. He wouldn't mention Nick.

"My apologies, I'm upset. I came to your parent's home before you disappeared. We were supposed to have a dinner date. When we were together on my sailboat, I felt there was a massive connection. I'm not usually wrong in the dating or women game."

Emily stirred the lemons.

"Life is not a game, Shane. I'm impressed with your knowledge of women."

"Emily, please don't argue with me. I wasn't bragging. You know I wouldn't."

She did know. Shane was angry with her. She led him to believe they would start a relationship together.

"I'll try to explain. There were feelings between us. I will admit that I was flattered by your attention. My plans were set. I was going to accept your job offer."

"What happened?"

Emily's mom came into the kitchen, found some fruit, and returned outside.

"I don't know how to answer. Somehow, my plans changed. Then they changed again. There are complications that I can't go into with you."

Emily didn't want to tell Shane she and Nick were lovers. He was hurt enough by her disappearance. Her heart was soft. She did care.

There was silence between them. Shane didn't want to ask the next question. He couldn't let it go.

"You're in love with him?"

Emily sighed.

"The word love is maybe too strong. Strong does mean indestructible. I find myself in the water and over my head."

Shane was finding her answers difficult to understand. He took the water analogy to mean Nick was in hot water.

"You could take my job offer. I still have the position open."

"I called your father about your company's charges against Nick. I hoped that he could persuade you to drop the major charge. I'm upset that the lawyers are moving forward."

Emily looked at Shane.

"Nick broke the law."

"He did."

She was now angry at him for being harsh. Shane could drop the theft charges against Nick. Their friendship wasn't enough for Shane to want to help.

Emily made her decision. Some of her other issues were not important for Shane to know. His disloyalty broke her trust.

"I am declining your job offer. There are some decisions in my future that are mine to make."

Shane assumed she was talking about Nick.

"Please reconsider."

"I can't."

He stood up to leave. Emily walked him to the door.

"If you need anything, you will call me?"

Emily lost her nerve and couldn't trust her voice.

He turned back to Emily.

"Our business is booming. With all the publicity, we've purchased a second sailboat. The sailboat is used and will need modifications. Next season, the second boat will be ready for cruises."

"I'm glad. My cruise with your company was unusual and interesting. The scenery and companionship were awesome. Plus, I learned to sail from a competent man."

Shane leaned toward her and kissed her on the cheek. She nodded goodbye. Shane didn't want to leave her but knew their differences were too much. He left feeling used and guilty about filing charges.

The door closed behind him.

34 Michigan Courtroom

Emily stayed at the cabin for two months when she wasn't in the courtroom showing her support for Nick Kent.

The lawyers questioned Emily Erin, Cyrus Allen, and Aiden Hanigan.

The three agreed before the court date that they were not stranded on the beach. Nick left them with food, water, and a very expensive dinghy loaded with gear. They made a pact to block the kidnapping charge.

Shane's lawyers were forced to drop that charge. This behavior from Shane's own kin and friends made him angry. His father should support the company.

His father told him to *bugger-off*. The company was originally Aiden's company. The only change was a larger sailboat and a new CEO acting strange.

The lawyers argued their cases before Judge Watkins.

It was time for the judge to retire to his chambers for an assessment of the stolen sailboat case.

"I do have some questions for the *survivors of the ordeal* as the plaintiff's lawyers have called the three people involved. My memory is fine. Three times I got their message. Ten times is a little too many gentlemen. I won't use survivors when I question the witnesses. Mr. Shane Hanigan feels the sailboat escapade might harm his business."

The judge asked Mr. Cyrus Allen and Mr. Aiden Hanigan if they felt threatened or stranded by Nick. Both men told the judge they always knew their exact location. The water and Lake Superior's shores didn't scare them. Their familiarity with the area was excellent. Occasionally, the weather turned bad. Even the weather didn't pose a threat. Nor did Nick threaten them. The fishing in the area where they went ashore was also good. They made the decision to move Northwest to find better fish. The Shane A. Hanigan Company sailboat cruises are popular and always filled stated Mr. Hanigan.

Cyrus spoke, "With the new mermaid lure they purchased at a marina, the sturgeon fish were easy to catch. They were larger by three pounds, your Honor."

The plaintiff's lawyer wanted the last comments stricken from the record because they did not relate to the theft charge.

"Stricken," said the judge. He motioned the defendant's lawyer closer and whispered.

"The mermaid lure is at which marina?"

The defendant's lawyer went back to the table with his clients. Nick pointed at Cyrus. Cyrus scribbled a note. The defendant's lawyer returned the note to the judge.

The judge pocketed the note and looked at both sides in his courtroom. There were seven people on each side. Two lawyers on one side for the defendants and six lawyers from the plaintiff on the other side. He noticed the tension and possible feud between a father and son. Mr. Aiden Hanigan's loyalty was not given to the plaintiff's company.

When Ms. Emily Erin was questioned, the judge heard the same story. The judge didn't like hearing a repeat version. He was glad there were only three witnesses and not ten. He wanted to know if she was upset when Nick Kent sailed away in the Shane A. Hanigan Company's sixty-foot sailboat.

Emily looked at Nick in the courtroom.

"Sixty-five-foot sailboat, your Honor."

Judge Watkins shuffled his papers.

"You are correct, young lady. My question remains unanswered."

"No, Nick knew how to sail the boat. I wasn't worried about his safety."

"Were you worried about your own safety?" asked the judge.

"I liked the sailing cruise. Also, I enjoyed the camping experience onshore. My understanding is that we camped a little longer than what was shown on our schedule. The meals, singing, and dancing in the sand was fun. We found cairns and knew our way. Shane appeared so we didn't have to use the road. That's why I finished the cruise. We were sailing again."

The judge said, "Cairns, like in marker stones?"

"Yes, your Honor."

"If Mr. Shane Hanigan hadn't come along, you would have followed the cairns and traveled the highway. But he did appear and put an end to your beach camping. Instead of going home, you finished the cruise. Would you go on another sailing cruise with his firm?"

"Yes, your Honor."

"The sailboat incident with Nick Kent won't deter you from using this company again?"

"No, your Honor. The Captain or Mr. Aiden Hanigan and Mr. Cyrus Allen are very experienced and capable crew members. The two used to race sailboats with DiMarco in Australia. The captain can turn a sailboat on a dime and miss a tanker with her anchor line out."

The judge looked heavenward toward the ceiling of the courtroom. The other people in the courtroom gazed at the ceiling.

Judge Watkins motioned to the defendant's lawyer to come forward and accept a piece of paper. The words on the paper were *Your autograph, please.*

The lawyer handed the paper to Captain Hanigan.

The captain signed the document and gave the piece of paper back to the lawyer. The judge pocketed the paper.

Judge Watkins frowned, "The tanker wouldn't by any chance be the *Dublin Darcy*?"

Emily could only shake her head.

Aiden intervened, "Aye, your Honor, the tanker is the very ship in front of us when we came around the sharp bend in the shoreline with a spinnaker on our boat."

"Thank you, Captain Aiden Hanigan. I would have liked to have seen you turn that sleek, ahem, sixty-five-foot sailboat on a dime. I read all sorts of books about the water and accidents on Lake Superior."

The judge looked at the cover of his next case regarding spoiled food which read *Dublin Darcy vs. Tanner, Thore, & Sons*

Shipping. He turned to Emily seated at the witness stand.

"Your experience with the Shane A. Hanigan Company has been exciting."

"Absolutely, your Honor.

"I see and completely understand."

The lawyers for the plaintiff watched Shane. He didn't look happy.

The judge took his glasses and disappeared into his chambers. There would be a recess for two hours.

The courtroom dispersed.

The judge read the evidence papers from each lawyer three times regarding the events before and after the sailboat incident. The coast guard was called into the search. Calling the coast guard was a serious business. He noted the sailboat was only missing a secondary blow-up dinghy which was later found onshore amongst some trees. A small computer from the sailboat was found in a waterproof compartment.

There were damages requested for a thorough boat inspection, haul out and haul back into the water. A second request for payment to the coast guard. Also, a request for damages to their company name was requested in the amount of three hundred fifty thousand dollars. The judge knew how much a used sixty-five-foot sailboat would cost.

The last request was a payment for the plaintiff's legal fees.

Reappearing in his courtroom, the judge looked at the young man called Nick Kent. There was only a small incident on the young man's records in college regarding a young woman. He looked at Ms. Erin who sat between Mr. Allen and Mr. Hanigan. The three people looked healthy and fit. They were a combined force of support for the young man.

Thinking to himself, the judge saw two old men with a huge and spectacular racing background supporting a Generation X couple. He looked at Shane Hanigan sitting with his lawyers. There was no young woman by his side.

The judge came to his conclusion quickly. He would choose the lesser sentence.

Nick was convicted of theft from the Shane A. Hanigan Company and would be sent to prison. His father couldn't buy Nick's way out of the charges or the sentence. Emily saw tears in the eyes of Nick's father. She wanted to cry but wouldn't show defeat. The payment was granted for the coast guard rescue. The damages to the Shane A. Hanigan Company name were not awarded. The legal fees were granted to the plaintiff.

Shane tried to talk to her before leaving the courthouse. Emily wouldn't listen to any of his words. She walked rapidly in the other direction. Shane was going to follow her when the captain blocked his path.

"Leave her be; you've done enough."

Shane turned angrily on his father.

"Nick is guilty."

The captain spoke, "You never took nor stole anything in your life."

"No," said Shane.

"How unfortunate! Some of us have. The thrill might have changed the person I see standing in front of me. This was a huge prank by a young and very spoiled rich man's son. I see the person. You don't. The law will make sure he learns his lesson. Is it justice you wanted or revenge?"

"He took her."

"She wanted to go with him to California. Her actions were her business."

"Nick interfered in my life."

"I see you've turned jealous and paranoid. By the way, Nick's father can buy your company any day of the week. Let's hope you don't encounter further problems in the business world. I would be more careful in the future whom you target."

Cyrus and the captain went back to their homes. Shane went back to his business.

Emily went home to her parent's house in LA.

35 Prison Visit

When she found the name of the prison Nick Kent was sent, Emily flew back to Michigan for a visit.

She wore a long black wool sweater coat over her white blouse and black slacks. A red silk bow was under the collar of her blouse. Her gold watch and bracelet showed on her wrist.

"There is a chill in the weather and a cold within these brick walls."

Emily sat in the hard chair and looked through the small booth-like window of hardened glass. The room space was private except for the guard who brought Nick into the barren room.

Nick sat down. He looked defeated and sad.

"Em, I knew you would come. You look good and very professional in black."

She was pleased to see him. The sign read, *no touching.* Nick's hands were laced together.

"I need to give you an update. The murder charges were dropped regarding Mara Peters due to insufficient evidence. Instead of drowning, the autopsy showed strangulation. I was on the boat at the time of her death. The captain verified the same information to the police because he saw me

258

enter my bunk. I went swimming later and that is when you believed I originally boarded."

Emily swallowed. "I'm pleased something is working in your favor. I wish we weren't in the marina that day. A killer took advantage of us and placed her in the water close to our mooring spot. The move was calculated and destructive. I hope they catch Mara's killer."

Nick wore a strange look on his face. "About that."

He stopped. Nick might know the killer or at least, he had developed some theories. He would keep Emily out of the loop.

"What do you have to tell me?"

"I mean this jail time for the borrowed sailboat is not good. The lawyer assured me there would be little jail time. He was wrong. My father will appeal to my case. I don't believe anything will change. In the meantime, you need to move forward with your life. Don't come back here. Living this way for a minimum of four years would be difficult."

She tried to interrupt.

"Let me speak. Continue using the cabin for as long as you wish. There will be a gardener and cleaning lady to help take care of the place. I owe you that much until you find a job. I'll get my dad to send you a car. The police will be taking the white truck."

"I'll come back. Why are the police taking the truck? You told me the vehicle was purchased from an old man."

"No, don't come. You heard me."

Emily shook her head.

"I have a written receipt. I left cash on the table. The problem isn't the truck. The old man, Mr. Whipple is missing. I was maybe one of the last people to see him alive. There was a note on his refrigerator. I told them the old man went fishing. My father is going to fight this next charge."

"They are charging you for Mr. Whipple's disappearance?"

"What can I say? I was in the wrong place. My fingerprints were in the man's house. The police found out I'm in jail. They jumped to their own conclusions about me being the bad guy. Luck isn't following me anytime soon."

"How long for stealing the sailboat?"

"I borrowed the boat so I could reach shore further down the coast and closer to the highway. They didn't believe me."

"Nick, I heard your speech in court. How many?"

"Eight years, maybe half that for good behavior. The judge could have given me more time. My lawyer thinks my time will be three and a half years. This facility is one of the nicer ones per his firm. I'll get used to being here. Then I will go to Africa."

Emily's eyes grew even wider.

Nick left his chair and signaled the guard. He didn't look back.

Emily didn't understand. Nick was being difficult. There was only an empty room with florescent lights. Her time was over. She walked outside and left the prison.

Flying to Santa Rosa, California, she hired a driver to take her to Nick's family cabin in Mendocino. The white truck was gone, and a new silver vehicle was parked in the spot. The vehicle would come in handy for moving boxes. She opened the small SUV doors. The title was in her name and the keys were in the ashtray.

She made no further contact with Nick after a package was returned unopened. Emily tried to send him a poetry book. The book was returned by his father's secretary in Chicago.

The police found Mr. Whipple's body. He was dressed in fishing gear and the autopsy showed he had a heart attack. The police dropped charges against Mr. Kent.

XXXXXX

In ten months, Emily moved into an apartment in San Francisco and found a job. There was calm in her life.

Days were spent going to museums and taking walks. She ate at the wharf frequently and stared at the seagulls. They looked the same as the ones on Lake Superior. They weren't. Even the sky was a blue color, only paler. Watching the sailboats skim across the water, she thought about the days spent on the catamaran. Nick's tanned and muscled body was part of her memories. His smile when he saw her in the morning still moved her.

"There's no denying the obvious. I was in love."

Dell sent her the photo taken on the marina dock from their sailing cruise. Everyone looked normal. Nick was standing behind her. She remembered he lightly touched her waist to step behind. The touch was more a caress. Emily missed so many signals coming from Nick.

Her life after that day was chaos. She placed the photograph in a photobook of her sailing adventures. She shut the cover on the book and thought about Nick.

"Was he remembering their time together?"

A year passed since she saw Nick at the Michigan jail. One day Cyrus called.

"How wonderful to hear your friendly voice."

She closed the bedroom door so she could hear him undisturbed. He told her they missed her and wondered if she wanted a free cruise. He told her about the dropped cruises. The sailboat passed inspection, but the bottom needed to be scraped and repainted. The paint job took three months because of the waiting line and rain. Then they looked at the props. They special-ordered two from a company in Sweden. Winter came early. The props did get replaced, and the boat was put in storage.

Emily listened. The Hanigan company didn't make much money for the period the sailboat was out of the water.

Cyrus told her that the boat was back in the water again and ready to sail. Emily declined the free ticket and was told the hatch on the sailboat would always be open to her. She thanked him.

The captain called her the next day and reiterated the invitation. He told her Shane went to Nick's parole hearings after the first year. The captain went with his son.

Emily was shocked. She wondered if Shane was developing a change in viewpoint. Nick Kent wasn't the bad guy.

"Interesting," said Emily.

"Cyrus and I thought he would never come around. We've been working on him. Nick helped when he was on the sailboat cruise. We kept reminding Shane."

Emily was thankful. She hung up the call with Shane's father.

There was a reason for keeping contact with the people in her past. They were her connection to happiness. Cari, the captain, and Cyrus remained friends and called her frequently.

She didn't call Shane Hanigan. Her mind wasn't in a forgiving mood. Her life was occupied elsewhere.

On occasion, she would fly to Los Angeles and stay with her parents for a week. They were always delighted to see Emily. Their travel days were over because their health was waning. Her parents showed her pictures of the places they visited. Emily saw a green palm tree after another and sunny beaches. She was glad they could hold onto each other and their memories.

Emily knew she would do things differently. Including a child in your life was very important. Somehow her parents missed the nurturing part. Because she was older, there wasn't any need to remind them.

36 Waiting for Nick

Three years later, her parents died, and she drove to Los Angeles to handle their estate. Her employer let her telecommute.

The movers came to take the parent's furniture to an auction house. Her furniture was in storage.

The little girl sat at the kitchen table drinking her milk and eating a chocolate chip cookie. A stuffed kitty was in the other hand. Her legs were swinging.

"Mommy, my hand needs a washcloth."

Emily brought the wet rag and wiped her hand and face.

"When am I going to be four? I can get a real kitty when I'm four."

"You'll be four after we move to Michigan. We can get a kitty there."

"What color?"

Emily stopped.

"We don't know. It depends. There's a magazine that has pictures. We can look together. I'll try to buy the cat magazine at the store. You remind me, okay?"

"Yes."

Her friend, Cari, knocked on the door. Emily let her inside and poured hot tea. The house was almost empty.

"Elizabeth, how are you?"

"I'm getting tired. My eyes hurt from watching those men move the dish chest."

"She means the hutch. I'll take her to the downstairs bedroom for her nap."

Emily returned.

"Elizabeth has grown so fast. Her hair is longer and she's taller."

"Yes, we have added shopping to our list for new clothes and a magazine about furry cats."

Cari looked at her friend. Emily looked thinner. "My husband knows some breeders. I'll text you their website names. Maybe Elizabeth can receive a kitten from them. I can take Elizabeth to a few specialty stores for some play clothes. That leaves one person left on my agenda. Emily, how are you doing?"

"We are almost ready to leave. The lawyer will handle most of the rest."

"Did you ever tell Nick about his daughter?"

"No, only my parents knew."

Cari's life was moving in a good direction. Her husband was working for a large engineering firm. She worried about her friend.

"Whatever happened to the Shane person? I really thought he was the one."

Emily looked at her friend.

"There were times when we clicked. We came to a disagreement about Nick and his defense. The wedge pushed us apart. To be truthful, my affair with Nick wasn't exactly perfect timing."

"I don't know how you can call a few indecisive moments an affair. Wait a minute. The Kent name is English while Shane's name is Irish. The countries fought back in the sixteenth century. It appears there's still animosity on both sides."

Emily remembered her history classes.

"However, you look at my past or theirs, my decisions locked my future. Men no longer are the highlight of my days. I don't care what country or century they came from. There's someone more important. I have a little person who needs me."

"Yes, but she needs a mom who's well-rounded."

"I'm well-rounded. I gained ten pounds and lost them."

Emily fiddled with the silver necklace around her throat. Cari found the kettle and poured more hot water.

"I wish that my metabolism matched yours. I gained twenty pounds and lost two. I like your new necklace. What's the stone?"

"The rock is a black diamond surrounded by chips. I was going for the single blue diamond heart, but the color was over my budget."

"Really, at least the necklace is a start at buying something for yourself. My recommendations are that you keep treating yourself with tender loving care. Make a list. Write down number 1, get back into being a fun woman; number 2, go play; and number 3, find a date."

"Speaking of the list, do you remember the dating list we made in college."

Cari laughed. "I do. Your list was impossible for any man to meet the criteria. The swing was so far and wide. Let me see. There was good-looking or not, rich or poor, wild or not-wild, rugged, but not too rugged, brilliant but sociable, and so forth. Sound familiar?"

"Was my list that bad?"

"Your list sounded like the qualifications for a pirate."

Emily brightened.

"That is bad. Do you know of any pirates for a blind date? I'm beginning to see the error in my judgment. I've picked the wrong guys to date. Nice is thrown out the window."

Cari said, "Oh, heavens. I shouldn't have brought the subject to your attention. This is where we remain friends. I don't answer and go home. Seriously, *think* about my recommendations. Maybe you'll find the guy who will buy you the blue heart or build you a house."

"I will."

Elizabeth awakened and came out of the bedroom with her suitcase. She looked at Cari.

"I'm ready."

Cari held out her hand.

"We'll have fun with a stayover. I'll bring you back in the morning."

"Okay, bye, Mommy."

The two of them left. Emily cleaned the dishes and finished packing the small toys. She made a last trip around the home to make sure all the toys were out of sight. She wanted all trace of Elizabeth gone.

"Did I create a war between Nick and Shane? Oh, god, I did. Somehow I messed with fate. I should have known better to start the fire between us. The ignition was already lit like a pilot light. The warmth was waiting. The love between Nick and I was ignited by me."

Emily realized she is responsible for what has happened in her life. Everything was her fault in wanting the sailboat cruise. She wanted to find love.

"I did. He touched me and my body responded."

There was a knock on the door. She saw the seahorse float on a pool chair. Emily dumped the plastic in an outside garbage can and ran to answer the door.

Shane was standing there with a small vase of flowers.

Breathlessly, she said, "Come in. The boxes are still here and there's a cleaning crew coming tomorrow."

Shane watched as Emily put more water in the vase. He stood standing. The visit would be short.

"Nick was released a while ago. He has been granted parole. I stopped here because I wanted to deliver the message in person. You might have already heard from him?"

Emily sat down.

"I didn't know his release happened. He has my phone number and my parent's number. Their phone will be disconnected next week."

Shane knew she didn't answer his question.

Emily jumped out of her chair.

"There's some cola left in the refrigerator."

"No, thank you. I'll be going. It was nice to see you again."

Shane left her parent's house for the last time. He didn't ask her where she was moving. Her future living arrangements were not the reason for his visit.

Emily went outside, removed the toy float and deflated the toy. She stuffed the item in a box and sealed it with tape. Taking the marker, she wrote *water fun*.

Emily looked at her phone and checked her parent's messages. There were no calls from Nick.

"Where are you?"

She waited for two months. She didn't have any way to contact Nick. She dared not call his father. The father would want custody of Elizabeth if he knew about her. One day, Emily stopped looking for messages. She changed her phone number.

"Africa, you've gone there without talking to me first. Why?"

Her life continued with her daughter. The decision was made on the color of the cat and breed. Elizabeth wanted a golden-shaded British Shorthair. The choice was easy. The color matched the child's stuffed toy. Emily contacted a breeder.

37 New Job Location

The house she purchased was across from Lake Michigan in Traverse City. She hired painters to redo the outside a gray with white trim and navy-blue shutters. She planted pink and red roses in the front of the home. Her furniture was modern and there were wooden floors throughout with colorful blue and red wool rugs.

The kitchen was updated and massive in size. Stainless steel and marble were evident. The large island was big enough for baking bread and cookies. She bought herself a good mixer and pasta machine. Tiny garden pots grew small tomatoes and herbs.

The road to her home was marked as a dead-end. Emily wanted to have the city change the sign to a private road.

There was one other large house in the area. An old man lived in the house at the end of the road. He was hard of hearing when Emily met the man. He did bring her cucumbers cauliflower, and squash from his garden. Her den window gave her a nice view of the open water.

Emily closed her computer and stared. She was lonely. Her job was working superbly. The nanny brought Elizabeth into the den.

272

"She's been the best child and we've had a good time today. The school took the children to the park with the beach. The sketchbook you gave her is full of drawings. There's one picture she's ripped out. The picture is a present. I must get my sister's dry cleaning. I'll leave and rush out the kitchen door."

"No problem. You must be as glad as I am that tomorrow is Saturday."

"Yes, ma'am."

Elizabeth gave her mom a hug.

"What did my sweet six-and-a-half-year-old draw for me? I'll bet it's an orange-colored kitty?"

"No, not this one. I left the kitty and rabbit inside my book. There's also a fairy," said Elizabeth.

"Let me guess. The drawing is a tree."

"No, I always do trees when I'm home. Guess again."

Emily threw up her hands in surrender. Elizabeth showed her the drawing.

"I drew a picture of your story. Your photo book has boats."

Emily gasped in delight.

"You've drawn a sailboat on the water."

"The boat is a big one."

"Yes, the boat is at least sixty feet."

"No, you told me sixty-five. I remember the numbers. I put the numbers in the corner on the paper."

Emily saw the pencil smudges of numbers.

"Elizabeth, you have a very smart brain to have remembered."

Emily rubbed her daughter's hair. The daughter giggled.

"We brought cheese pizza on the way home. The pizza is on the counter in the kitchen."

"You did. I'm so hungry. Let's go cut a slice."

Elizabeth raced from the room. Emily took a magnet and put the picture on the magnetic board. Stepping back, she saw a stick lady and two men. One man wore the captain's hat and one wore a cook's hat.

Emily almost wept. She missed her friends.

After pizza and a review of the other drawings, Emily stopped. There was a drawing of a blue diamond heart. The lines were a little oddly shaped. There was light and darks as if someone showed her how to color the stone.

"I wonder," said Emily.

"You like hearts. I remembered."

"Yes, I might have mentioned the blue color."

They closed the book and she gave her daughter a bath, helped her with pajamas, and tucked her in bed.

She went to her master bedroom made a call to her two old friends. Satisfied, Emily fell asleep exhausted.

About two o'clock in the morning, Emily was awakened by motorcycles on the private road. She listened. The motorcycles didn't come back. A creepy feeling came over her. She would check on old man Withers in the morning. The onions in his garden were ready. Emily would have an excuse to visit.

She was fixing her daughter's breakfast when the motorcycles roared past. She looked out the window. One rider saw her. Emily didn't recognize the man on a dark green motorcycle. There was a large dragon on the back of his jacket.

The nanny took her daughter to school and she walked toward Mr. Withers' house. She saw a campfire at the end of the road and strange burn marks on the earth.

"The marks look like crosses. How strange."

She assumed the bikers camped on the county's property for the night. Walking toward Mr. Withers' back door, she saw him sitting in his rocking chair on the porch. She could see the county property and the swamp grass.

"Mr. Withers, it's Emily. I picked some green onions."

She showed him the onions and he nodded his head. Emily left some of the onions on his kitchen counter and returned to the back porch.

"Did you see the bikers on the county's property?"

"What?"

"The motorcycles were on the land with the swamp grass."

"I own the land."

"No, there were people here on the county's property."

"People, no, never saw anyone."

Emily looked again at the swamp grass. He must have seen the bikers. There was a set of binoculars on the small table next to his rocker. He must have his reason for keeping quiet.

"If they come again, you should call the police. I don't know why. They make me feel strange. Maybe it was the biker with the dragon. There were the others. I guess I've lived alone too long. My anxiety is kicking in."

"I saw the dragon, too."

She smiled and took her green onions. She waved at Mr. Withers. He did the same.

Upon reaching her house, she saw footprints around her back door.

Now she was alarmed. Her driveway showed tracks where motorcycles turned around. There was a burned "X" in her driveway. She called the police and filed a report.

They told her there were bikers in the area except they seemed to have left the vicinity. Emily thought no further about the incident. A new security system was put in place at her home. Her daily routine wasn't interrupted again.

38 Sailboat Cruises

For two years Emily and her daughter were booked on Hanigan's older sailboat with the captain and Cyrus for a back to back six-week cruise. They used a fictitious name for the two guests. The men didn't want Shane to see her name on the roster of guests. He was busy with his new girlfriend and didn't bother too much with the cruise agendas. Shane's new manager was capable and handled the newer second boat.

Emily grabbed their large duffle bags.

"Don't forget your fanny pack."

The doorbell rang and the three women ran around the house trying to catch the cat. They corralled the British Shorthair in a room and used the broom to scare the cat out from under the bed.

"Gotcha."

Emily let Elizabeth kiss her favorite creature. The cat was deposited in the carry bag.

"Don't you worry, Elizabeth. This cat loves my place, especially the greenhouse. There's butterflies, bugs, and birds there for the chasing. She won't know you are gone."

"Thank you, Mrs. Breen. We need to hurry."

278

Elizabeth was the first one to make the dock gate. Cyrus saw the young child and held out his arms. After a big hug, she saw the captain.

"Well, hello, young lady, I forgot your name."

She giggled and gave him a hug.

"We recovered the bunk space. Let me show you the new bedrooms."

Emily dropped her two bags. Cyrus picked them up.

"Welcome aboard, old friend." Emily squeezed his arm.

She knew the trip was going to be a good one. Her daughter was becoming very knowledgeable about boats and maps. Sailing was also fun on a small craft stored below deck for her when they stayed on the beach.

The rest of the guests arrived. Emily and Elizabeth were introduced as the Parkers. They kept their first names to make things easier. At first, Emily wasn't fond of the change in their last name. The hard part was convincing her daughter.

Emily finally told her.

"I know the owner of the boat. We don't really get along."

"He might not be happy."

"Exactly."

"Okay."

Emily looked at the captain. He told her the young figured things quickly. They took complicated and turned them into simple. Little girls did those actions better than boys.

"Complicated, uncomplicated, I give up."

The first cruise was the normal pleasurable ride for three weeks. The mother and daughter were fit and tanned. The sailboat moored at her original berth. The boat would take three days to get ready for the next cruise. There was a cancellation by two people unknown to the captain. He would be surprised to see his son and his girlfriend step onto the boat.

Emily wasn't due back from the ferry until the next day. Cyrus disappeared to leave Emily a message on her cell phone.

Elizabeth tripped and broke her arm while they were ashore in town. Emily was required to take her to the doctor's office.

"I don't see any reason why your daughter can't remain on the cruise. The arm should heal. I would stay away from handling the lines and take things easy."

Emily looked at her daughter's hopeful face.

"There's a prescription for antibiotics?"

280

The physician handed her the note and the authorization for her daughter to continue with the cruise. Emily noted the authorization form showed her last name, Erin.

They spent their last night at the hotel eating soup and ice cream. The prescription and pain pills were in her purse. Emily didn't check her phone.

The two females arrived at the sailboat. Cyrus saw them and ushered them to their quarters. He was very agitated. Cyrus ran off to get them a cola. The captain came back with the two cans.

He handed Elizabeth her can and gave his sympathy regarding the arm. The captain told Elizabeth that Cyrus was waiting to show her a new knot. The little girl disappeared.

"Emily, we have a slight problem."

She opened her can and took a sip.

"You've overbooked the sailboat."

"No, I wish the problem was so easy."

Emily looked puzzled.

"There were some dropout guests. Usually, we require a week's notice. For some reason, Shane let them have their money back."

Emily wasn't surprised. "He would refund a guest's money."

The captain knew he was taking too long. Guests would be boarding.

"Shane will be on the cruise."

Emily didn't move.

"He will be with his girlfriend."

Emily couldn't help herself. She started laughing. The captain decided to join her. The door was opened. Shane appeared.

The captain stood, "Excuse me and left the two alone."

Shane started to speak and stop. Emily waited.

"Your name is not on the roster. I would have remembered."

"You might try Parker. We've already paid for our cruise."

Emily exited the small bunk area. She needed air. Seeing her daughter with Cyrus, she relieved him of her care.

"The conversation didn't go well?"

"No. I'm staying."

Cyrus was delighted. He shuffled off to greet the new set of guests.

Emily took Elizabeth to the front of the sailboat to watch the seagulls. Her daughter knocked on the boom for good luck.

"The white boom. Which one told you about the knock?"

Elizabeth threw an apple slice into the water and watched the seagull dive.

"There was this lady. She wasn't on the other cruise."

Emily knew the lady was Shane's friend.

"Maybe we should get off the boat?"

Elizabeth cried, "No, I want to stay."

Shane approached and looked at the two guests.

"You should stay. The owner would like you to continue with your cruise. I promise the sail is worth the journey."

Elizabeth remembered what her mom said about the owner. Shane was the person her mom didn't really like.

"See, mom, he asked us politely. Please!"

Emily looked at her daughter and Shane. He now knew about Nick's daughter.

Shane echoed her request, "Please."

There was no condemnation in his eyes. Emily looked away.

"I looked at the menu. We are having cheese balls. I know someone who needs a treat before supper. She deserves the treat because she has been a good girl."

"Thank you, thank you."

Elizabeth scrambled to meet the other guests.

Shane was still looking at Emily.

"I know this is awkward for you. We do need to be civil with each other. I'm at the helm tomorrow morning. Meet me there."

"Okay, tomorrow works for me. I'll have Elizabeth do some of her reading material in the galley. She likes to read about boats."

Shane looked at the birds and stepped away from her. He went back to his guest. Emily joined the others.

39 Holding the Helm

Settling Elizabeth at the table in the galley, Emily went topside to the helm.

Shane was steering the sailboat.

"Hold on, I'm going to tack."

After checking his position and the sails, he turned to her.

"Tell me about Elizabeth."

Emily was still holding the railing with her right hand. Her left one was beside her side.

"She is Nick's daughter and mine."

"I guessed that part. Tell me what she likes to do for fun."

Emily was startled. She thought the conversation would have gone a different track.

"She loves cats, birds, anything that is furry and moves. Water is special. She swims like a fish and loves to sail. Her ballet lessons are hilarious. She makes her own steps which frustrate her teacher."

He smiled.

"She's like her mother. I see strong, intelligent, independent, and beautiful."

"Thank you, I think."

Shane held the wheel with his left hand and took her hand with his right. He kissed her hand.

He kissed her a long time ago on this sailboat. Emily felt his love flow toward her. The feeling was one she recognized. She glanced at him. He looked happy.

"The wind is perfect. The moments with you beside me bring back memories. We feel good together at the helm."

"Yes."

They sailed for twenty more minutes. He reluctantly released her hand to tack again. People were beginning to enter the top deck. It was time for Emily to go below to check on her daughter. Cyrus saw the two people hold hands from the hatchway before the guests awoke. He informed the captain.

The rest of their sailboat cruise was filled with days of pleasure. The girlfriend remained below most of the cruise due to seasickness. The opportunity for Emily and Shane to get reacquainted and talk again was all they needed. Their friendship bloomed.

Her daughter noticed their laughter and told her mom she liked Shane.

"I do, too, honey."

One evening was misty. The guests were bored with being in their small cabins and went topside in their rain gear. Cyrus and the captain made hot chocolate for the guests. One of the older women on board was an opera singer. She started singing her song.

When she was finished, everyone clapped and wanted more.

The woman began a swan lullaby. Emily looked at her daughter. Last year, the song was one her daughter's dance team won a medal in ballet.

Elizabeth took off her rain gear and did her ballet routine on the deck. Her plaster cast arm was mostly behind her so the guests would only see her graceful hand movements with the good arm. Her legs were lifted high and spins were slower than normal because of the wet deck. Otherwise, the routine was top-notch.

The song and dance ended. Elizabeth and the woman bowed while the others cheered. Shane hugged Elizabeth and congratulated the woman. He would hire them both for any cruise they wanted.

The others began dispersing for the evening. Cyrus took Elizabeth below for apple pie.

Shane came over and spoke, "You've done the world a great service by teaching your daughter. I'm not easily impressed. This evening was more than special."

His eyes looked brightly at Emily. He made a move to kiss her. She stopped him.

"I only wanted to say thank you."

"I know. Sometimes emotions can get carried away. You're with someone."

"I am. However, she seems to be missing from all the activities on a sailboat. I didn't realize she wasn't a water person. Our relationship could prove difficult. I want a wife who can travel with me. I'm not expecting perfection. It's just I'm not having a very good trip."

"Does she have medicine?"

"Oh, yes," said Shane.

"I would have thought the medicine would be working by now."

Emily felt sorry for Shane. She leaned over and kissed him on the lips and went below to eat pie.

Shane went to the front of the sailboat to watch the anchor and clouds. The clouds were breaking apart. He could see the stars. The kiss back from Emily was unexpected. His mind was reeling with thoughts. Her soft body touched his heart afire again. He asked himself if he wanted to go down the same road.

He knew the answer.

"Will she want to go with me?"

Shane turned and was startled by his girlfriend in rain gear.

"Rhonda, you're feeling better. Come see the stars."

"No, I get dizzy when I look over the side. I think you need to help me back. My legs are stiff from fear."

288

Shane took her into the galley. Emily and Elizabeth already went to their room. Cyrus was washing their dishes. There was some pie left on the table.

Shane cut Rhonda a piece and poured her a hot chocolate.

"I heard music earlier. I got dressed. I must have arrived too late."

She ate the apples and left the crust. Cyrus disappeared. He was on the first security watch for the evening.

"I'm glad you are feeling better. There was music and much more."

"Aren't we stopping at a marina tomorrow?"

"Yes, why do you ask?"

Rhonda took out a small map.

"I want to get off this boat. There looks to be a car rental of used vehicles here. I'm well enough to drive home."

Shane couldn't believe she wanted to depart.

"We're two weeks into the trip. There's only one more week to go. We have hardly spoken at all."

"I'm not staying. Don't bother me. You need a shave."

His girlfriend stomped off to their room. Shane rubbed his day beard. He needed to shave tomorrow. Emily didn't criticize his beard. She didn't even notice when she kissed him.

"What a mess?"

LINDA MCKOWN

40 Charity Run

Nick was in Chicago visiting his father's offices. The pot of coffee in the breakroom was full. He poured himself a cup and added the cream. He stirred his coffee and went to a small table.

Opening his briefcase, he reread the real estate papers. The lawyer hadn't yet arrived. His father was transferring some of his properties to his son. The transfers were part of Nick's bonus package.

One of the properties was the cabin in California. He planned on tearing down the cabin and replacing the structure with a large storage building. A new home would be built closer to the beach.

Putting the documents away, he flipped through the pages of a brochure on a new catamaran. Another worker came into the breakroom and turned on the television. The worker left.

Nick glanced at the runners in a charity race in Michigan. The camera moved to a lady announcer who interviewed a blonde woman.

"Em, you're on national news?"

He turned the volume up and listened.

"Emily Erin, the spokesperson for the Tennison Trant Company. We're glad your company is one of the large four corporations putting on this event. Tell our viewers what you hope to accomplish today."

"My company sponsors hospitals each year who are searching for funds on a building project that will benefit the community and help fight cancer."

"They particularly help children," said the announcer.

Emily thanked someone who handed her a towel and a glass of water. After wiping her brow, she took a drink.

"Sorry, I was thirsty."

She coughed.

"Yes, my town is building a new wing in their hospital for cancer research and to help the fight for children to receive proper care."

"We appreciate their efforts very much. The other sponsors will be interviewed next. If anyone would like to donate to this event and cause, please call the 800 number which my news station will post at the end of our program. Thank you, Emily."

Nick turned the television off and sat down.

He hadn't seen Emily for a long time. She looked very good. Nick knew she moved to Michigan. He followed her movements because she was important.

Nick asked himself why he didn't go see her on this trip while he was in the States. He had time in his schedule. The house plans for California were being designed with her tastes in mind. She liked the water and watching the sunset. There would be large windows and a huge deck overlooking the dock.

He shook himself.

"She probably won't ever live there."

His father's secretary appeared.

"The lawyer is here, and Mr. Kent is ready to see you. I've ordered sandwiches for lunch."

Nick followed the secretary.

XXXXXX

Another person in Michigan saw the news channel coverage on the charity race. He recognized the woman's face and name. The woman knew Mara.

"The lady on the large sailboat lives in Michigan. I believe she might know where to find Nick Kent. The other bikers might want to join me. First, I need to make a visit. Hopefully, her name is in the local phone directory."

The man looked at his last bank statement. He would make a call to Susie after his visit.

The motorcycle was filled with gas and an extra pair of underwear was placed inside a plastic bag. The bag was put in the leather compartment on the bike. The man looked at the funds in his worn wallet. He took a brief smell of his shirt.

"Still smells clean."

The man saw the oil stains on the shirt. He drove home. Taking his shirt off, he looked in the cracked mirror on his bike and made the cobra tattoo dance. Going back into the house, he pulled a shirt out of the dirty laundry pile.

Finding a less stained shirt, he pulled the green shirt over his head. The shirt image was a reptile mating. The black jacket covered the male.

"No sense in scaring women I might meet on the road. If I find someone this evening, I can always turn my shirt inside out."

He stored his cigarettes and a small bag of white powder. His knife was on the table. The knife was dropped inside his pants pocket.

The black bandana tied to his head was faded. The scarf went with his faded jeans.

"No need for a helmet."

The man only wore one in the winter to cut the brutal cold. He wondered if they made chains for motorcycles. He could ride his bike longer.

"The salt on the road rusted his bike. Maybe I should get some new used tires."

He kicked a wheel.

"Don't need air."

Stopping at the local gas station and parts garage, he asked about the price on a pair of rubber wheels. The garage monkey told him their pair of treads looked better than his. The price quoted seemed high.

"You'll take less?"

The monkey shook his head. "No."

The biker walked away and was ready for a road trip. He looked around for any cops. None were in the area. The man flipped his stub of the cigarette into the wet ditch. Pulling out his map, he found the town.

"I must have to go through Duluth."

He turned the map upside down. Mara told him to get help if he couldn't figure the map. He stuffed the map in his bag.

Stopping at a different gas station was required. He didn't trust the monkey at the other one who gave him a bad price for the new rubber. The attendant wrote down the highway numbers for him.

Dean stole the yellow highlighter when the attendant wasn't looking. He didn't have seventy-five cents in change in his pocket and didn't want to break his new twenty-dollar bill from the bank.

Then he saw the corn dogs with hot sauce. The twenty was given to the white-haired girl seventeen years old at the counter.

His mouth opened and shut. He never saw someone so pretty.

"Here's your correct change, douche bag."

"What did you say?"

The white-haired girl leaned over the counter. "Do you need a bag?" She chewed her gum and blew a bubble.

Dean watched the bubble and didn't count his money.

"No, I don't think I do. Well, maybe I can take a bag."

She bent over and Dean watched. She slowly handed him the plastic bag.

He read the words on the bag, *Don't Litter.* Down the road, he would realize she short-changed him. The girl better not be there when he drove back.

"Traverse City, here we come."

He threw his wrapper and the wind swirled the paper with the hot sauce. The piece landed on a stop sign. He tossed the paper bag that disintegrated when it hit the electric fence. The horned cows ran away from the sizzle.

"Frisky freaking buffalo."

41 The Biker

The grocery store was two miles away from Emily's home. She looked inside the refrigerator and wrote bread, eggs, milk, peanut butter, and jelly on her list. She planned to stop at the chicken place. Her daughter was craving fried chicken wings with mashed potatoes.

Emily picked up the cat.

"You get to go to the veterinarian for your annual shots while I'm shopping."

She placed the noisy cat in the carrier.

"I know you don't like to go there but we need to take precautions to stay healthy."

The cat meowed.

At the last minute, she took her laptop computer and put the item in her carry case. Her daughter's drawing book was in her case as well. She would work for an hour in her car in the store parking lot until the store owner opened the doors.

Emily saw the doors swing open when a woman went through them. Emily noticed there were other vehicles in the lot. Closing her computer, she called the vet to see how her kitty was doing. She was told there was an emergency, so the appointment time was pushed back two hours.

Emily wondered whether she should get her milk now or wait. She decided to work for another hour. Glancing at her clock, she stopped working. The parking lot was almost full.

Emily groaned. The checkout lines would now be longer. She entered the store and deposited the few items in her cart. Moving down an aisle, another cart blocked her path.

She tried to move around the cart. The man blocked her path again. Emily watched the man's face.

"Emily Erin, from the fancy sailboat. My, my, you live here. Mara told me you were money."

"You must be related to Mara or a friend? I'm sorry about Mara's death. We were saddened by the news."

"The name is Dean Jesse Peters. I bet you were sad, like maybe five seconds."

Emily remembered the man's name from reading a newspaper online regarding Mara's funeral. The bandana looked familiar. She thought about the group of bikers on the county's property.

"That's rude."

The biker ignored her comment.

"You were in California on a catamaran having a good time with Nick Kent. I saw you and him on the news channel.

Where is Nick? We've been looking for him."

Emily wasn't sure if she should talk to this stranger. He seemed to know about her life.

"I don't know. We lost contact."

The biker took off his kerchief and tied the fabric around his hand. He held up his fist.

"Nick is free to walk this earth now that he is out of prison. My sister is dead in the cold ground. Someone has got to pay. I aim to correct that little problem."

Emily didn't like his mannerisms, tone of voice, or nasty words. Obviously, the man hated Nick. Nick wasn't here to explain or defend himself.

She made a move to turn her cart around. The man grabbed the metal handle.

"Get out of my way or I'll scream for help."

Dean didn't move.

"You are lying. Nick is around the area. One of my people saw him. Is he hiding at your home on Elm Street? Maybe I should look around again."

Suddenly, she knew he was part of the motorcycles that burned the mark in her driveway. Emily didn't want the man anywhere near her place.

"If you trespass on my property, I will call the police and get a restraining order. They have my report about the fire mark on my land. Your group of people did the damage."

"Oh, like I'm afraid. The fancy lady has power."

A salesclerk approached the two stalled carts. She was a large woman with muscles.

"Junior, your cart is blocking the aisle. Read my lips. She mouthed the letters p, o, w, e, and r. The word is power in case you missed a letter. You see this patch. Maybe you can't read either. The patch says *Security*. That word should make your small frame stand at attention." The salesclerk raised her voice ten decibels higher than a normal conversation. "Now, you move this cart or else!"

Dean turned to the salesclerk. He pointed his long black-gloved finger at the large woman.

Stella didn't budge. The man's eyes reminded her of an Aye-aye lemur she once saw at the Denver zoo. The lemur was white-faced with dark ears.

"Go away, this is a free country. I'm talking to this person."

The salesclerk looked at Emily.

She shook her head in a negative fashion.

"Miss Erin is a regular customer here. Her credit is good in this free country. By the look and stink of your clothes, dirt poor comes to my mind. Or else you've been working at the cow farm eighty miles south of here."

"They were buffalo," remarked Dean smartly.

"Your sense of direction is off. There aren't any buffalo in Michigan. They live in Montana and Colorado. Now if you have a dime on your person, I'll be surprised."

Dean dug a quarter out.

"Here, go away."

The salesclerk was getting testier. She saw the manager looking down the aisle. She gave him an okay sign with her fingers. Rolling her sleeves, she talked.

"This store is private property. There is nothing free inside. I asked you nicely to leave.

"What are you going to do about my cart fat woman? I'm not moving," said Dean.

"White boy, when I come back, you better not be here."

"Humph!"

Dean turned to Emily. She bit her nail having watched the episode in front of her for the last five minutes. She was starting to get anxious.

The salesclerk marched off and came back with a metal bat. She raised the bat over her head.

"Okay, okay, I'm leaving the store. Your prices are too high, and the bananas look rotten. What is with you people in Michigan? All I did was come to this store to buy matches for my cigarettes. This woman's in my way. You trash talk to me. You're picking on poor me, a civil white man. That's harassment."

Whack!

The metal bat hit Dean's cart handle and broke the red plastic. The cart vibrated against the metal.

"Ow, the plastic hit me. I could sue."

The entire store's customers stopped in their tracks and there was dead silence. The store manager's voice came over the intercom.

"Don't worry folks. There's a special on bananas today at forty-nine cents a pound. We have a customer who will be leaving the store from aisle ten. Give the man some room."

Dean swore.

He looked evilly at Emily and the salesclerk. He squinted at the patch on the fat woman's uniform. He was going to push the cart into the two women.

The salesclerk raised the bat a second time. He left the empty cart and ran out of the store.

The customers dispersed. A few of them went to the section for bananas.

The salesclerk moved the empty cart out of Emily's way.

"There you go Ms. Erin. Civil, my ass."

"Thank you, Stella."

"No problem. I like to remove garbage from this store."

Emily checked out of the store and went home. She deposited her groceries on the kitchen counter. Her phone rang. The cat was ready for pickup. She looked at her watch.

Calling the nanny, she left a message that she would collect her daughter from school.

Emily paid the vet bill and deposited the carrier in her car. She went to the chicken place and purchased two dinners. Then she drove to the school and waited. The bell rang. Floods of children exited the building. Her daughter saw Emily.

"Hi, Mom, you have the cat and chicken."

"I thought we could go to the park and eat. The cat can stay in his carrier and watch the birds."

The two females went to the park. Emily was glad she didn't have to cook. Her computer was in the car. The cat was safe. She and her daughter were bonding. The day was beautiful.

Elizabeth said, "Do you think my dad will ever want to see me?"

Emily looked pensive. Today was a challenging one. The man at the store rattled her confidence. Her daughter's questions could go on and on.

"I wish I knew."

"Maybe he feels bad because he went to jail."

"Yes, I'm sure he feels bad about what he thought was a stunt. Actually, the result was very serious."

"Now that I'm older, I thought he would want to talk to me. Babies are hard to understand."

"You're only nine, going on twenty-one."

Emily hugged her daughter. She thought about the comment the biker mentioned. If Nick was in the area, why hadn't he contacted her? There were many questions swirling in her brain. She didn't know his reasons for leaving Africa.

"Let's go home."

42 Emily's House

The private road to Emily's house was blocked by police and a fire engine. Emily pulled over to the side of the road.

"Stay here. Do not get out or let anyone inside the car."

Emily rolled the windows down a short distance for air. She could smell the smoke. She approached the nearest fireman.

"Hi, Mark, what's happening? The fire truck is blocking our road."

"Miss Erin, we have bad news. Your house has burned to the ground. The garage also collapsed. The security alarm didn't go off. We believe someone torched your home. The smell of fuel and the extent of the fire damage are important clues. You'll need to wait for the fire department's final report for the insurance company. Do you know of anyone who might have started the fire?"

"There has been no one in my life who would do such a terrible thing. There's a stranger in town who did harass me today at the grocery store. Stella scared him off."

"Yeah, she has been given the job of security and takes her new assignment seriously. Did she pull her gun or use the bat?"

"Stella banged the bat."

"Whoever did the burn was a professional who knew where to drip the gasoline. They also knew where to cut the security wires and disarm the system. We checked on Mr. Withers. His granddaughter was let through to stay with him. Do you have the biker's name or know where this stranger is staying?"

"The name is Dean Jesse or Dean Peters. My mind is going around, and around. The name is a combination."

"We'll find him and bring him in for questioning."

"Oh, he has a motorcycle and usually has a gang of bikers with him. I think he was the group that burned a mark in my yard two years ago."

The officer wrote down her information. He informed her she could look at the property once the police reopened the road.

Emily went back to her car and drove into town. She stopped at the office where they were leasing new condominiums. Elizabeth carried the cat carrier inside and sat in a chair in the small café. Emily disappeared with the leasing agent. After an hour, Emily appeared with keys in her hands.

"We're in 109."

Elizabeth followed her mother. Once inside their two-bedroom condo, Elizabeth found one of the rooms.

"Can I have this one?"

Emily looked at the small space. Her daughter liked cozy. The room would do fine.

"Why did someone burn our house down? We could have been hurt. There isn't anyone at my school that dislikes me."

"Oh, Elizabeth, the fire wasn't your fault or mine. There are bad people in this world. We have talked before about the crazies."

"Yeah, the person was crazy. I hope he falls down a big hole and breaks a leg."

"Now, Elizabeth. Let's try not following the rabbit down a hole."

"The crazy man isn't a furry rabbit. He's a slimy green lizard."

Emily threw up her hands and went into the kitchen, took the water and food container out of the cat's bag. Next, she unzipped the lower compartment and took the small bag of disposable litter out. She found the broiler pan and dumped the litter inside. The pan was placed in the bathroom with the cat's food and water. She unzipped the carrier. The cat came flying out and prowled the rooms.

Elizabeth handed her mom a pop can and a bag of chips. They sat on the living room floor. Emily needed a moment to calm down. She was fighting an anxiety attack. She did her breathing exercises. Her daughter was quiet. She knew her mom needed space.

The cat came over to Elizabeth and sat down with her.

"Without a house and yard, we can't buy a little lamb."

Emily looked at her daughter.

"I didn't know you wanted a lamb."

The book from my school library was burned in the fire. I was going to show you the lamb. She was so cute in the picture. The face and feet were black with light-colored fuzzy fur. I don't remember the name. The librarian told me they were originally from England."

"I know the name. They are Suffolk sheep. They are quite docile."

Elizabeth said, "What's docile?"

Emily rubbed her eyes. They seemed to mist over at all her daughter's questions. Elizabeth remained quiet. She didn't want to upset her mom.

"Your lamb would be good for children."

Emily thought about the little lamb her daughter envisioned.

"We someday might buy a little lamb and live in an area with a proper barn and place for the animals to graze. You and your need for fuzzy animals are strange, indeed. We can see if there are any farms with sheep to visit. Petting them will help us forget the fire disaster."

"Okay."

"For now, we'll stay here. I've signed a six-month lease on the condominium until the insurance is solved. Then we'll decide where we want to live."

Elizabeth brightened. "We can live on a sailboat if we can't buy a lamb."

Emily knew her daughter was overcompensating. She wanted to find a sheep farm and buy five lambs to love on her daughter. Emily knew she must move slowly and find a new direction. Moving in with Shane would be too easy.

"We could, except the winter is too cold."

"I forgot about the ice. Ice would hurt the hull like the rocks," said Elizabeth.

The captain must have told her daughter about the structure of the earth around the Great Lakes.

"I didn't forget that most of my toys are gone. I only have two tiny ones on my backpack."

She showed her mother the bag. One was a mouse toy for the cat. The other was a fairy. Emily touched her daughter's hair.

"We were going to donate some of them anyway. Most of the toys were never played with. There were only a few that you really liked."

"My stuffed kitty is gone."

"You have a real furry cat and your drawing book."

Elizabeth calmed down.

"We can be brave and accept change. I'm sorry you couldn't have kept some favorites. We can keep our land for now. This will give us time to think and dream about a new future. I don't know who was responsible for the fire. We'll trust the fire department and police to take care of the investigation."

The next day, Emily contacted the captain. He offered his place to them. He explained Shane was in California or else she might have stayed at his home in Sault Ste. Marie, Michigan. Emily gave the captain her new address. She also called Mr. Withers' house and talked with his granddaughter. The old man was glad they were safe. His garden was not touched by the fire. The daughter would bring her some vegetables.

"Thank you. We appreciate Mr. Withers' kindness at this difficult time. I probably won't rebuild, and we'll stay at the new condo building."

After her business was completed, the two females went shopping for bedding, food, and new clothes. A few toys were purchased. Emily bought makeup. They ordered furniture and received a date for delivery. Supper was at a restaurant close to the water.

A short school break was granted to Elizabeth so Emily could get more of her affairs settled.

Shane called and talked with her for over an hour. He was worried about her well-being. He was upset the biker, Dean, harassed her at the store. He argued she should press charges.

"This dude sounds like he should be in prison."

"He didn't touch me at the store, and I don't know if he was involved in the fire."

Emily only wanted the incident to go away.

She agreed to meet Shane for a fancy dinner. He told her the outing was way overdue. She might need a fancy dress and shoes. The restaurant was five star and expensive. Most everything Shane bought was pricey. Emily was pleased by the turn of events.

He also told her there was something he wanted to ask her. He wouldn't talk about the subject over the phone. Emily was mystified. She called Cyrus to find out new information regarding Shane.

Cyrus told her that Shane broke off with his girlfriend a few months ago. The two men were quite elated by the news. Emily was sure there were good reasons for the break. Rhonda didn't seem his type.

"I only met her once and she was depressed to be around."

Emily wondered what type of woman Shane liked. Obviously, she was going to find out. Emily was glad she overcame a problem when she was eight. She understood Rhonda's issues.

"Fear of deep water."

43 Tanks of Gas

The man watched the biker and his friends leave the property. The one dog was chained and left with a tin of water. Taking the hotdogs out of his pocket, the man approached.

"Mr. Pooch, they left you all alone with no food."

The dog barked.

The man yelled, "No!"

The dog growled and the man waved the hotdogs. The dog smelled the baloney-type meat. His lips dripped with saliva. The pooch whined and the man waited. The brown dog rolled over.

"Good boy, here's one."

The dog wolfed down the meat in two bites. The man gave him half the other hotdog.

"I'll check the property and come back. You can have the other half when I'm done. Do we have a deal?"

The dog wagged its tail. Nick explored the dump of a house. The garbage barrel was full of trash. He didn't find anything inside the house nor around the small buildings. There was one older gas can.

Nick looked around the property. There were single tire tracks that knocked down the weeds. He followed the track into the trees. The cornfield in the back was high. He pulled a cob off and looked at the corn.

"Nice crop."

He watched the birds in the trees. There weren't any birds in one tree. He wondered why. As he moved closer, he could smell the gasoline spill.

The six empty cans were in the weeds. The labels were the same as the local hardware store.

"I believe we have found some items of interest. The real question is where things go from here. The biker wants to do more damage. The fire was only the beginning of his attack against me. Cheap shot picking on the innocent ones. Emily only saw Mara twice. She didn't deserve to be your target."

Nick was calm. There was no need to report his findings yet. There was more investigating to do. He tried to figure a way to get the other bikers to leave.

He saw the pump handle where the bucket stood. There was a house a couple of miles down the road. He noticed the well and pump people putting out a sign.

Nick went back and hopped on his small motorcycle. He drove to the house with the water problem. The well and pump people were gone. He felt good. They placed two signs. Grabbing one of them, he drove back to the dumpy house.

Planting the sign next to the pump, he threw the dog the other half of the hotdog. Nick drove a distance down the road, stashed his bike, and put mosquito repellent on. He waited.

The line of motorcycles went by. He counted the number of bikes and waited hidden in the grass. He wanted to get closer to hear their conversation and plans. The danger level was too high. These bikers were armed. He saw their knife sheaths. Even the women carried knives. Nick touched his old wound. He wasn't getting close anytime soon.

He was glad the afternoon air was cool. It wasn't long before the roar of engine sound came closer.

Crawling on his stomach, he took pictures of the bikers as they drove past. When they were gone, he counted the bikes. He didn't know his plans for the pictures until he zoomed on a couple.

"Shit, Mara told me about these two people. She even showed me their pictures. Well, ladies and gentlemen, we have Susie and her muscle man, Henri Ortiz. They used to be flame throwers in a circus until the place went bankrupt. Now they hire themselves to whoever will pay. Co-conspirators in crime. I imagine Emily's condo building will be next."

Nick lay in the grass feeling powerless to stop the onslaught against Emily. One of the bikers used the black sailboat rope to try to frame him for Mara's murder. That plan backfired. Now they were targeting what they thought was Nick's woman. He hoped his brain worked better and faster than the group of nasty human beings he ran across today.

"There are three miserable bikers left at the house."

He looked at the red motorcycle. Remembering Mara, she mentioned a guy named Mike. Mara never liked the man. Mike drove a red bike and was rough and mean to women. His hands were large, and he was a mechanic. Mechanics made good money around a marina. Nick wondered where Mike was when Mara was murdered. He saw the red bike leave. Waiting for a half-hour, he saw the dark green bike leave. The man wore a jacket with a dragon on the back. Nick took a picture. He didn't know the man's name.

"I'll lay odds which bike is still there. Yes, sir, the black one with the rusted fender. The man is lazy and cheap. He sponged off Mara for years and can't seem to buy spray paint at the hardware store. There he is in full panoramic color. Leader Dean is the person

318

staying. He more than likely has a stash of beer to quench his thirst. I'll need more hotdogs."

Nick drove back to town. He asked the attendant if he could use their copy machine. The man told him there was a library just a short distance and they had a copier. Nick placed the bag of meat, a large envelope, and stamps in his bike pouch.

Going to the library, he printed the images taken. He wrote the names he knew of eight of the bikers. The gas can picture was the first one on top. He included the picture of Emily's house before the place was toast.

Nick scrolled through the frames of pictures on his cell phone. He touched the face.

"Sorry, Mara. I hope they catch him."

He printed the picture. It was the selfie picture with the diamond necklace. He wrote Mike Nichols's name. Nick believed the man might have kept Mara's necklace as a souvenir. His hunch was a long shot. If the police were smart, they would do their research. Just in case they didn't, he included Mike Nichols's bike photo next and drew arrows to both pictures.

The stamps and addresses were ready. The incriminating pictures were inside. He hoped the police would appreciate the photos.

The next morning, he drove close to the house. The dog and lone bike were in the yard. Nick ate a bite of his egg sandwich and drank black coffee. The time was around seven-thirty in the morning. About nine o'clock Dean came out of the house and filled the water dish.

"Where's the dog food?"

The food dish was empty. Nick shook his head. He would need to call the dog pound for a rescue. He looked up the number and saved it on his phone.

The biker took his shirt off.

"Put the shirt back on. I'm not impressed with snake tattoos."

Nick saw a cobra in India. The snake charmer was impressive. He didn't need to watch another show. Once was enough.

The biker was scratching his chest and smelled his underarms. He saw Dean look at the well water pump and head back into the house. The bare-chested man came out and went down to the riverbank for a swim.

"I wouldn't take a swim in that stream. The water is an ugly green that sort of matched the other man's motorcycle. There's cow slime upstream. Oh, well, maybe that's why the other well went bad. Slime for slime. Stop wasting breath, Nick, and get moving. It's now or never."

He took the meat packet and pulled his knife in case he was forced to defend himself. Running to Dean's motorcycle, Nick shielded himself by the bike and peeked across the lawn. There was no movement.

"Hi, boy. I'm glad you didn't bark or growl this time. You're a good pooch."

He threw the hotdogs. The dog was scurrying around trying to reach the meat. One was out of the chain distance.

"Aah, I'll get the morsel."

He tossed the wiggly meat in the air. The dog jumped and swallowed. The chain rattled.

Again, Nick watched the lawn. While the dog was eating, Nick checked the bike. The biker leather bag was full of chains and metal tools. He saw the brake line and examined it closely. He pocketed his knife and saw the hotdogs were all gone. There was no need to leave any of his prints. He scraped the ground with his gloves and backed away. The dog closed his eyes content with a full belly.

Nick jumped at a sound. He was forced to turn. Running like his pants were on fire, he found his motorcycle where he left the bike.

Dean walked over the lawn, barely missing the trespasser. Nick let out his breath.

"Too close. You aren't as fast as you were five years ago."

Again, he watched. After an hour, Nick saw Dean turn the bike around, start the engine, and drive on the road. He followed and kept a safe distance. Dean drove out of town on the winding highway. There were hills and no passing zones. The trucks sucked his motorcycle toward them. Nick hung on. He was determined to watch a dangerous person.

44 Nick's Appearance

Emily finished her coffee at the small shop outside. She heard a chair scrape at the next table. A man sat down.

"Hello, Em."

The voice was familiar. She wasn't sure she wanted to see the man. He moved his chair closer to her table. She was forced to look up.

"Nick, really, now you pay me a visit. What's with the long beard?"

"I know. Don't go getting mad. There is a reason I've stayed away. My work has kept me in Africa. However, I've been in Chicago recently visiting my father. We talked about some of his properties. My job perks are very good. My father has decided my work should be paid in the way of benefits. Some properties were transferred into my name."

"I'm glad you are getting along better with him. Owning real estate is a new one for you. Still, the beard?"

Emily figured the properties were in Africa. Nick was drifting all over the continent. She wondered how he managed to traverse the country. Evidently, the beard was important.

"The beard helps me look fierce."

"I'll bet."

Nick was silent. He wanted to touch her but didn't. Emily was still angry with him. He knew her comment wasn't necessarily about his beard. He decided to confess.

"You were on the news. There was a charity run. I was in the breakroom in my father's offices."

"Yes, did you notice I was number one hundred ten. There were one hundred and nine people ahead of me."

"No, I only saw tanned and gorgeous."

Emily became quiet. She didn't want to connect with Nick. He felt her mood.

"I've been following you to make sure you and Elizabeth were safe. There's a group of nasty bikers in town. Normally, bikers are a great group. These are hardcore and dangerous. I have sent their photos to the police."

Emily didn't understand the secretive nature.

"You've been following me, like in sneaking around?"

He sighed. She was not understanding.

"The sailboat drawing. I met our daughter in the park and helped her draw the boat. She doesn't know who I am."

324

"How did you know she was ours?"

"I do remember a special evening and can count. She told me her name, birthday, and age. Besides, Elizabeth looks like you and rolls her eyes the same way."

Emily was upset her daughter talked to a stranger and didn't tell her. The nanny must have been in the bathroom.

"She wants to see you."

Nick looked in the distance.

"I know. My plans don't work for a visitation. I am returning to Africa once my business here is done. I've been working at one of my father's offices. I was out of the country."

"I could understand if your home were on the moon. But then, there are the satellites. There also are many mail systems; and let's not forget, cell phones do work. Africa has roads with jeeps or elephants to ride. I forgot the boats. You do know about water transportation?" mentioned Emily.

Nick grabbed her glass of water and took a swallow.

"You're still very upset and more than mildly disappointed. I've been terrible about communicating with you."

"Really. There is a brain actively working."

Nick was getting mad.

"Stop it, Emily, I'm here today. Today counts. The only thing I forgot was to send money. I'll pay the support money."

Emily shook her head.

"We don't need your money. I make a reasonable salary. A college fund would be appreciated."

"I'll have my lawyer send you the documents."

Emily was silent.

"The fire at your home was instigated by Dean. I saw him several times lurking around your home. He hired some professionals. They are a couple who deal in the underground as hired arsonists."

Nick explained his actions over the last week.

"The fire was an act of revenge. When people go out of their way to make me mad, I return the favor. I lurked around the place Dean was staying. In some trees behind the house, I found six empty and new gas cans. The can tags looked familiar. I went to the hardware store and talked to a young man. He described our biker anti-friend to a perfect tee. Dean came in three times to purchase the cans. He paid cash."

"Why burn down my house? I don't know this person or any of his group."

Nick didn't want to answer.

326

"I thought by my leaving, there wouldn't be a connection. I was wrong. You were associated with me. The group believed I was responsible for Mara's death."

Emily was more confused.

"I lied to you. On the catamaran, I wanted there to be an *us*. I made up a story. Part of the story is true. We fought. She wanted money. This was the first time she asked me. I guess it was the way she asked. Mara hinted that sex should be paid for by a rich boy. I was her stupid rich boy. She made me mad. I wouldn't give her any money. I might have called her a name. She shoved me. I shoved back. Mara fell and hit her head on a rock. I took her pulse. She was breathing. I left."

"Is this story true?"

Nick sighed.

"In a way, I'm responsible. I should have taken her to the emergency room. I don't know what happened after I left her."

"Someone else killed her."

"Yes, my thoughts are Dean. He boasted about getting some money after her death. Then, there's this Mike person. I have no evidence, just a hunch."

"You should go to the police."

Nick looked at her with a screwed-up face. He sent the photographs to the police. The pictures were all he had.

327

"Getting back to Dean, his bike brake line showed a small dent. While he was swimming in the creek, I felt the dent. His brake line was brittle. The man didn't take care of his method of transport. If a bike is the only way to get from point A to B, you'd think he would get the cycle into the shop. There wasn't any money spent on normal maintenance. His tires looked worn, too. We should be glad about his lack of mechanical skills. You don't need to worry about him anymore. There was another biker that seemed peculiar. He was on a green motorcycle and wore a jacket with a dragon. I hope that I didn't miss anything."

"I think that I saw the green biker ride by my house with the other motorcyclists before the fire."

Emily let the waitress refill her water glass. Nick was maybe not a good person after all. She couldn't trust him. He conned her once. She wasn't sure she believed him.

Nick saw her pull away and felt bad.

"When we made love on the catamaran, my feelings were real. There was no darkness in my heart. You need to understand because our daughter will ask. I'll always care."

Emily remembered the moment vividly. The catamaran and the water. She wouldn't stop caring either. She touched his hand. He decided to tell her.

"I was following Dean yesterday. I knew the police questioned him and let him go. I couldn't believe they didn't lock him away. They locked me so fast, my lawyer didn't have a chance to blink twice. My dad paid a hefty fee to get me out before the trial. This vile biker gets nothing. When I was thinking of how unfair the world can be at times, there was a sharp turn in the road. I saw him try the brake. There was no smoke from the tires. He went over the cliff."

Emily's face watched Nick.

"I pulled over. There wasn't anyone on the road. I tried to look over the cliff. There was too much brush. I yelled and no one answered."

"And, what happened next?"

This was the part and reason Nick stayed away from his family.

"I wanted him gone. I drove down the same road for fifteen miles. When I went back, there was an ambulance with a tarped body. A wrecker was pulling the bent bike from the sand and rocks."

Emily was feeling no remorse. The man scared her and damaged her home. She wasn't safe with Dean alive. Her daughter could have been hurt. She wanted Dean gone but didn't know how to dispose of a body.

329

"Revenge stopped by a turn in the road."

"And a push from fate."

Fate or luck, Emily looked with alarm at her former lover.

"Nick, you didn't do anything?"

"No. I didn't need to do any damage. Now you know my reason for staying away and returning. I couldn't let Dean try again."

Emily was sure Dean would have tried.

"I'm not always a good person. You've seen me in action. Elizabeth needs a better role model. Also, there is a woman in Africa. I thought you would want to know."

Emily was relieved. She could now begin her search for someone else to love. She fleetingly remembered a kiss with Shane.

"You deserve a better life. I've moved along. You should do the same. Em, your ability to survive this long and properly take care of our daughter shows me there's no need to stay."

Emily wanted him to meet their daughter.

"There's one more job that you will do before you go to Africa. A change of plans is necessary."

"A change of plans. Where have I heard those words before?"

Emily wouldn't budge.

"You can be stubborn."

There was no need for her to plead. He must want the connection. Emily wouldn't be responsible if he walked away.

Nick gave in to her command, "Name the place and time."

Emily finally smiled at Nick.

45 Nick's Daughter

Elizabeth fidgeted with her new sundress. Emily grabbed the short white matching sweater and told her daughter to put the clothing on.

"The weather says balmy and the wind will be blowing in the park."

Her daughter put the sweater on. Emily took one glance in the mirror.

"Come on, mom, we don't want to be late."

They met Nick in the small drive and walked across the street to the park.

Elizabeth said, "I know you. The man in the park was my dad? I can't believe you didn't tell me. I get it. You wanted to see me but remain hidden."

"I was being careful. You weren't."

Elizabeth said, "I know my mom gets upset when I talk to strangers. You looked furry with your beard and lost."

"Your mom is right. Don't talk to strangers."

He took her hand.

"Let's run to the slide."

With pigtails flying, Emily watched her daughter with Nick race across the freshly mowed grass. They played on all the equipment. Nick's legs were squeezed on the rocking horse.

They ate a picnic lunch and Emily left the two people to talk. She took her cell phone and a bottle of water. Moving to the swing set, she swung gently.

"How come you didn't see me sooner? I was waiting and waiting," said Elizabeth.

Nick didn't know how to respond. She helped him along.

"My mom says people don't always act the way they should. People make mistakes even though they try hard. She told me you tried hard."

"I did. Your mom is wise. She's the reason why I returned. I went to jail for some time. Instead of coming to see you, I went to Africa. My head was maybe not thinking too well."

"My mom gets sick sometimes. She has medicine. I help her when she gets stuck."

"I've seen your mom. She rather freezes in one place and can't breathe."

"Uh, huh."

"I'm glad you are here to take care of her."

"The captain and Cyrus help, too. We met a new friend named Shane."

"I believe that I know those three people. They like to sail."

Elizabeth jumped up and down and waved her hands. Emily wasn't alarmed. She had seen the gestures before.

"I pretend that I'm on a sailboat and the waves push me through the water."

Nick laughed and hugged his daughter.

"You can sail. I didn't know. I'm pleased your mom takes you sailing. Let's get serious though. I must catch my flight. I'll make a deal with you. When I can, I'll send you postcards. That way, you know I'm thinking of you."

"Can I send a postcard back?"

"No, my movements and locations will change."

Elizabeth looked at her father.

"Okay!"

She danced over to the swing.

"Nick told me it was time."

Emily got off the swing and let Elizabeth get on. She walked to where Nick waited.

"I'll write. Here's my lawyer's card. You can reach me through him."

Emily pocketed the card.

"Our daughter mentioned Shane."

Emily kept silent. Her silence was enough. Nick bent down and kissed her. There were tears in her eyes.

"I hate when you cry."

He hugged her and left.

Emily gathered the blanket and basket. She walked over to her daughter.

"Are you okay, Elizabeth?"

Her daughter took her hand.

"Yes."

They walked down to the beach. Emily picked the flat white and black stones. Elizabeth picked the red and orange ones. They built a cairn close to the water's edge. There were four rocks four inches high.

"A marker so my dad can find his way back to me."

"Very good. What if we move?"

"We can build another one. We know how." Elizabeth stooped and brought another rock to her mother.

"You found an agate. This is a special rock. People come from miles away to find this pretty stone."

"We can put the agate in a box and send the rock to my dad because he is special."

"We can."

Emily saw a lone seagull fly and dip into the water.

"Look, mom, the bird caught his own fish."

"Indeed, he did. The seagull is most definitely not lazy. Maybe he's a part eagle."

Her daughter laughed with delight.

The two females went to the condo and the cat.

Nick sent many postcards. One time there were fifty cards at once. The cards were pictures of furry wild animals. A truck delivered some stuffed ones the next day. Elizabeth's room was full. They bought a net and strung the cotton along one wall. They were able to get twenty-five of the stuffed toys off the bed.

Once there was a card with a picture of Nick with a brown mongrel-looking dog. Scrawled on the card was, "His name is Pooch. I finally received him after the long wait of vaccinations, permits, etc. He's a good dog and where I found him is a long story."

Elizabeth approved. "He looks friendly. Nick told me about the dog. He likes hotdogs and baloney."

Emily shook her head.

"Your father found a lunch companion. He's an expert at making bologna sandwiches."

46 Green Bike

Old man Withers opened his door to get his mail. His granddaughter was gone for three days but left her phone number in case of an emergency. He was astounded to see a man with a motorcycle jacket at his door. Mr. Withers peered around the corner of the door to see a dark green bike.

"Hi, my name is Saul."

Old man Withers said, "I don't read the bible anymore since my wife died. The words are too little and the magnifying glass broke."

"Not Paul, my name is Saul and I have a pen and tablet."

"I don't need a pamphlet."

"Saul Dragonne." The biker turned and showed the back of his jacket.

"Dragon image. Pale with green tinges. The green matches your bike. What do you want? I'm not selling vegetables today."

The biker frowned. The man was hard of hearing and half-blind. Saul raised his voice.

"Here, take this pen and paper. I need Emily Erin's new address."

The old man took the pen and tablet and wrote down some words and handed the items to Saul.

The biker read the note, *the beans are all gone*.

The biker motioned for the man to come outside. The old man shuffled his feet slowly until he reached the edge of his porch. The biker pointed to the burned-down area of Emily's house.

"The woman moved."

Mr. Withers pointed at the fire and nodded.

"Bad fire, killed the rose bushes."

The biker threw up his hands in frustration. He would try one more time.

"New address, where does the woman live today."

"I don't know where she buys her dresses. Now go away and stop bothering me."

Mr. Withers went inside and slammed his door.

Saul went to his motorcycle. He would need to stay and watch the area to see if Ms. Erin came to visit the old man. It was a long shot, but he needed Emily's address. He drove his bike to the end of the private road and placed his one-man tent close to some swamp grass. Saul looked around. He remembered the first time his motorcycle group was there. Dean was the lead proponent in bringing the people known as the fire starters.

Mr. Withers took his binoculars from their worn leather case and watched. He looked at a picture Nick Kent sent him on his cell phone.

"Same bike."

He wondered if he should call his granddaughter.

"This isn't exactly an emergency; however, I don't like dragons and I'm not going to tell Saul where Emily lives. Let him think I'm deaf, dumb, and blind."

Mr. Withers made himself a sandwich, took a soda out of his refrigerator, and sat on his back porch watching the motorcycle man. He was glad the biker was close to the swamp grass and the deserted sewer line hole.

Eventually, tiring of seeing Saul set his gear and use a small cookstove to make his supper, Mr. Withers fell asleep in his recliner until morning.

All the next day, Mr. Withers watched Saul kick at Emily's burned ground and look toward his house. Saul never came back to Mr. Withers' door.

The granddaughter came home and visited the home.

"Grandpa, was there anything unusual happening while I've been gone?"

The old man turned up the volume on his new hearing aid. She waited and repeated her question.

"Did you see a green motorcycle at the end of the road?" said Mr. Withers.

"I did and a small tent. Is someone camping on the county's property again?"

"Haven't seen Saul Dragonne for two and a half days now. I think he went fishing."

Her granddaughter looked upset.

"Why didn't you call me about the trespasser? The police would have told him to move along."

"I couldn't find your emergency phone number."

"Well, I'll check on you in three days. Bye, grandpa."

The next day, Mr. Withers heard the motorcycle driving round and round the length of the swamp grass. The grass grew along the old buried line. He went outside with his fried egg and ham sandwich. He sat down to watch. He thought about turning on a horror movie and decided the live show was better.

"I wouldn't get so close to the swamp grass. If your bike drips gasoline, you might start a fire. This ground has been known to contain gas."

In the afternoon the old man decided to listen to a new audiobook. He put his earphones on and listened. While he was sitting in his recliner, he felt the ground shake a little.

"Probably the old sewer pipe acting up again. I've called the fire department enough times about the rumble. They told me to call the county. The county placed me on hold three times. I gave up. I wonder if the biker smokes. I saw he went into town and purchased a gas can."

He put the audiobook down, went outside to the back porch, and sat in his rocker.

"Nick, one of Emily's friends, told me to stay away from the biker people. They were dangerous to be around. Mr. Kent appeared to be an intelligent person. He told me about sailing with Aiden Hanigan. I know about Mr. Hanigan. He was a huge racing star."

Looking toward the swamp grass with his binoculars, he noticed a tiny light from a cigarette butt. The biker didn't stomp out the butt. The butt was next to the gas can.

He went inside his house to get his hat, heavy army jacket, rubber boots, gas mask, and free plastic sunglasses like the eye doctor gives a person after the eyes are dilated.

The tall grass near the pipeline entrance was now on fire.

Mr. Withers put on his thin sunglasses and the rest of his clothing gear. It wasn't long before the flames burst fifteen feet in the air and a loud boom shook his chair, house, and ground. He was glad last year the remodelers put new metal siding and roofing on his house and garage. The driveway was replaced with cement and five feet of rocks were around the buildings. All the brush was cleared away. The landscaping people mowed his lawn yesterday. The sprinklers kicked on this morning. His property was in no danger.

He watched as the entire length of the sewer pipe burst and shot up more flames almost as tall as the swamp grass. The bike gas tank blew. The sound was muted by Mr. Withers' hearing aid volume. There were no cars on the road. He could faintly hear the fire trucks and police coming in the distance.

Mr. Withers went inside. He answered his door when Mark, the fireman, appeared in the small window. Mark motioned him to follow to an awaiting fire department vehicle. Mr. Withers jumped sprightly into the large truck. When they were safely away from the area, Mark stopped the vehicle.

"We can take our gas masks off. I see you kept yours from when you were working at the firehouse."

Mr. Withers turned the volume higher on his hearing aid.

"We heard the explosion in town. Are you okay, Mr. Withers? At a quick glance around your property, there are small burn marks on your garage. A few new metal pieces of siding should fix the dent."

"I'm fine. The insurance company should cover the replacement."

"Did you see the person who owned the motorcycle?"

"A man came to my door about five days ago. He wanted to buy beans. He told me his name was Paul or Saul Dragoon or something like that."

"We found his license plate fifty feet away from the first blast so we'll have to see if we can locate the man."

Mr. Withers' granddaughter drove next to the red vehicle and stopped.

"Have a better day, Mr. Withers. You've seen enough fire and smoke. We'll let you know when the area is safe. The county will probably eventually sell the land to a developer who wants to build condominiums."

"Good day, officer."

Mr. Withers went to his granddaughter's apartment to live temporarily. He called Emily and told her she needn't worry about the green motorcycle or the dragon-man anymore. He told her the man wanted her address.

"Of course, I didn't give the man the time of day. The dragon on his leather jacket wasn't a good design. The dragon looked ill, almost gray like a corpse."

"I don't know much about dragons. I do believe I saw the man at the end of our road before my home caught on fire."

"He wasn't a good person. I did talk to your friend Nick. He told me to watch out for any strange bikers. He thought the green biker was dangerous to be around. Nick was right."

Emily paused. "I'm glad Nick warned you to stay away and thank you for not releasing my address."

"I'll be visiting with my granddaughter for a couple of weeks. There's a rumor going around about the county selling their land at the end of our road to a developer," said Mr. Withers.

"Your comment about the county is an interesting surprise. I'm also glad your new hearing aids are working better."

Emily hung up her phone. She read about the sewer explosion in the paper.

"Well, that explains Mr. Withers' phone call."

47 Planned Vacation

Elizabeth carried her own bag. She was ten years old for their next vacation. Emily handed her bag to the steward. They were the first group of passengers to board the ship.

The steward showed them to their quarters. Her daughter flopped onto the couch, opened her bag, and took out one of her books.

Emily said, "We should explore the ship."

Elizabeth kept reading. Emily took the book and put it on the side table.

"Look, every kid in the world wants to be on a cruise liner of this size and type. The pools, waterslides, and entertainment are stellar."

"I'm not your average kid. I don't care about a waterslide. There's sailing with friends. That's where I want to go on vacation."

Emily looked around the cabin.

"We can try to have a good time. The cruise is short. After two weeks, we can get off the ship and go home."

Her daughter rolled her eyes. Emily wanted to laugh. Nick was right. Elizabeth acted just like her. Now was not the time to make fun of her daughter.

Emily knew this cruise was a mistake. She didn't want to take the chance of running into Shane on the sailboat cruise. Emily was avoiding Shane.

"We need to have different experiences. This trip will add to your knowledge of this world. I need different."

Her daughter crossed her arms.

"Okay, but next time, we go sailing."

Emily gave into her daughter's wishes.

"I can agree to a sailing vacation next year."

Her daughter was smart.

"Sailing with the captain and Cyrus."

Now Emily was locked in.

"All right."

Her daughter stuffed the book in her bag. The two took a tour of the huge vessel. They bought juice out of the machine and packaged crackers. The cruise liner was towed from the port and the ship was on its way out to sea.

In the evening, they decided to skip the dinner and ordered a salad from the menu. A steward brought their trays with a basket of bread rolls and bottled cola.

The next morning, they went swimming before eating breakfast. When they came to their room, the trays were waiting. After showering and changing into their clothes, Emily looked outside. Her daughter came to the railing.

"This boat is slowing down. I don't hear the engine noise."

"Mom, I think you are right. We were going fast before."

Other patrons were gathered outside their rooms. The stewards seemed to be running around not quite knowing what to do. A worried look came over Emily's face.

The captain's loudspeaker came on.

"We have engineers looking at our engine problem. If everyone would please go about your business. The kitchen is still open."

Emily and her daughter went into their room. They ate their cold cereal and packaged roll. For some reason, Emily's daughter liked cereal.

After two hours, they heard the engine restart and the ship moved forward.

Elizabeth said, "This was a new experience."

Emily threw a pillow at her daughter. They played board games on the computer in the afternoon. Lunch was forgotten. Bags of chips and peanuts were eaten. Emily knew they needed to eat a full meal for supper.

When they walked to the restaurant area, they noticed most of the tables were empty. Emily thought the lack of customers was odd.

"Let's try a different restaurant. There's one a deck below this."

They looked at the menu board and decided on hotdogs. It was hard to mess with cooking a hotdog. The machine kept the dog at the proper temperature. Elizabeth liked her dog plain. Emily usually went with all the toppings. She chose a few condiments in packets.

"Do you want some fried macaroni? The frying part is new this year for restaurants. Usually, the ship's chefs made the stuff. I believe they buy the cheese macaroni frozen."

"Okay."

They went to their tables and watched as others came to eat. Emily received a text from Cyrus.

"How's the ship?"

Cyrus would be horrified about the frozen macaroni. He made his from scratch with five different kinds of cheese. She pocketed her phone. She would call him later.

Walking back to their room, the evening was serene. The ship was cruising fast to their destination.

"After watching some television, we can call Cyrus and go to bed. Our ship should be at the first destination tomorrow by noon per the schedule."

After talking with Cyrus and listening to her daughter complain, Emily thankfully tucked her in bed and crawled into the second bed. She couldn't sleep. Shane was on his original sailboat for the entire six weeks. Emily groaned. Tomorrow she would make their day more fun. She was hungry.

The steward brought their tray in the morning. Elizabeth opened the silver lid. Inside they saw undercooked eggs, dry hash browns, and greasy sausage. Emily knew her daughter wouldn't eat the meal.

"We can try the other restaurant. I saw frozen yogurt with fruit when we passed yesterday."

The two females ate their yogurt and again went to the pool. There were a few patrons in the water. Emily asked an old couple, "Where is everybody?"

"Our neighbor is sick. We decided to get some fresh air. We don't want to catch anything."

Emily agreed. She swam with Elizabeth until they were exhausted. By the time they left the pool, there were more people.

After showers, she turned on the news. The speaker was talking about a ship that was close to the port where many of the passengers were ill. Emily gasped. The ship was the one they were on.

Elizabeth heard the announcer.

"I should pack my clothes."

Emily turned off the television.

"I'll help you. Don't eat any food and don't touch the railings."

When the ship pulled into port, they exited. Emily watched for their taxi. They drove to an expensive hotel courtesy of Cyrus and the captain.

Finishing their two-week vacation, a tad earlier than planned, they flew home. After a week's time to wash their clothes, Emily dragged out their new soft suitcases. She threw the old ones in the trash.

Elizabeth entered the room.

"Where are we going?"

Emily hadn't told her daughter. Now was going to be the best time.

"Shane invited us sailing. He moved two clients to a later cruise."

"We really get to sail!"

"Sometimes change is a good thing. This time we do our vacation better. We go with our friends."

Her daughter went screaming with excitement. The clothes were stuffed inside in five minutes.

"Elizabeth, redo your packing."

She emptied the clothes and started over. The cat came out from under the couch and sat on the pile.

48 Potential Future

Shane met them at the ferry. He hugged Elizabeth and kissed Emily long and hard.

"Welcome back. We are going to have fun. I promise you the food and sailing will be better than your last vacation. My room is next to yours."

Emily was delighted to see the twinkle in his eye.

When they arrived at the sailboat, the two men were waiting to take their bags. Elizabeth wouldn't stop talking. Emily and Shane went to their favorite spot at the bow of the sailboat. They sat next to each other.

"Was your trip really horrible?"

"Unbelievable is more the word."

"My crew is glad you didn't get ill?"

"We ate mostly packaged or bottled items. They weren't exactly nutritional."

"I couldn't believe you changed your vacation with us. May I ask why?"

Emily looked at the seagulls. They were flying in groups.

"My life hasn't been easy. There's constant juggling. Nick was in my life and then was gone. He came back."

Shane looked at her apprehensively. Emily shook her head.

"He's in Africa now with someone else. Nick wanted to see me again. He didn't like my house burning down or a biker threatening me. He was only here for my protection and his daughter's."

"So, he knows about Elizabeth."

Emily nodded.

"We read in the paper about Dean Jesse. The police believed the man was in an accident."

"Nick found gas cans where Dean was staying."

"Maybe the biker accident wasn't exactly true?"

Emily didn't want to talk anymore about past events.

"Nick said the brake line was brittle because the man didn't take care of his bike."

Shane was quietly thinking about her silent messages. He knew she was done talking about Nick.

"We've known each other for a long time. I trust your judgment call. I'm glad you have your freedom. I'm glad I have mine. There's plenty of time for us to make new plans if you are interested."

Emily moved closer. Shane took her direction and did the same.

"When do you want to move in with me?"

Emily was speechless.

"Let's make it soon," said Shane.

Emily hadn't replied.

They walked together to the back deck to greet the newcomers. Elizabeth saw Shane touch Emily on the back. Elizabeth disappeared below to ask Cyrus how to make a wedding cake. Cyrus pulled an image of three tiers on his computer.

"We could go for three or two tiers. What do you think?"

The captain watched the group and lifted three fingers.

"Three-tier white cake with lemon and maybe a few strawberries."

"Perfect," said Elizabeth.

The rest of the sailing adventure was much like the trips in the past only this time there was an element of romance. The laughter flowed like gentle rain on a sunny field. There was no hesitation anymore. Emily snuck into Shane's bed when her daughter fell asleep. The men saw her.

There was much discussion of when the event would take place. The where was already decided. The sailboat would be decked out with running lights and flowers for the wedding. The honeymoon would be on the sailboat for an evening. Then Elizabeth and the others would join the cruise.

A move would be required. Elizabeth, Emily, and the cat would need to live with Shane. A change of address would need to be sent to Nick.

49 Prison Hazard

Susie and Henri Ortiz were in prison for arson. Someone sent a newspaper to Susie. The guard told her there was no name on the return address. The stamp was from Chicago and was sent priority mail. She didn't know anyone from the windy city.

"Only lawyers use priority mail."

She opened the newspaper and read the article that was highlighted.

A woman named Karen Kane was strangled in Michigan. The police knew a Mike Nichols was the last person to be with the woman. A security camera caught them together in a parked red motorcycle an hour before she died. The new cameras were part of the marine store's new security system. Mr. Nichols was unaware of the cameras. The police took out a search warrant and went to Mike Nichols's home.

There were pieces of jewelry and coins in his home. The investigation was lengthy. Mr. Nichols was found guilty of two murders and sent to prison.

Susie read the name of the prison. There was a second line indicating the original prison was changed to a new one due to the double homicide.

The second person he murdered was Mara Peters. The police found a diamond necklace in Mr. Nichols's home. There were also coins. They anonymously received the photo of Mara wearing the necklace. The photo was a tip from some time ago and the police didn't follow the lead. One of the police members remembered the photo. Ms. Peters wasn't wearing the necklace when she was found. The coins matched photos on Mara's phone and email notes describing her inheritance received from her father. They believed she was the owner of the coins because her father's name was also etched in the leather pouch containing the Morgan silver dollars. Mr. Nichols confessed to the crime upon the recommendation of his lawyer in exchange for a life sentence regarding Ms. Peters' death.

Placing the newspaper under her bunk, she waited until Sunday when her sister, Shannon would visit.

Susie asked her sister to contact Henri. There was someone who would soon arrive at the same penitentiary. She wanted

Henri's help. The cutout news article was given to the guard who passed the paper to Shannon. She accepted the paper and read the article. Shannon nodded. She would visit Henri.

After Shannon left, Susie sat outside in the prison yard. The day would be perfect if she was home. The female prisoners were exercising. Today wasn't going to be a workout.

She remembered Mara Peters. There were watery tears in Susie's eyes. The two women liked each other. They were friends for a long time. Mara could talk her into doing anything. Susie would cave and give in because the bond was strong between them.

"Mara, we're sorry we couldn't help you stop this person. You should be alive."

She knew Dean was dead. It was up to her to pass information to the other bikers who were in prison.

"Mike Nichols is being transferred to Henri's prison. They found him guilty of murdering Mara and another woman. He played us. He acted sad at the funeral and encouraged us to hate. The man is a joke and a cheap actor. He stole Mara's necklace and her father's coins. The money was a small bonus for him. How could we have known? There were no clues Mark was obsessed with women in a bad way. He was a strangler and thief among us. I'm in this prison because we believed Nick killed her and we burned his girlfriend's house. We were wrong. Now we get our turn for justice."

Instead of years in prison, the man's mattress caught fire during the night. Henri heard the fire alarm go off. Mike Nichols was transferred to the infirmary where things became easier for the biker gang. Mike met his end. He was found smothered between two mattresses.

Shannon came again to visit Susie. She brought her two cupcakes, one with no candle and the other one with cream cheese frosting in the middle. The message was received.

"The man was snuffed out. He won't hurt another woman ever again."

Susie was fortunate to be placed under a new program. She was given the opportunity to work in the prison's bakery to lessen her time.

Every day she made bread and delighted in throwing ice cubes into the hot gas ovens. The steam made the bread moist and taste better. Steam looked like blasts of fire smoke to her. Susie took cooking classes to become a chef when she got out of prison.

Henri worked in the kitchen at his prison grilling hamburgers. He and Susie agreed no more arson attempts. The pay wasn't worth the time. Money from Dean was never received due to his untimely accident.

Because Susie's prison sent Henri's prison homemade hamburger buns, he decided on their next plan. They eventually would open a burger joint near the marina. The marina was expanding.

Henri liked the taste of his wife's bread. He started working on a ketchup sauce. The library cookbooks took over his desire to start a fire. The prison let him use the canner, glass jars, and special lids. With pride, he wrote his name in black marker pen and labeled the sauces.

The rest of the prisoners enjoyed the sauce. No one bothered Henri.

The prison sold his sauces to other prisons. They paid Henri in credit. The credit could be used to reduce his large arson fine.

50 Hesitation

Emily's anxiety attacks increased. She called off the move into Shane's home. Their wedding wasn't canceled but simply placed on hold. She and her daughter stayed in their condo.

The two elder men from the sailboat retired and let a younger set of crew members manage the sailboats.

Shane grew increasingly impatient with Emily and his living arrangements. He couldn't understand her reluctance. He couldn't pinpoint what was wrong with their relationship. He began working weekends.

The shoreline became a familiar place for Emily. The water was either still or not. Her hesitation created doubts about Shane. She knew he would one day pressure her for more.

Life moved along slowly. Emily agonized about her choices. She realized that she was unhappy.

Time passed; Elizabeth turned eighteen and wanted to visit Nick. Emily flew with her daughter to Africa. Emily didn't quite trust Nick with reality.

Her time in Africa renewed an older relationship. He purchased a larger catamaran with better navigation instruments. The two women met Martin. He was Nick's young assistant and second helmsman. Sailing on the catamaran gave Emily feelings of real joy. Nick noticed how she was the same person he fell in love with.

Emily became friends again with Nick. When it was time for Emily and Elizabeth to go, he hesitated.

"Maybe I should kidnap you again."

Emily couldn't believe he said the word kidnap.

"That is a crazy thought."

He let her go a third time. This time he wrote to her frequently. She wrote and kept every letter.

When Elizabeth started college, Emily was alone. The same friendship existed between her and Shane.

Their annual vacation date arrived. Shane invited Emily to a cruise on the sailboat. When she loaded her bags on the boat, he seemed nervous.

They sailed most of the morning and stopped earlier than planned. She knew he was up to something.

She watched as he lowered the dinghy and brought the small craft around. Emily knew they were going to the beach. She saw the steaks and champagne in the galley. There were candles as well and a large basket of food. She grabbed the expensive caviar. One can of caviar did fall into the basket. She didn't see the light can slide off the table.

She was standing near the railing in her new azure blue bikini. Shane was walking along the side. He reached out his hand.

Emily backed away.

"I don't trust you. You look nervous and edgy. Maybe you've been smoking marijuana."

Shane gave her a look that said he never smoked. He motioned with his hand that she should come to him. Resigning herself, she slowly gave him her hand. He pulled her toward him.

"You are soft. Closer, Emily."

She complied.

"Feel my heart and tell me your reaction."

"You are very warm, and the beat is strong."

"Do you love me?"

Emily couldn't help but laugh.

"Yes, you're the best friend ever. There's always the light-colored caviar on the boat for me."

"Good. I'm at least someone smart enough to have written down your favorites."

He caught her off guard. Shane picked her up, stepped over the railing, and they both went into the water. Emily couldn't believe he carried her overboard. She was spitting out cold water when he swam over to her.

"No, you don't."

He grabbed her hand, "Now feel my heart."

She complied.

"You're cold."

She splashed him with water.

"There's a load of food that needs to go ashore."

"I forgot the food."

"Before we get the food, look toward shore where my security man awaits on the beach."

Emily looked. "You bought a sailboard for the cruises. The sail is a pirate's flag. How wonderful!"

Shane laughed.

"Cari told me about your dating talk."

"Every woman wants one."

Emily swam away from him. He wasn't sure she meant the sailboard or the pirate flag.

"Emily, wait."

They swam to the dinghy and crawled up the net. Loading their supplies, they were ready.

"Let me take the load and I'll come back to get you. I have another surprise later. This one is more impressive."

Emily watched the small craft move toward shore. She went below to make sure all the items were gone. She saw the caviar can.

Taking the can with her, she went through the hatch and turned toward the sound of an anchor chain dropping. A catamaran was off the starboard bow. She watched as the vessel came closer.

51 Starting Over

Emily watched in amazement. She knew this large catamaran. As the boat came closer, she saw the man at the helm.

Shane returned to the sailboat. By the excited look in her eyes, he knew Emily's heart belonged to someone else.

"Do you need a ride or are you going to swim?"

Without hesitation, she jumped into the cold water. She opened her eyes and saw massive bubbles. This time she remembered to use her arms and legs to reach the top of the water. Coming through the warm layer of water, she surfaced. Taking gulps of the sweet lifesaving air, she swam toward the catamaran as if her life depended on it. The catamaran waited.

Shane stood on the white boom and watched Emily's powerful swimming strokes. He made sure her lover pulled her aboard.

"Love stops for no one, except for you, Emily. Fly my beautiful one and touch the stars for me," said Shane. He knew she wouldn't look back.

A life preserver was thrown her way from the catamaran. Emily held on as the strong man pulled her toward the boat. Martin was at the helm.

"Em, fancy finding you in this wonderful large lake."

"Nick, you shaved. How nice? But you are more than crazy."

"I believe that's a compliment. You should have said wild and crazy. I have a wonderful dinner planned. I ordered takeout. Our meal is in the refrigerator."

Emily held up the can of caviar. "I love takeout and have an appetizer."

Nick took the can and the windbreaker was offered in exchange.

"Very expensive. I would have stayed if he has more cans of this brand."

Emily hit him. He picked her up and kissed her.

"You could have steered closer or do you always park your car one hundred yards from the curb?"

The anchor was raised. Martin turned the boat into the wind. Sails filled with the warmer air. Once the boat was stable, Martin turned the helm over to Nick.

Nick tacked a couple of times. Satisfied, he put the tether on the wheel and looked at the ripples on the screen. He had only moments. He picked her up to return her to the water.

She was laughing. Her dig about the car hit home. She remembered their man overboard exercise. Emily knew that he wasn't going to throw her back. He gently put her down.

The catamaran bounced and Nick quickly undid the tether. He steered the vessel. Emily was by his side.

"Let me have the helm."

Nick stepped aside. She rocked the boat even further.

"This one is touchy. She's heavier which is good. I'm not used to the way this boat turns on these waves."

"I'll show you."

The look in her eyes said everything.

She stood in front of him at the helm. She lightly held the wheel and followed him through several tacks. He caressed her body and pulled her close. The evening stop would be appreciated by both. Their warmth and love for each other were redeveloping. Memories of their past cruise, the shark, and their loss in between fueled their desires.

"This is the perfect way to sail."

Nick pulled her tighter.

"I get to kiss you. Your hands are busy elsewhere."

They sailed the catamaran together.

"Should we let Shane know about us? You know, the permanence thing."

"He knows. This was your surprise."

Nick looked at his woman. He would remember Emily swimming toward his catamaran. The distance was exactly a hundred yards. No woman ever did that move for him.

"He'll be fine. Watch the boom. Our computer course will take us where we want to go."

Emily stood at the helm with the love of her life. There was no turning back. The surprise Shane wanted to show her was the best.

She watched Nick handle the wheel. Emily turned her body to face Nick. He held her with one arm and steered the catamaran with the other. They sailed into deep water holding each other.

Martin appeared, saw the two lovers, and checked the sails. He gave Nick a thumbs-up. The two lovers separated. Martin would take over and sail them to their stopover.

Emily knew they were traveling fast to reach another spot on the beach before the evening.

Nick showed her the point on the computer.

The winds would take them to wherever they should live in their future. She wanted the freedom of casually drifting in her dreams. Nick was always part of that dream. Emily knew her heart.

Nick held her in his arms. He would protect Emily always. He finally realized one day; she was the only one with whom he wanted to hang around.

Martin was ready to take over the helm. Nick released the wheel and Emily went with Nick below deck.

"I'm crazy about you," said Nick.

"I know."

After they went below, he gave her a beautiful pearl necklace and matching ring in a white velvet bag. Emily's eyes grew misty. The necklace was important. The ring was a bonus. She tucked the bag in the windbreaker until morning. She suddenly realized her clothes were on a different boat. Nick saw her hesitation.

"I bought some clothes that are your size. Also, a pretty pair of white pajamas."

He opened the door to their bedroom and a brown dog came bounding out to greet her.

"Pooch?"

"Meet my old dog."

"Hotdogs and baloney must be in the refrigerator."

"Of course. You don't mind the dog? He likes to swim and run the beach. Pooch has been in the impound place. I couldn't leave him with my father. He sleeps on the floor."

"The dog will be fine."

The dog didn't sleep on the floor because he became very attached to Emily. Her soft heart let him sleep at the foot of the bed only when she gave the bed a pat with her hands.

Nick was appreciative. He didn't want to share Emily when they first went to bed. His other plans required space for play.

They sailed with Martin's help to their next destination and the next. The rest of their journey would be wrapped in twilight dinners by the water.

Time passed. Their daughter graduated from college.

Their love deepened and solidified into permanence. Emily was still as unpredictable as a wife. Nick didn't care. The adventure with Emily was worth every moment. He wasn't going to miss any more valuable time.

XXXXXX

Occasionally, they lived in Sausalito or San Diego. The other places where they lived were mostly in the United States. Emily visited with Elizabeth. She was surprised at the extent of the properties they also owned.

They sold their property in Africa. The distance was too far to travel with the cat and dog.

On occasion, Elizabeth went with them flying over the water and sailing with the wind when they were in Sausalito. Her skills matched Nick's abilities.

Elizabeth learned about love and life by sailing on different shores with her parents. She watched their love unfold into joy. They told her a little bit about their first cruise. She wasn't upset. Cyrus and the captain told Elizabeth the real story.

Elizabeth brought her cat with her on some of her visits. The cat watched from his cage. The seagulls and their spiral act fascinated the cat.

She took the cat out of the bag when they were moored.

"See the boom. The metal looks pretty but the swing can dump you in the water. You don't like water. Pooch is just the opposite. He's at the pound for a week while my mom and dad are on vacation."

More meows.

"I know you sort of like the dog. He really thinks you are pretty. I see him watching you all the time."

The cat looked at the white metal, walked a few steps on the deck in the life

372

jacket, turned around, and laid in her lap. She petted the soft fur and snuggled closer.

"Good kitty."

Emily saw the feline and her daughter together. The world seemed a safer place with her daughter and cat on board. Nick was her rock. She no longer felt anxious.

Nick was fixing breakfast. The two females saw smoke and heard the fire alarm go off.

"We'll have to eat out. I burned the sausages."

Emily and Elizabeth walked into the galley. The cat was in his bag purring loudly. They looked at the warped pan and totally black cinders of string. The spray foam covered the top of the stove.

"Ewe," said Elizabeth.

Emily found a rag and mopped the foam into a bucket. She was glad they installed two fire extinguishers in the galley.

"I vote we eat at the wharf today," said Elizabeth.

"I'm in," said Emily.

Nick threw the spatula in the sink.

"What are we waiting for? Let's get going!"

They brought the cat with them to their favorite restaurant in San Francisco.

The waiter recognized Emily and Nick. He was excited to meet their daughter.

He stammered and finally wrote their order down. Elizabeth saw Martin arrive and waved him over. She was smiling brightly.

Emily and Nick looked at each other.

Love surrounded the table.

After lunch, Elizabeth went with Martin.

The catamaran carried the two back home close to the house on a hill with a view of the water. The harbor was a safe place for their boat. They lived in Northern California in Mendocino for the rest of their life.

She told him about a memory that was suppressed previously. Emily told him about the words she heard under the water at age eight.

Nick knew fate stepped in and brought them together. Emily waited for him. They were both meant to be together.

"What do you want for our anniversary?"

"Which anniversary?"

"I like to count from the day Cyrus made us the most delicious three-tier wedding cake and you wore an exquisite white gown. The lights on the sailboat were nice but you were the star."

"The white cake with strawberries was delicious. I also liked our wedding vows, especially the promise forever part."

"If you will recall, I told you forever a long time ago. Em, you didn't answer my question about a gift."

Emily's eyes twinkled.

"Surprise me."

52 Surprise

Nick led Emily blindfolded to the field at the back of their home in Mendocino, California. She wondered what her husband built for her anniversary present.

She opened her eyes and there was a new white barn that dotted the landscape. They entered the barn and there were two horses in the stalls. They looked like riding horses.

"We'll probably get a few more horses later. We'll need them to round up our sheep."

He took her across the barn to a stall that held a female and baby lamb. The male was in another stall. Nick enjoyed her hug.

"They are Suffolk sheep like we saw in England. We're really going to raise sheep?"

"Elizabeth gave me the idea. She and Martin want to give up city life and move to the country. I've set aside some acres for them to build a home. They will move closer to us. We will hire people to care for the animals."

"Thank you. I love this part of my surprise."

They walked toward the barn office and one of their workers was holding a new puppy. Don handed her the small sheepdog.

"He is so cute. Do we have a trainer for him?"

"We do and a very nice dog area in the barn. His area is insulated more and has a warmer light for the winter."

She rubbed the puppy's head.

"What about pooch?"

"They've already met and seem to have found instant companions."

Emily walked with her husband arm-in-arm to their home. On the dining room table was a blue velvet box and a bouquet of pink roses.

"Mine?"

Emily smelled the roses. Nick picked up the box and opened the lid.

Tears brimmed in her eyes.

"Did I guess wrong?"

"The necklace is perfect. Wait a minute, you helped Elizabeth draw the lines and the color on her blue heart picture a long time ago."

In the box was a platinum necklace with a blue heart-shaped diamond. There was nothing more to say. Her life was complete and less rocky.

"Guilty."

Emily snuggled closer to Nick.

"Happy now?"

He always knew what was close to her heart. It just took him a little longer than planned.

"Yes!"

"Good, I'll get the expensive light-colored caviar. The glasses and champagne are in the bedroom."

"I forgot your present."

Emily handed Nick his present. She collected his poems, went to a printer, and bound the pages professionally into a hardcover book with his name in gold letters. He was delighted until he turned to the back. His picture was photoshopped as a pirate.

"Wait a minute, you're not going to try to run away?"

Emily did a dart and dash with her tanned legs moving the chairs. He chased her around the table into their bedroom. She screamed. They fell into each other's arms on top of the soft layers of down and satin.

They were on safe shores. Nick threw his shoes at the door closing the world out. The bedding was tossed onto the floor.

He slowly kissed Emily in her beautiful curves. She felt the high wind swirling around them and waves crashing on the shore. His kisses would fuel and fill her night. They welcomed the heat between them before the sunset.

The star array blinked in the distance forcing the moon to reach high on its journey to a specific place in the atmosphere. The outrageously glowing moonlight shown on the water about five hundred miles along the California coast.

The full moon showed brighter because the exact angle existed between the earth, moon, and the sun.

Emily moaned, "Perfection."

Nick smiled.

"The moon or me?"

"*Yes, maybe.*"

Nick grabbed her. She wasn't going to get away with the word, maybe. He and the night were filled with passion. Nick needed her to choose him. He pulled her closer.

Emily laughed, "Yes, Nick, my love."

He was pleased.

"I still worship you."

Her eyes sparkled. She saw their reflection bouncing off the patio glass. He turned to look.

Emily memorized a poem he wrote. The date was after their shark experience and while he was in prison. Now was an appropriate time to recite. She spoke softly.

Two people bathed in light
watch seagulls drift amongst a cloud
whilst a white boom does its swing.

WHITE BOOM AND THE SEAGULLS

A man is caught in between a shark fight.
The woman sails to form a hard shroud turning wide the boat's protective wing.
Two lovers saved to live the magic night.
Wait for me even though my head is bowed.
We're frozen in time until our hearts can sing.
Someday love, I promise you, we will reunite.

www.ingramcontent.com/pod-product-compliance
Lightning Source LLC
Chambersburg PA
CBHW070400260626
47161CB00001B/209